Northumberland's Harvest

by

Amanda Hawken

Eloquent Books
New York, New York

Eloquent Books
An imprint of AEG Publishing Group
845 Third Avenue, 6th Floor – 6016
New York, NY 10022
http://www.eloquentbooks.com

ISBN: 978-1-60860-298-8

Printed in the United States of America

Book Design: Bruce Salender

ACKNOWLEDGEMENTS

First and foremost, all the glory goes to God and to him alone.

I would like to thank a myriad of people who have helped me produce this book from the ether of my thoughts and dreams.

Thank you to my darling husband who encouraged me to keep going when it would have been so easy to give up. And to my children and their spouses whose constant interest helped me along.

My Mum and Dad…thank you for taking me on your travels when I was little, visiting castles and museums of the world. The seed of my story started then.

To Maree Cutler-Naroba, a prophetess in the nation of New Zealand, thank you for sharing your visions, which I still aim for.

Thank you Tony Aldridge, my writing tutor, if it hadn't been for your encouragement, I would never have taken the step.

Lastly, but most importantly, to Sally, if it wasn't for you, none of this would have happened! A million thanks!!!

PROLOGUE

Border Country, 1500 AD

A horn sounded. Its mournful wail shattered the peaceful stillness of the morning. Her eyes darted about the barren fields surrounding her home. She watched, waiting. Nothing moved. An icy north-easterly suddenly rose up and blasted across the bleak wastes, scouring the landscape, clutching at her clothes and stinging her face. It died away as quickly as it came. Silence, uneasy silence … not even birdsong.

Then there he was: a speck on the hill. A young scout was racing back to Dunningford Keep as if all hell was on his tail. The sheep and cattle spread wide on the slope before him, like water before the bow of a ship.

The Keep watchman sounded his horn again from the ancient buttresses. It now carried the pitch for alarm!

As the scout yanked his sturdy pony to a stop at the bottom of the stone Keep, which straddled the stream from whence the old castle got its name, she saw many black dots crest the hill on the horizon behind him. They then proceeded to roll down the slope like stones in her play pit, in which she now crouched. Her face and hands were smudged with dirt as she hunkered; Meggy, the rag doll, was rigid in her frozen grip.

From the periphery of her vision, there was a flurry of activity. The women were shouting as they grabbed their children; the men, too, as they herded their loved ones into the Keep. She heard her name being called, but she was mesmerised by the approaching marauders, who seemed to grow legs with hooves and arms with swords.

Tucked down in a hollow in the ground to the side of the Keep, her blonde hair appeared like tussock grass tugged by the wind.

The sound of a fierce battle cry swelled in the crisp autumnal air. Men fell from the steep steps leading into the Keep proper. They fell like her doll Meggy did when she didn't balance her right. Her name was being called again. Through the flapping laundry, she saw her mother running towards her. Before she could raise herself, something flew overhead and lodged in her mother's chest. Without a word, her mother flailed backwards, a dark stain spreading across her bodice.

Suddenly, the sun darkened as an ecliptic shadow fell over her world, leaving her no time to comprehend what she had just seen.

She froze instinctively. Her little heart slammed into the sides of her chest; her eyes widened. Her breath became quick and shallow.

Time felt suspended.

The air became instantly heavy and still. It shimmered silver, like a mirage, with waves of heat emanating from above.

Flaring nostrils, almost as big as her face, snorted, blasting hot moist air over her head. A velvet muzzle brushed the soft, silky locks of baby hair. The mighty horse snorted again as the fine, fair strands tickled its nose. Spats of wetness landed on her head and the ground shook several times as the great animal stamped its feet.

After an eternity, the shadow passed over.

A destrier, a great warhorse, the spoils of another skirmish, and its rider, picked their way through the billowing washing.

The screams of those attacking, the cries of those attacked with the clashes of steel on steel slowly died away. After an eon of time, a plume of smoke arose from the Keep. It fell, drifting wide in the cold, still air, hanging over the thatched hamlets to undulate like a menacing ocean. An eerie quietness shrouded the Dunningford holdings.

The sun arched and fell.

In the fading twilight, the marauders regrouped with their booty, including the hundredfold livestock, and headed south, leaving the land bereft of the last vestiges of lordship it would know for the next few hundred years.

The little girl looked up. She could see the first evening star winking in the deepening sky.

Night was coming.

CHAPTER ONE

France, Summer 1521

The voice, which came suddenly from behind, spat malice.

It came with rough hands, gripping her right forearm and taking it behind her back like prison irons.

"I see you with your new friends, Mademoiselle Percy, those religious reformers of the Meaux Circle. I heard them speaking treasonous words that you don't need a priest to hear from God! Reading literature from that upstart Martin Luther! What would your Catholic benefactor think about that?"

She felt the hiss of his breath specked with spittle on the back of her neck. "You'd better be careful, I'm watching you."

Stunned at this violent and unexpected embrace, Isabel Percy swallowed nervously, her clear eyes wide with fear, unable to comprehend her predicament.

Another strong hand held her neck forward, so she was unable to see who had grasped her. She was assaulted with hot, sour breath at her ear. It made her start in terror. Was it possible to be more terrified?

"You could be charged with treason back home, my dear."

"P–P–Please s–sir?" Isabel tried to move her head and look around, her pupils almost as large as her irises. She was desperate for someone to intervene, but she knew she was undone even at the thought, for she had chosen this secluded spot in the upstairs gallery to have privacy to read her letters from home, Alnwich Castle, in Northumberland, England.

Amanda Hawken

"Please, indeed, Mademoiselle Percy. You may get away with your religious leanings here, but the Earl of Northumberland would never stand for it! How disappointed he would be to find his ward abusing his trust."

"Wh–what … what do you want?"

"I'll let you know in my own good time. You remember I'm watching you." The owner of the raspy voice tightened his grip on Isabel's arm and took it to near breaking point behind her back. Isabel was really frightened now as her pain level increased tenfold. An involuntary sob escaped her lips. Tears gathered and spilled from her storm blue eyes; some clung to the blonde tips of her eyelashes, glittering like crushed diamonds.

The offending mouth moved in closer to rest on her smooth, pale cheek. The moist breath was revoltingly warm on her skin. She shuddered.

"Nay, don't be afraid. Just do as I ask and all will be well."

Isabel's body tensed as her private space remained invaded. Her left hand, hanging at her side, gripped the letter opener she had used only moments before. In a fraction of a second, her attention swung like a lead weight from the threat behind to the instrument in her hand that might buy her freedom.

Instinctively, without thinking, Isabel followed a routine of quick, decisive movements practised in early childhood.

When she could, after her morning lessons, Isabel would escape her tutor's clutches to spar with her cousin Henry Percy in the list stalls. Enjoying the freedom of this physical exercise, which would have been frowned upon if she had been caught, and trying to win one over her cousin was pure joy.

Isabel now swung around with all her strength, her skill none the worse for years of disuse and plunged the small dagger into her blackmailer's neck. It was totally unexpected – from both parties.

She turned and stood back trembling from head to foot as the heavily cowled body sank to the floor. Her hands flew to her mouth, fingers fluttering like doves at a dovecot. Words

10

tumbled out incoherently, "Oh, dear God! Jesu! Jesu! I've just killed someone!"

The crumpled form, with the hood covering its face, moaned. Isabel could see blood seeping between the fingers at its throat.

She fled, the wake of her departure scattering the leaves of unread letters, which had landed at her feet.

Isabel was shaken to the very core of her soul. She had just committed an act that was against the very nature of her being. She had murdered someone! How could that be? One moment she had been a God-fearing, genuine-hearted, conscientious young woman, always eager to please God and believe the best of people. Now she was a cold-blooded murderer! Isabel felt bile quickly rising from her stomach as the world she knew, values she lived by and everything that she thought she was, crumbled into rubble within her soul. She crashed down a spiral staircase, her hands grazed by the hewn stones as she tried to stop herself from falling headfirst down the narrow steps. At the bottom, she bolted haphazardly through a door that led into a walled garden with just enough time to clear her damask skirts and vomit into the thyme topiary.

CHAPTER TWO

England, Autumn 1521

At the same hour, across the miles and over the sea in another country, a tall, dark, swarthy man with dark eyes stamped his feet in nervous anticipation.

Nobody noticed as the antechamber in Greenwich Palace was a busy place. He was jostled this way and that as people continually passed by. The occasional acquaintances bowed their heads or tipped their velvet, bejewelled caps. He noted others at small gaming tables throwing dice while they waited for an audience with their king. Still more lounged against window casements reading books to while away the time.

"Sir Thomas Boleyn!" a voice boomed, accompanied by a stamp of a halberd on the wooden floors, polished by the tread of thousands of feet.

Sir Thomas started and pulled himself up. He hadn't even seen the doors of the king's presence chamber open, although he had been watching it all day.

"The king's out hunting," John Fisher, Bishop of Rochester, had said when he had passed some time ago with eyes rolled to the ceiling. "Nailing the king down to deal with the affairs of this country on a fine day like this, is like trying to keep water in a leaky cistern," he vented. "Never mind that you are fresh from Ireland with important correspondence. How does that compare with the chase?"

Sir Thomas had laughed lightly with those around him as the aged theologian passed but was inclined to agree with him. Compared with his father, where Sir Thomas began his life at court as a page, Henry VIII was far too fond of pleasing himself.

Now it seemed, the king had returned.

He straightened his doublet and walked through the path people made for him as they stepped aside.

The king was surrounded by eight members of the privy chamber, as per protocol: four esquires of the Body and four gentleman ushers. He saw his brother-in-law, Thomas Howard, the Duke of Norfolk, leaning nonchalantly against the window, picking his teeth with a hazel twig, displaying his usual superior confidence. It irked Thomas considerably, though he hid it well.

They locked eyes in silent greeting.

"How now, Sir Thomas?" called the king heartily from across the room. Sir Thomas Boleyn affected an exaggerated bow, doffing his hat to the floor.

"Your Majesty!"

The young king was as fair as Thomas was dark. His startling blue eyes danced with merriment. He was the picture of health and vitality, his red hair more gold than auburn, his tall, well-built frame fit and honed.

"You look well, sire."

The king shot him a twinkled glance as he spat out the last pip from the fruit he was eating. He dabbled his fingers in a bowl of rose water and pressed them into a square of lawn. "Glad tidings, Sir Thomas! We have just received most welcome news from the queen's apartments! She is in a delicate way again. Pray God a brother for the Princess Mary. We are pleased!"

"Wonderful, Your Majesty! Wonderful news indeed!"

"Celebrate with me!" Henry nodded to his cupbearer for wine all around.

Sir Thomas saluted Henry with his goblet raised. "To a safe delivery and heir for England!"

13

"Hear, hear" was echoed all around, but God save us from another miscarriage or stillbirth was the silent prayer.

Furtive looks were hidden from the king as the men buried their eyes in the business of sculling.

Henry slammed the gold goblet down with relish. "Now, to business! Norfolk, take this correspondence from Tom; we have other matters to discuss at this juncture."

The king motioned for Sir Thomas to be seated on the stool next to his chair of state as the Duke of Norfolk took the leather satchel filled with important parchments. Thomas tried to catch his brother-in-law's eye again for any information in advance. The duke kept his eyes down in seeming deference, leaving Thomas none the wiser and making him more irked at his brother-in-law than before.

The king perched himself on his magnificent chair of state, which was placed upon a low dais. He chewed the inside of his cheek as he fidgeted mindlessly with a tasselled gold dorsal hanging at the side of his armrest. With a sigh, he then pursed his lips and thrummed his fingers on a hard muscled thigh.

Thomas' heart sank, though a shadow never touched his face. He meant to deliver bad news and didn't know how to serve it.

Henry stilled himself and faced Thomas squarely. "This matter of these Irish lands," he waved his hand ineffectually as if he were casting off a minor irritation.

"We may be at war with France soon, Tom. So keeping peace with Ireland is desirable. I am aware of your claim to the Butler titles through your mother." Henry shifted uncomfortably in his seat and continued. "If it was up to me, you could have them. But I must think and rule for the good of all England and not just a favoured few. Your mothers' relations in Ireland hotly contest this suite of yours. And so, a strategy of peacekeeping would be prudent."

Sir Thomas inclined his head, as to concur, but felt the celebratory wine in his stomach sour.

"You have another daughter, as yet unengaged; do you not, Sir Thomas?"

"Yes, Your Grace, my daughter Anne."

Henry sat up and spread his hands expansively upon his thighs. He grinned broadly.

"I give you a consolation prize! Offer her to Sir Piers Butler's son. He is currently residing in England, methinks. Think on, Thomas. Moses didn't enter the Promised Land but the *children* of Israel did."

"Well said, Your Majesty, well said," appraised Wolsey from the side.

Thomas didn't see the Cardinal to the side of the room. He looked at him now. He sat like a comfortable, benevolent toad, his heavy jowls resting on his red velvet robe.

How did a butcher's son rise to such elevated status? Thomas asked himself, already knowing the answer. By being shrewd! By granting Henry's every need, even to the point of knowing beforehand what Henry was looking for in an outcome and giving it to his sovereign on a silver platter!

Yes, Wolsey was very clever and I must be just as clever, he admonished himself. What does Henry need that I may provide?

Thomas bowed his head toward Wolsey in acknowledgement, not only of his presence, but also in thanks for informing Henry for him of his plight with the Butler titles. Thomas was hopeful of Wolsey's influence on Henry to produce a favourable outcome. Wolsey's return look was one of commiseration at this worst-case scenario. He'd done his best.

Turning aside, Sir Thomas knelt and kissed the hand of his king in an appearance of total obeisance, his blood boiling with disappointment. Once again, he stood like a poor country cousin beside his brother-in-law, the Duke of Norfolk. He pushed down feelings of humiliation at being turned down. His voice, when it came out, was full of self-control, even a hint of warmth.

"Thank you for your goodness, sire."

They both rose together and Henry grabbed him in a bear hug.

Thomas could see that Henry had found the situation awkward by the way he displayed his relief in his abundant affection. Thomas glowered inwardly, trying not to pull back from his sovereign's embrace.

You so hate confrontation! Why don't you have some of your father's backbone? he fumed within.

Henry withdrew and threw an arm about Thomas's shoulders as he walked him towards the door.

"Stay close to court, Tom. When we have details to hand about France, I may need you to carry some correspondence for me across the channel."

"Most certainly, Your Majesty. Hever is only an hour to the south of London. I shall keep my man Stafford here, should you need me."

Henry smiled cheerily and pounded him on the back with affirming fervour. "Till then, Tom."

Sir Thomas Boleyn made his way back to the stables. He did not see the faces of the people he passed. His thoughts were turned inward as he stewed in his frustration and anger.

Why was it that God saw fit to give people titles and influence on a plate but he had to work hard and manipulate to get a tiny foothold? Well, if that's the way the game is going to be played, let the games begin!

He felt his heart shrink and harden as if an iron fist had closed around it. It didn't make him feel uncomfortable; in fact, it seemed to offer strength to his newfound determination.

There had to be another way to advance his ambitions. There just had to be! Marriage into the infamous Howard family had not brought him where he wanted to be. Yes, he married a duke's sister, but he was still left as a lowly knight. It was true that he and Elizabeth had married for love. It was just convenient for him that she was also nobility, from one of the most powerful families in the land. And he had hoped to glean more titles and status from that, but none had been forthcoming.

What does Henry need that I can provide for? he asked himself again. *Maybe that is the key to promotion. It has worked well for Wolsey, clever man,* he thought, smiling grimly.

He clenched and unclenched his fists at his side, his eyes dark with focus.

His character was that of a stream in spring melt, infinitely calculating for advancement. If the natural course of the flow was obstructed, it should then flow over, under or around, in order to find another path.

CHAPTER THREE

Northumberland, England, Winter 1521

"Mary! Come away from the window! Remember your complexion. You'll be as brown as a nut with that sun on the snow!"

Lady Mary Talbot lingered, her pale, almost lashless eyes trailing the black, meandering ribbon of the River Aln as it slid past the majestic edifice of Alnwick Castle, the last bastion of English defence in the north.

Her stepmother was right. Keeping her complexion fashionably pale was a constant battle. She stood out in neither beauty nor accomplishment, but in this she did try to strive.

Sighing, she went to move her slight form away from the great, long casement, but suddenly two lots of movement caught her eyes simultaneously. She stalled as she watched.

A lone rider was coming in fast from the south. Even from this distance she could see that he was well travelled.

His cloak sailed out from behind him and the dry mud on his steed drifted out like a cloud in a strong wind as the hooves hit the road.

Also, just coming into view from the west were her father and their host, back from "the king's business," as her stepmother had put it. The king's business was delivering pensions to those in the north who were now retired from the king's service.

Her father, the Earl of Shrewsbury, Lord Steward of England, and the Earl of Northumberland with his three sons clattered noisily into the courtyard with their usual entourage of well-mounted and caparisoned attendants.

"Mary! I won't tell you again!"

Her stepmother's voice set her teeth on edge but Mary quickly obeyed. She missed her dead mother. This visit was to be one of the most important moments in her life and she wished that she could take comfort from her mother's quiet, calming presence. Her death a year ago had been devastating to her. They were a close family by society's standards. Tears pricked behind her eyes as a wave of self-pity washed over her.

Her stepmother, Elizabeth Walden, had insisted that they accept this invitation from their neighbour, the Earl of Northumberland.

Her father had been reluctant, explaining that he was in the north on the king's business and didn't have time for the frivolity of visiting. He had left the room at their home in Sheffield quickly not wanting to argue in front of his eight children with their governesses and nursemaids. Not to be subdued, her stepmother had rushed after him leaving the door slightly ajar.

Mary rose as if to close the door but kept it open a crack to eavesdrop. She ignored the raised eyebrows of disapproval from the servants and laid her ear to the door.

"He's asked for Mary to come, too. Why do you procrastinate over her future? It is time she and Henry were betrothed. It is a good opportunity for Mary and Henry to meet one another."

Mary could imagine how her stepmother's eyes were glinting with expectation at being related to the great Northumberlands!

Mary had only been introduced to Elizabeth Walden when her father brought her home as his new wife. And even in the short time she had known her, she could plainly see her stepmother's ambition to squeeze the most out of life. She was quite extraordinary and Mary had never known anybody quite like her. She didn't know whether to love her or to hate her.

Mary was pulled between two different but equally strong emotions: her resentment towards Elizabeth for taking her mother's place in her father's affections and displacing her, or loving her ecstatically for supporting her marriage to Henry where her parents seemed reluctant to do so.

"How powerful will your grandchildren be with these two estates joined together, Sheffield and Alnwick?"

George Talbot was silent. Mary could hear the turmoil in her father's mind by the agitation in his footsteps.

"George!"

Mary turned her eye to the scene.

She saw her father look at his new wife. She was younger than her mother, fierier and self-willed, sleeker and more youthful. Mary could see her father's resolve melting as his gaze rested on her stepmother's flushed cheeks and at the rise and fall of her full breasts.

Mary had never seen her father look at her mother like that. It shocked her. For the first time in her sheltered life, she saw her father in a new light. He was not only her father. He was a man—a man who lusted after a woman!

His eyes bright, her father moved toward his young wife. Mary could see that Elizabeth was triumphant but hid it by dipping her head as his lips fell on her breasts.

Mary had closed the door quietly.

Too much information was running around in her head. She dazedly stumbled to the nearest window seat, mindless of her brothers and sisters at play on the floor, and stared blindly out through the diamond panes into the Sheffield countryside. She had never felt so alone or alienated in her life.

Now, aware of the purpose for their visit here at Alnwich, Mary, more resigned and composed, fluffed out her new gown that Elizabeth had insisted on. It was yellow, which only made her pale colouring appear washed out, but her stepmother had insisted upon it so that it would compliment pearls and topaz from her mother's inheritance that she wore at her throat.

She wanted to sit very prettily for when the Percy brothers walked in. She wanted to make a good impression. She pinched her cheeks and bit her lips while her stepmother and Catherine the Countess of Northumberland weren't looking. She had seen other women do it when they wanted to make themselves look pretty. Unbeknown to Mary, it only caused unsightly red lumps to rise on her pasty complexion.

Some giggling at her side revealed that her actions had been observed. Lady Margaret and Lady Maud Percy held their little hands up to their faces. Mary poked her tongue out at them, which made them laugh all the more.

Mary decided to ignore them, as one does small children, and lifted her chin into the air.

The blotches on Mary's cheeks bloomed at their height when the men and boys entered the room.

Lolloping wolfhounds and racing mastiffs preceded the men as they skidded on the polished flagstones and jumped up on each other in play. Their sharp barks, yips and growls hurt her ears but she laughed out loud with delight at such a display of unruliness. Scenes like this were never seen in her home. Her father and mother had run a very strict, regimented household where quietness was encouraged for godly meditation and dogs were for hunting only, therefore they remained outside the house. Her stepmother was subtly changing their household. She had brought her pet dog with her to Sheffield when she had married her father. That he allowed it was amazing to her and made her realise what an influence she was over him.

Much shouting ensued as the two younger Northumberland sons, Thomas and Algernon, pulled them up and ordered them to sit by the cavernous fireplace where massive ash and beech trunks were ablaze. Thomas was handsome, Mary decided. He had dark, curly hair with the same lashes to frame his lively blue eyes.

Algernon had lighter colouring with sandy hair. He was thin and gangly with the sudden upward growth of young men leaving boyhood.

Peace reigned at last as the dogs appeared happy to settle and they were soon fast asleep after their morning's rigours.

Servants appeared quickly, divesting the men of their over-coats, furs and riding cloaks, while the Countess of Northumberland oversaw the dispensing of mulled wine to grateful waiting hands. Wafts of cinnamon, orange and nutmeg tantalised the senses, making mouths water.

The new Countess of Shrewsbury was the first to speak. The question was directed to her husband. "Last pension delivered safely, my dear?"

George Talbot put his back to the fire and stretched his hands out behind him to feel the heat.

"Yes, Beth dear. Old Bassett has become quite frail, but still able enough to drink to his Majesty's health … and still able to regale us with stories of his service to the king and his father!"

Laughter flowed easily around the room.

Mary looked up as the Countess of Northumberland, Catherine Percy, called her eldest son to her.

"Henry."

Henry had his back to everybody, stoking the fringes of the fire absently with an iron poker.

He dutifully set the poker on its stand and coming from behind his father, turned to his mother.

Catherine raised her hand to Mary, who now rose awkwardly from her stool, embarrassed that every eye was upon her. Mary flicked up a quick look at Henry and she blushed a furious red.

Oh, he was beautiful! Achingly beautiful … a delicious thrill rippled through her. She wanted to drown in it.

Long, leggy and lithe, with the same strong jaw line as his father, Henry Percy, the heir apparent, held himself with a quiet, unassuming grace. His unruly blonde bangs hung rakishly over his eyes. He tossed his head to reveal shy blue eyes.

"Henry," said his mother. "May I present the Lady Mary Talbot?"

Mary's stomach did somersaults and her knees felt weak.

Henry came forward and elegantly bowed over her shaking hand in greeting. "Lady Talbot."

"Call her Mary, please," interjected Elizabeth, her chest fluttering with eagerness to please the powerful Northumberlands.

Henry gave Elizabeth one of his most engaging smiles, revealing a set of even, white teeth. "But of course, madam," he said.

Both Mary and her stepmother felt their insides melt.

As Henry drew aside, Mary became aware of an awkward silence. The Earl of Northumberland was trying to lock eyes with her father, but her father would not meet them. Her stepmother choked on her wine. When Elizabeth looked up, Mary saw fury on her face.

The entrance of the house steward interrupted the moment. The ancient man bowed stiffly, his calcified features barely moving. "A messenger, my lord. He bears the Cardinal Wolsey's livery, my lord. Shall I show him in?"

Northumberland, still handsome and virile despite his years, turned his gaze from Shrewsbury and said with his usual commanding presence, "Indeed. Show him in."

A travel-stained messenger came forward and bowed low.

"I come from London, my lord; from the presence of the Cardinal Wolsey himself, my lord."

He then produced a piece of folded parchment with the Cardinal's seal from his weatherworn cloak. Northumberland broke the seal and read the contents.

"Well, well," he mused. Then he looked up to his house steward. "Ah, give this man," he motioned to the messenger with his forefinger, "some rest and refreshments. I'll reply directly."

As the house steward and messenger departed, the earl looked at Henry expectantly.

Henry straightened up. "Father?"

"Well, my boy. You are favoured."

Henry's brow frowned with a question. "Father?"

The earl beamed the smile of a proud father. Mary could see that Henry was not moved by his father's sudden admiration. Indeed, he almost looked apprehensive with it.

Puzzled, Mary mirrored his frown for different reasons.

"Your presence is required at York Place, in London," announced the earl to his son. "The Cardinal, it seems, desires a page to assist him there. You are to leave after the Christmas celebrations. Catherine, my dear, you may have him ready to leave after the snows have melted. Hopefully you won't be impeded by bad weather." The smile continued, but his tone had changed. It sounded like a warning rather than an affirmation. "You'll do us proud, won't you Henry?"

Henry didn't answer. Whether he hadn't heard or chose not to hear, Mary didn't know for Henry looked stunned at the unexpected and exciting news.

Mary could see the excitement beginning to grow in his eyes as he began to get used to the idea. Go to London! See the king's court! See the world! Advance his prospects for a great future! *Why wouldn't he?* thought Mary. *Who was she to hold him back with a "maybe" betrothal?* Nothing had been mentioned to solidify the deal between the families during their visit that she was aware of.

For the first time in her life, Mary could see what she wasn't.

How could she, a plain, unsophisticated girl, just out of the schoolroom, with no real knowledge of the world keep a young man of his calibre interested? The intimidation of her fantasy of court life and the well travelled people who dwelt there pressed unbearably in upon her.

Henry remained speechless, a dumb smile hanging off his face as everybody crowded around. There were slaps on his back, hands pumped till they were about to fall off and wet kisses applied to his cheeks. Only Mary held back. Her mind had quickly spun into an emotional vortex with the sound of the excited voices in the room fading far away.

The brilliant elation felt by Henry Percy was equalled by the utter devastation in Mary Talbot.

***

George Talbot and his wife Elizabeth lay in each other's arms after a wonderful session of lovemaking. She sated him more than his first wife, Anne, ever had. As they lay back on the huge embroidered bolster in the guest apartments of Alnwich Castle, he ran his hand over her abundant breasts, and he could feel himself stirring again. He had loved Anne dearly and they had a loving relationship that transcended many other married couples that they knew of. Their love for each other and their similar values that they held in life had flowed down onto their many children creating a very harmonious environment. Elizabeth, though, had drawn out that secret place within him, that wild place to step out into the unknown, to actually experience things that before were only a passing thought, to be fulfilled mind, body and soul. It was a place of scary fun, not only sexually but also in all areas of life. She ran ahead of him in the running of his household, his position at court, even in church matters, encouraging him to tear down his boundaries built by tradition and insecurities. It excited him and it challenged him. Most times he emerged from his old mindsets reluctantly, like testing bath water with his toe. This situation was no different: the marriage of his oldest daughter to the son of a man who lived life on a knife-edge.

He was aware of Northumberland's offences against the crown. He was a man who liked to be a law unto himself. It was only money and position that kept his head from the spike. What kind of future was that for his daughter?

"Good. Keep thinking those thoughts my beautiful brave husband."

"Eh?"

"You heard," said Elizabeth playfully chucking him on the tip of his nose.

"It is not an easy decision, my love."

"You cosset Mary too much. You have sheltered her to the point of stunting her maturity. I have seen the signs of it in her, a tendency to dwell on herself more than is healthy. I understand that you love her and that you want to protect her but now the time has come for a husband to replace you. She has to be released to grow and find out what life is all about. It is the healthy way, the natural way. You know our Lord said that a wife must cleave to her husband. Young girls are not to cleave to their fathers for the rest of their lives."

George frowned keeping silent. He knew it. He knew it his heart. She was right but could he trust the son of a man that pushed the laws of the land to the limit? Perhaps finding his daughter a safer family to marry into would be the more prudent thing.

"You have to think of your unborn grandchildren," said Elizabeth reading his mind, as she was wont to do. "What better family could they be born to than the Northumberlands? They would never want for anything. You would never have to be overly concerned for their welfare. You will visit them, bearing gifts and speaking wisdom into their lives like grandparents do. All will be well, my love, just you see."

Elizabeth turned her face up to his and pressed her delicious body up against him. "My love, you know that I am right. Like has to marry unto like. You have to let Mary go and trust that she can make her own way with her own husband."

He smiled down at his wife to placate her but he couldn't shake the uneasiness he felt in his heart.

CHAPTER FOUR

Calais, English France. Winter 1521

One month on, in an alehouse on the docks of Calais, two travellers sat hunched over their warmed tankards. Although not as inebriated or jocular as those around them, they did toast to their success. Their plan was well under way.

Their table was accidentally bumped as a bustling old woman dressed for travelling moved through to the hearth at the back of the establishment. So as not to lose his cap placed on the edge table, the older man grabbed it and folded the worn leather, thereby hiding the little amber vial that had just fallen into it. He looked around furtively, under a heavy brow, to see if he was being watched. Nothing caught his attention. There were only well-wrapped bodies, head to head with each other, intent on eking out the warmth of good ale and companionship. He relaxed and turned his own head back to his cup.

Contented and unhurried, they firmed up the next leg of strategy set a few months ago.

As the sun started to list from its zenith, they knew that the tide would be turning soon. They threw down the last of their ale and wished each other Godspeed. As they stood up to go, the door to the inn banged open by the wind. A dark figure stood in the doorway. The convivial chatter froze, as did the temperature of the air as all the warmth was sucked out. The lone man entered the room and recognising the two standing, went to join them. As they sat, eyeing each other the conversation slowly resumed as people relaxed.

The newcomer spoke in low tones so that they wouldn't be overheard. The faces of the other two men grew grim. The news took a while to settle. After some silence, the older man came to a decision and gave the younger one instructions to follow. They then stood and made their way to the door.

Outside, black and white storm clouds scudded across a vivid blue sky. Sea birds wheeled and swooped with piercing cries. The wind was strong and gusty, carrying with it the tang of the sea. It whipped away the collar from the younger figure as it followed the older into the raucous causeway of sailors, peddlers, merchants and ne'er-do-wells. Their fleeting visitor, one of their scouts, had disappeared as though he had never been.

Daylight revealed that the stab wound to his neck had healed into a nice scab.

The blade must have been clean for no suppuration had set in. Also, by some grace or favour, no vitals had been severed.

Both hands found the flapping collar and hooked it to its fastening.

They separated, disappearing into the throng.

CHAPTER FIVE

France, Winter 1521

Laughter exploded in the upper salon.

Marguerite de Valois, Duchesse d'Alençon, the king's sister and her gentlewomen were almost bent double in ecstasies of mirth as they tried to contain her dogs. What had started as a little tug-o-war with an unravelled bolt of cloth over the end of a table had now grown into a full-blown war with casualties. The servants had rushed in with spectacular dives, careening into each other and upending the furniture and spraining limbs. Lengths of cloth twirled like ribbons and the barks of the dogs, which were now worked into a frenzy, were deafening.

"Joliet! Russo! Sousou! Minette!" Marguerite called to her spaniels as they skidded passed and dove under a settle. She pointed to Anne Boleyn as Russo dashed past her skirts. "Grab him!" she shrieked. Anne spun, then dipped and found herself sliding on the polished floor with said dog safely captured. She came to rest at some long, blue-hosed legs.

Very quickly the room fell silent, bar the puffing from exertions. Anne's eyes travelled up the well-turned legs into the face of the King of France.

"Francois! Your Majesty!" Marguerite exclaimed, and immediately, with everybody else in the room, sunk to her knees.

Francois' dark face wore a look of smug amusement as his black eyes surveyed the scene of carnage before him. "Marguerite, ma soeur. I thought to surprise you a week early."

"Well," gulped his sibling. "Surprise you did my brother!"

Laughter exploded again; then Marguerite encouraged decorum by setting to and regaining some resemblance of order to the room before greeting her brother with a warm kiss and embrace. Everybody rose and busied themselves to help.

The King of France lowered his hand and brought Anne to her feet. A servant, bowing low, took the wriggling Russo from her lap.

"Mademoiselle Boleyn, is it not?"

"Yes, Your Majesty," she returned in perfect French without a hint of English accent.

He held her at arms length, critiquing her this way and that. "What a fine French beauty you have grown into. How long have you been with us now?"

Anne kept her eyes lowered. "Almost seven years, Your Grace."

Her life in England, then in the Netherlands with the Archduchess of Austria, seemed like another lifetime.

The king walked around Anne, his experienced eyes roving up and down. Her beauty was not conventional, that being blonde, ethereal and well rounded. Anne was as slender as a willow and had the colouring of her father with large brown eyes, so dark that they appeared black and a wealth of shiny, luxuriant black hair.

"She is not at all like 'la hackney,' isn't that so, Marguerite?"

Anne blushed at the derogatory name with which the king had described her sister. *Mary has brought it on herself,* Anne thought, being far too free with her favours. Even so, it was not an easy thing to hear. God willing she would never be called such names. She must make sure of it!

"So, mademoiselle, what has my sister been teaching you? Teaching you how to run wild, I can see." He gave his sister a playful wink. Marguerite gave him a grimace then threw him a kiss. Their sibling intimacy, fostered by their loving and ambitious mother, was understood in court circles and obvious to all.

He plucked at Anne's sleeve, noting its unusual design. "One of your creations?"

Anne lowered her eyes, her black silky lashes brushing the deep cream of her cheeks. "Yes, Your Majesty. Your sister has taught me many things, art, music, design, masques. I have been a keen pupil, but I have yet to attain her level of skill."

"Ah, Mademoiselle, in your design of the cloth you are already there."

The king's eyes appraised the simplicity of her red velvet gown.

Anne had designed the square cut neckline to push up her small breasts, making them appear bigger than they were. Her long elegant sleeves covered her hands to the second knuckle, to hide an embarrassment: the protrusion of another nail on her little finger.

She pretended to pluck some dust off her skirt with this hand drawing his attention away from it. Francois gathered the other and held it to his lips. Her skin was dewy and fresh under his breath.

Anne could feel his attraction towards her. Having no affection for him in that way but not wanting to rebuff, she teased him by gently disengaging her hand while holding him with alluring eyes, a skill she had caught rather than was taught by the ladies of his sister's household.

She loved the feeling of power. She was amazed to find that by tilting her head and casting a seductive look, she had men dancing like puppets. It was not unlike a fisherman casting his net and catching a haul.

She suppressed a laugh of delight at her own emerging confidence in herself and what she could do to turn even the head of a king!

"How is Queen Claude?" asked Anne, knowing that turning the conversation to his pious deformed wife would dampen his ardour.

She was successful for the light in his eyes shuttered like a Venetian villa in the midday sun.

"At Amboise, of course." He dropped his hand from hers and rolled his eyes up as if he were bored. "Almost ready to pop the next whelp."

Instantly disinterested, sucking the inside of his cheeks as if he had eaten something distasteful, he walked away.

Anne hid her alarm at the king's lack of love and compassion for his wife. She knew him for an uncouth and unfeeling man at times, but it didn't take away the feeling of horror it must be for Queen Claude to be married to one such as him, though, like all true royalty of the blood, she never showed it.

God keep her from an uncaring, philandering husband! *For as God is my witness,* Anne vowed to herself, *I could never stay quiet about it!*

***

Isabel Percy heard the laughter and barking as it floated up on the frozen air from the first floor. She sat on a window seat in her bedchamber, her eyes staring vacantly through the open casement, the leaves of an old Gutenberg bible fluttering in her lap.

Before her, the French countryside nestled quietly under its blanket of snow. The clouds above looked bruised behind the black skeletal trees and appeared to huddle in on the landscape for comfort.

Fear had bitten Isabel like a serpent since the assault, paralysing her from enjoying everyday life. She jumped at every shadow and was suspicious of every movement that entered the periphery of her vision.

Who had seen her talking with the gentleman of the Meaux Circle? she asked herself. Everybody had seen her, and lots of others besides. It was nothing to question. The king was well known to be quite relaxed about religion and the housing of intellectuals with their theories. His sister encouraged intellectual discussion with her women on all subjects that surrounded them in life.

Martin Luther was a spearhead for spiritual theory. His revelation of scripture was discussed with animated freedom.

Why had she been singled out? What did this person want with her? Had she offended someone? Had she seen something she wasn't meant to see? No, she didn't think so. She knew her own heart to be changing by Martin Luther's revelations of God's word. The revelations that came from the discussions with the people who belonged to the Meaux Circle were life changing. They were all of the opinion that she could have a relationship with the Holy Spirit without the intercession of a priest! Her outward actions had not changed, except perhaps to start talking to God like she might talk to a friend. Her friends of the Meaux circle had said that that was actually prayer! She couldn't quite get her understanding around that one. Does God truly hear you without being on your knees at a church altar? She was sure nobody had seen her in this activity as she often whispered her words under her breath. She shivered as an icy finger of winter wind caressed her neck. Only days ago, she had been in ecstasies of delight when she had heard from Brother Yves Briconnais. He had said that God loved her as literally as a loving earthly father loves his child. She'd never known her father and although the Earl of Northumberland was indeed a kind benefactor, how could it compare to having a father of your own? Ever since she could remember, she had been taught that God was to be worshipped but mostly to be obeyed, as one would quickly obey a harsh master so as to avoid retribution. She would kneel obediently at the altar, gazing upon the statue of Mary and baby Jesus, wondering if God really did hear her prayers. She would often look up at the sky and wonder if God was really there at all. Now she could feel an intimacy growing between her and God; that was quite apart from the religious observances that has surrounded her from birth. It was like the developing relationship with a friend. But suddenly, since the assault, it felt like that life belonged to someone else. It was as if God had withdrawn himself from her. Maybe that bad, evil man was right. The Northumberlands would never accept her way of thinking. Anything other than the Roman Catholic way of worship was heresy. And heretics were burned at the stake. Isabel shivered again. This time it was not the chilled drafts that eddied through a window casement but the imagined fingers of a horrifying death, slithering across her mind, causing her skin to crawl.

She had confided in no one about her assault. She didn't know in whom she could trust.

There was Anne Boleyn. She had been a wonderful friend—two English girls away from home supporting each other. But over the years, she could see that while Anne was a lot of fun, her mercurial moods could turn on you in an instant. Anne's first priority was always herself.

No, she couldn't trust Anne, as much as she loved her like a sister—not with a burden like this. Anne wasn't keen on her relationships with her friends of the Meaux Circle and she could see Anne using this scenario as a tool to criticise and pull down the good things that meant so much to her.

Then there was Anthony Browne. He had joined the French court from England a few years ago. *No,* she thought. He was still too much of a boy. He was always playing the jester and making them laugh; she wasn't sure if his character would go deep enough to do the right thing by her.

As far as she knew, she hadn't created any enemies. How she wished she could unburden herself to someone. Maybe Brother Yves Briconnais, the young scholar of the Meaux Circle? He had said God would answer her prayer directly, that she didn't have to go through a priest. Suddenly it dawned on her what that meant. Her cheeks flushed heatedly with embarrassment and she spun her head around to make sure she was alone. It was as though her thought had just been shouted out aloud! She could still feel it reverberated off the chamber walls. She had no training in the ways of a priest.

Nervously, taking a deep breath and feeling really silly she said into the cold air. "God, I need your help. Who is this person who attacked me? Why did he attack me?"

Silence resounded in her ears. She waited with baited breath, expecting a clap of thunder or a loud voice but there was nothing, only the sound of the fire crackling merrily in the grate behind her.

Weak in faith, Isabel was suddenly deflated and tormented when there was no instant answer. She pushed away her heavy blonde tresses, which fell in loose, silky curls over her shoulders, from off her face. She let go of faith and instead of pressing in to God, gave herself up to the torment of doubt.

I stabbed a man! Despite the icy cold biting into her flesh from the open window, the thought of it bathed her in a clammy sweat. Dread consumed her until she was trembling.

God forgive me! God, you knew I didn't mean to kill him! He would have killed me first! Why, why, why? Why did this have to happen to me? Isabel banged clenched fists at her temples.

She started to give in to the worry of it all and tears soon started to roll unnoticed down her cheeks.

Is he dead? What will happen to me now? I have sinned. Murderers do not enter heaven. They go to hell. She'd heard it from the pulpit! *God forgive me! God forgive me!*

Isabel tried to rein in her thoughts. She sniffed, sat up straight, wiped her face and smoothed out her gown with long, white, trembling fingers.

Another thought flew into her mind from nowhere. No dead body had been reported found in the gallery alcove! Maybe, just maybe, her attacker was only maimed? Perhaps he was still alive? He had gotten up and walked away? A wave of relief washed over her only to be dammed up by sudden doubt again.

Deciding to push all her thoughts out of her head, she took the Gutenberg Bible in both hands and raised it to her face to help focus her mind. It was opened at 1 Kings and the words her eyes rested upon burned like a flame into her soul. It was as if the Latin words had elevated themselves above the page and floated there. They seared into her heart and she knew that God was talking to her. She re-read the words to deepen and clarify their impact.

"How long will you halt between two opinions?" she read. "If the Lord is God then follow him."

Follow you God? Am I not following you or trying to? What do you mean? There was no answer. Her desperation seemed to hang above a cliff.

A knock at the chamber door made her look up and drop the Bible to her lap, the intrusion shattering the intensity of the moment.

It was Anne.

"There you are! You've missed all the fun!"

Isabel smiled tightly, but it still produced the dimples in her cheeks that endeared her to everyone she met.

Anne wended her way around the cots and pallets where the Duchess of Alençon's ladies slept and plopped herself on the window seat next to her. Isabel noted the cold, dismissive look Anne gave toward the Bible. Anne was as God-conscious as the next person, but she walked the broad highway so as not to draw attention to herself in that way, for survival she had said. Suddenly, Isabel received a flash of revelation. She followed God for love. Anne followed God because that was what society dictated. Anne continued to let her know that she didn't approve of her meditations on manuscripts that could cause trouble. *Well,* thought Isabel, *if this is what seeking God means, disapproval of her fellow men, then God strengthen me to do so.*

The bristly, frigid moment, which had nothing to do with the winter air, passed as Anne lifted her eyes to smile at Isabel.

"Brrr! It's freezing, Isabel!" said Anne speaking English but pronouncing her name the French way, *Isabo,* with accentuation on the long sounding *s.* It was the only time they were free to speak their native tongue, when they were together alone.

"Let me close this window." She leaned past Isabel and latched the leaded casement.

"How are you faring? Do you still have your bad head?"

Isabel's defined mouth curved wanly. "I'm better," she lied.

Anne took Isabel's hands and rubbed them warm between her own.

"Look at you, your nose and cheeks are as red as pomegranates," she laughed. "Listen, I have some news."

A spark of interest alighted in Isabel's heart-shaped face.

"What?" she said, wiping her nose.

"The king is here!"

Isabel sat up surprised, eyes widening. "Here? Under this roof?"

"Yes!"

"But he is early. He was not due for …"

"Yes, I know—a week from now."

"Why?"

Anne shrugged her slender shoulders, rolled her eyes, then leaned in close in a conspirator's whisper, "I suspect that he is out for some fun while his poor wife is confined!"

She pulled away. "Anyway, he is here. I don't know if the entertainments will be the surprise that Marguerite wanted."

Isabel was inwardly shocked that Anne referred to their French benefactor by her first name, even if they were by themselves. On further self evaluation, she realised that she was slightly envious of Anne who had a natural ability of weaving herself into people's affections. She wished that she had that ability. But she couldn't contrive words to manipulate. She was too honest and too respectful of people to flatter for self gain. *Come now,* she scolded herself, *Anne was Anne and she didn't always flatter for gain.*

"The king walked in on the costume designs!"

"Oh, no!" Isabel put a hand to her mouth. "All our weeks of preparation!"

"Oh well, we shall have fun despite it all, I expect."

There was another discrete knock at the door.

A petite maid entered. Raven black, corkscrew ringlets bobbed about her head as she curtsied. Her slight frame could have been made for a bird. She extended a silver platter towards them. "Correspondence from England, Mademoiselles."

Anne reached out and took the letters.

"Merci, Claudette. How are you finding your way around our wardrobes?"

Claudette was new to the châteaux and her duties were the Waiting Ladies wardrobes, overseeing the maintenance and laundry of some ten to fifteen women.

"So many beautiful clothes, Mademoiselle! What a pleasure!"

The maid curtsied again and left. Anne turned the heavy parchments over in her hand.

"One from father and one for you, from your uncle, and one from your cousin Henry." Anne laughed. "I recognise that scrawl anywhere!"

Isabel laughed with her. Over the years, they had shared in Henry's letters, living, laughing and crying with his ordeals back home at Alnwich.

They both settled onto the window seat, side by side.

Silence ensued as they broke the various wax seals and started to read. A crow cawed its lonely cry from a bare copse beyond the châteaux.

Anne burst out loud as her eyes scanned her father's elegant penmanship.

"Oh, *mon deux*!" exclaimed Anne like a true French woman.

"We have been called back home … War with France? How ridiculous! Father will be escorting us back to England within the month! He will be in Paris on business …"

Isabel's eyes darted across her pages written in the bold hand of the Earl of Northumberland. "I am to go into service at the English court as one of Queen Katherine's ladies … pending negotiations on a marriage settlement with a Sir Roland Tavistock who has estates bordering on Alnwich. Oh, my goodness! And my cousin Henry is at court! He is now in Cardinal Wolsey's service as a page …"

Anne looked up, her eyes dreamy. "I am to be the next Countess of Ormond …"

Isabel's face lit up with a genuine smile, her pain, for this moment, forgotten. Joy radiated from her face for Anne like rays from the sun. It was their life's work to land and forge a good marriage.

"Oh, Anne! I'm so happy for you," she hugged her.

Anne hugged her back.

"As I am for you, Isabo!—Lady Tavistock!"

They looked into each other's eyes, clutching at each other's arms, sharing each other's excitement, then both burst out laughing.

They chatted an hour away, talking of all the new possibilities, of their shock and sadness to leave France and their French family so suddenly, of entering into the mysteries of marriage, and of living in England, which now appeared as new and strange as France had to them more than seven years ago.

"Come," said Anne, hauling Isabel to her feet. "We should tell the Duchess of our news."

For the first time since her attack, Isabel felt lightness in her step. As much as she loved it here in France, perhaps going back to England would be the best thing. It will leave behind bad memories and bad people, whoever they were. Yes, a fresh start will be just what was needed and the timing couldn't have been better!

***

Thousands of beeswax candles and hundreds of bodies created a stuffy heat in the large dining hall. The many course dinner in honour of the king's visit was over, and the musicians had struck up a courante to start the evening's revelries. The courante was a slow, formal dance, but in typical French fashion it allowed closeness between partners to the point where lingering touching and even kisses were enjoyed. As it was the first dance there was much play-acting and innuendo to stimulate inhibitions.

Everybody was masked and dressed in their chosen winter deity.

Isabel saw that Anne had paired off with the king for a few steps. The tips of their fingers touched as they performed the intricate toe movements.

"I hear that the moon is about to wane over France and wax over England," said Francois, giving the appearance of concentrating on his footwork. Anne also gave the appearance of deliberating on her steps, though a smile touched her lips. She was dressed as the goddess of the moon, wearing a silver mask, but nothing could disguise the long black hair worn loose, falling freely to her hips.

She shot a glance at the king. "That is true monsieur Dieu du Blanche."

The king was dressed all in white and no amount of disguise could have hidden him either, as he stood head and shoulders above everybody else in the opulent hall.

"That is true," Anne continued. "But the moon waxes and wanes in cycles, does it not? It shall wax over France again, God willing."

They parted to touch fingers with their next round of partners.

Isabel felt wonderful, as light as air as she bowed to her next partner, who stood about her own height, dressed in black.

Their formal goodbyes had been exchanged with the Duchess that afternoon. She and Anne would be riding with an escort first thing in the morning, to be met with Anne's father in Calais. She looked forward to leaving the unpleasantness of the last few months behind. She looked forward to serving Queen Katherine who she had heard was a good Christian queen and loved talented young people about her. She would miss her friends of the Meaux Circle though. Would Queen Katherine allow open speech like the Duchess of Alençon?

Isabel couldn't remember much of England. She had come to France at the age of nine as part of Princess Mary Tudor's bridal retinue, as a "child of honour." She remembered the trauma of separation as the ship left Dover.

She had kept her eyes on the Earl and the Countess of Northumberland, her benefactors and the only parent figures she had ever known, until the sea swallowed them up. Life with its comforting routines and certainties was gone. Although Princess Mary's ladies took her under their wing, it was Anne, another child-of-honour, the same age as herself, who had made life bearable. In the same predicament as her, being far away from home and family, they had stuck together like sisters, even writing letters when they were in different households.

The dance ended with a dramatic flourish from the horns in the open gallery above. Her partner, instead of relinquishing her hand, held it for the next dance, which was a lavolta. She looked at him questioningly but could see nothing through his black mask, depicting a stag, only the occasional glint of light reflecting from his eyes.

He bowed in answer to her look. "Shall I be your quarry, Mademoiselle?"

Isabel relaxed and laughed, for she was indeed dressed as a huntress, with a bow and a quiver of arrows at her back.

"My pleasure, Monsieur le stag," she said easily. "I promise to keep my weapons intact."

"I doubt that," he said smiling roguishly.

Isabel had no time to respond but her heart skipped a beat as her partner swept her off her feet with the first note of music.

Isabel loved the lavolta. It was an energetic dance where, if done in the Italian way, the man lifted the lady above his head. He seemed to know the Italian style of the dance and he held her up with ease. His strength impressed her. He brought her down, slow and controlled, close to his body. She could feel the heat of him as he lowered her to the floor.

She searched his face to find something to recognise him by, but the mask covered everything bar his lips. She glanced at these, trying to take in as much detail as she could without giving way her interest. They were full and well chiselled and set above a firm square chin with a close clipped beard. She didn't recognise him from her acquaintances from the French Court. She studied his hands, warm and gentle upon hers. They were tapered, square and strong at the ends.

They swirled around each other back-to-back, arms entwining in the air. Isabel's eyes shone, not only with the physical exhilaration of the dance, but also with the anticipation of good things for the future. As the men moved up one to another partner and an elf king took her hand, she forgot the stag. Her mind quickly flew to the morrow. *I go home in the morning! I'll see Henry again! How exciting!*

Marriage. Children. What will this Sir Roland Tavistock be like? Would he be kind to her? Would there be love?

Marriage, she knew, was mainly a business contract between families. She couldn't imagine her uncle letting her marry for love. As his ward, it would be her duty to repay him his kindnesses by being obedient with whomever he had chosen for her. And she would be dutiful and obedient because that's part of who she was.

She found herself back with the stag as the lavolta finished with arms raised in a clap. They bowed to each other, smiling and slightly breathless. Isabel felt invigorated.

"Some refreshment, Mademoiselle?" inquired the stag.

"Please."

Her masked partner guided her to a refreshment table. She took side-glances of him, intrigued. She was disappointed again. All she could see was his dark brown curls on a white cambric collar.

A goblet of wine was produced before her. She accepted it and took a large mouthful. The smooth liquid slid down easily and warmed her insides.

She smiled up into her partner's eyes. She still couldn't see their colour. The mask obscured everything accept the glint of reflected candlelight on their liquid surface.

He offered her his arm. "A stroll, mademoiselle? It is so very hot in here."

Isabel acquiesced with a nod of the head, feeling the sheen of perspiration upon her face and neck.

"Shall we finish our drinks here?" he asked.

Without waiting for a reply, her partner finished his wine in one swallow. Isabel stared at him in momentary surprise, and then consented to do the same. It would be better to stroll unencumbered.

She downed her wine in two long mouthfuls.

Outside the night air was icy but refreshing. Their frozen breath drifted like white gauze about their heads.

Muted conversation, sprinkled with the occasional laughter drifted to them from other couples and small groups wandering across the frosted balconies.

Isabel looked up. Heavy clouds lumbered across the full moon, their fat bellies pregnant with more snow. They compressed themselves onto the horizon.

"More snow," said Isabel.

"Yes. Are you cold? Would you like to go in now?" her new friend asked.

For the first time, she noticed a faint accent in his French. She looked up at him again to see if she could read more. As she did so, her head swam.

Alarmed, she instantly dug her fingers into his arm. She stumbled and almost fell as she tried to shake her head of the dizziness. A strong arm was already at her waist. She went to apologise, but her lips and tongue felt like they belonged to someone else. They became slow and thick and the words wouldn't form.

His face spun before her as he leaned forward to help.

Gaining control of her faculties was now taken over by panic and nausea.

Her struggle was short.

She collapsed into his waiting arms.

CHAPTER SIX

Clouet Abbey, Normandy, France

He hadn't thought of her as a person. He never did think of them as people with their own lives. He had been taught not to from a very early age. But he hadn't been with a woman for a long time and he had never been this close to a gentlewoman, almost nobility, before. Her clean fragrance invaded his senses. Her soft, supple, refined body, with skin like a baby's, had stirred his manhood. It surprised him. He had tried to brush the feelings and thoughts away. He had a job to do. His clan were counting on him.

He looked down at her now and hesitated. Her soft, full lips, slack in unconsciousness, had parted to reveal even, healthy teeth reflecting pearl in the moonlight. *The product of a privileged life,* he thought bitterly. Her breath trailed out like silk into the frozen air. Despite his bitterness, he felt an overwhelming urge to kiss her, to taste the softness, the sweetness, and the cleanliness that surely would take him to that wondrous place of fulfilment and release.

Suddenly, the vision for his mission crumbling, he threw caution to the wind and he broke the rule.

He could hear his father's voice as he levered the mask off her face. He knew it would weaken him but he told himself that he was strong enough to take it.

He was tired of rules and self-discipline. What was it all for in the long run? He loved his father and understood what drove

44

him. It drove him too, but it had been too long, too long without warmth, too long without a woman's touch, too long away from home. Where was his home now? He'd been to so many places to do his father's bidding that he didn't know who he was anymore or where he belonged.

"Don't get close to the subject. Don't see them as people. As soon as you do, you will be undone!' His father's voice echoed around in his head.

He didn't care anymore. He just wanted something for himself. He wanted his soul to be soothed. A sigh escaped unnoticed from his lips as he gazed at the face before him. There he saw vulnerability, innocence and beauty. It was something he recognised, but subconsciously didn't think he was worthy of being a part of.

He replaced her mask gently unaware that in those few seconds, a strategy, months in the planning, began its slow but sure demise.

***

Murmuring intonations brought her up, out of her black void.

Noises emitting from her throat alerted those supporting her that she was coming to.

Her eyelids were still too heavy to open but the sounds around her were getting sharper by the minute.

Strong arms, both from the left and the right, were holding her up. The words being spoken were in Latin. They were questions. Someone answered in English. More Latin. Someone at her side jabbed her in the ribs. Her eyes flew open as she cried out.

She could hardly see. The lighting was very dim.

She tried to take stock of where she was and what was happening.

Before her stood a dishevelled priest. His robes were dirty and his sparse hair stood out in all directions. The alcohol and garlic emitting from his mouth almost made her gag.

She twisted her head away.

The priest was very nervous.

Suddenly her left hand was grabbed and a ring was being pushed onto her third finger. Shocked, she realised that she stood before the altar of a church ... and she was getting married!

The priest finished his hasty, slurred lines with, "I now pronounce you man and wife before God. Amen."

Isabel tried to pull away from her captors in protest. This wasn't happening. She was dreaming. A nightmare! Her muddied mind was aware that her fresh, awaited future was now slipping away into some sort of madness. Some papers were hastily signed then sickly sweet wine was being plied to her lips. She choked it down, coughing it from her lungs. Her head spun out as she felt herself tumbling back into oblivion.

An older man gave directions without sentiment.

He left with a parting comment that was supposed to encourage. "You can leave your brother to me. He won't interfere. I'll see to it."

He left very briskly with a man who had held her at her left side.

The other man that stood at her right lifted her from her feet and whisked her away along an unlit corridor.

The priest was left alone. He tottered about the altar in a drunken daze and then fell plum onto his backside wondering where he was.

Deeper into the labyrinth of the ruined abbey, the man, with Isabel in his arms, hesitated at a turn in his route.

He looked at the little oak door at the end of a dark corridor to his left. There, a horse and groom waited for him on the other side.

After another moment's hesitation, he kept going forward until he came to a narrow flight of spiral stairs on his right. He ascended, the soot on the stones bearing witness to why this part of the abbey was not inhabited. As he came into the tower room, moonlight flooded the charred floor. A fire had eaten away half the turret.

He would have been happy to lay Isabel on the floor but he was delighted to see a cot pushed against the inner wall. It was damp and the edges encrusted with ice crystals, but it would be serviceable enough.

He set to work.

His actions pulled Isabel up from the depths of her drugged abyss. She was aware of being tugged. Hands were gripping her waist then thighs. A voice was speaking English again. Her eyelids flickered as she tried to break the surface of her consciousness.

The young man didn't see. His head was raised toward the celestial display of heaven through the dark clouds.

"I can't let him take what's mine. I don't trust him. I have to make sure … God forgive me, but it's for your own good!" Grunt.

The tugging, Isabel realised, was not tugging at all, but penetration! Her legs were wide apart and he was violating her. Isabel's shock and horror knew no bounds!

She had heard of things like this, but never once dreamed that it should happen to her. Her mind refused to own it. Anger rose within but her body couldn't respond.

His riding her came to a peak. She felt his body shudder its release.

Spent, he sat back and collected his breath.

Isabel tried to break through her drug-induced fog by forcing her eyes open. They were so unbelievably heavy.

She felt him peel off her mask. He seemed to linger and then she felt him trace the side of her face from her brow to her mouth with a finger.

She wanted to shake him off. At last a moan escaped from the back of her throat.

She felt him climb off her and straighten her skirts.

Isabel's eyes finally fluttered open. Immediately she tried to push herself up. She winced as a hot gush of fluid burned between her legs, wetting her undergarments.

Her rapist knelt before her. It was her dance partner with the stag mask.

"Here. Drink!" he insisted angrily. He thrust a small vial into her face.

She shook her head, moaning, trying to fend him off. Her movements were as weak as a newborn kitten. She felt like she was trying to wade through honey.

"No … No …"

Her bottom lip trembled and the tears pooling in her eyes began to roll down her cheeks.

Despite her own predicament, Isabel could tell the man was uncomfortable in his skin by his shifting stance. He lifted his masked face to the sky, as he appeared to struggle with inner conflicts.

"It's all right," his eyes avoided hers as he tried to placate her. "We are married now. Please understand. I had to consummate the marriage to make it valid, to keep you from him—to keep you from harm."

She understood his words, but she couldn't understand why any of this had to happen.

She tried to reach out and implore him to undo his actions. Her voice was weak and she sounded breathless.

"But I am to be married in England. My … my uncle …"

His voice cut her off, his venom barely controlled. "Yes! I'm well aware of your uncle!"

Without another word, he decisively plied the vial to her lips, tipping its contents down the back of her throat.

Isabel choked and coughed again as she fought for breath.

"Don't worry. All will be well," said her captor tersely.

Isabel got no comfort from his words. She could feel the effects of the drug pulling her into its black, numbing arms. She didn't want to fight it anymore. She no longer cared. She wanted to sleep and never wake up.

She held the eyes of the masked stag until the blackness consumed her. Amazingly, she could see them. Just as there was a break in the clouds and the bright moonlight revealed, another golden light grew from the side to bathe them both. She heard a soft voice far off in the distance. The golden light grew. It was as he turned his head to answer to the voice that she saw his eyes. They were the colour of amber, mesmerising amber. The colour of amber held up to the firelight.

***

Her name was being called from far away. She could barely hear it with the storm that raged around her. Violent waves rocked the boat. She turned to get a better grip as the rain and sea spray lashed her face. Blinking, she tried to clear the water from her eyes. In a moment of clarity, she saw a wall of water rise before her. Immediately she knew that she wouldn't survive it. There was nothing she could do. As she watched, the wave, its size beyond comprehension, tipped the boat, tossing her into its salty, cold depths. The icy slap of water on skin at velocity woke her up.

She awoke to being rocked awake in her own cot.

"Isabo! Isabo! Wake up!"

Isabel's relief was huge. Only a bad dream! She tried to focus on the face, which had planted itself in front of hers.

Anne.

"Isabo!" Anne shook her shoulders again. "Isabo. Wake up. You should be dressed. We leave in one hour."

Isabel groaned. Her head throbbed something terrible and her throat felt like a goat had slept in it. "Water ..." she croaked.

Anne threw back her head and laughed. "Too much wine, methinks!"

Nevertheless, a cool goblet touched Isabel's lips and she slaked her thirst. She was helped to sit up and some bread and cold beef were thrust into her hands.

"You look awful," Anne commented as she helped Claudette pack the last of their wardrobe.

Isabel didn't bother to reply. She ate despite her ragged feelings. The food tasted terrible. She felt very disoriented, like she'd lived a hundred years in the last twenty-four hours.

Nothing felt right. Her body, her feelings and her surroundings felt like they belonged to someone else.

Perhaps it was just the lingering effects of the bad nightmare. As she sat up to dust the crumbs of breakfast from her coverlet, a dull burning sensation flared between her legs.

She sat stock still as fear paralysed her again. All the past night's memories flooded into her consciousness. So, it was no dream. Isabel felt devastated as the nightmare of her real circumstances overrode the fading horror of her dream.

She leaned forward, drew her knees up and hugged them to her chest. Numbness veiled over her soul as she refused to let the memories venture out any further into her mind.

She was going home today and that would be an end to it! He or they wouldn't find her again!

Isabel tossed all negative thoughts aside, lifted her coverlet and rose from her bed. The sudden movement made her head throb. She held it in her hands until the pain abated and the black spots in front of her eyes disappeared.

Her mouth was dry again like she'd stuffed it with sawdust. Claudette was instantly there with more water and a travelling gown over her forearm. She dressed Isabel in silence with quick nimble fingers.

As Isabel stretched her hands forth to receive her sleeves, she saw the wedding ring. Another witness to the truth of the night before!

The ruby, like a large drop of malevolent blood set in gold, glowed sullenly, brooding.

Isabel ripped her arm away from Claudette's ministrations and flung the ring across the room. It pinged off the lead casing on the window and fell spinning on the floor to disappear under a cot. She rubbed her arm as if a snake had bitten her.

Claudette paused momentarily then continued her fastenings without an exclamation or a sideways glance.

Isabel appreciated Claudette's integrity in her serving. No doubt she'd seen worse character displayed over the years of serving the Duchess's waiting women. Maybe.

Finally, with hair coiffed and netted, Isabel lifted her soft kid gloves from Claudette's hands and followed her out of the room.

Out into her new future, which she realised, she was determined to have!

CHAPTER SEVEN

Spring, Westminster Palace, England 1522

Spring had nudged out winter early this year. Not that Isabel could see the whole bounty of it on water steps of Westminster Palace by the River Thames. Looking up, she could see the duck-egg blue sky dotted with clouds tinged with yellow, floating like dollops of clotted cream. Along the banks, she saw primroses and violets making room for themselves where they could, between habitations and causeways of men. On the opposite bank, willows trailed their new verdant fingers on the downstream currant. The river itself was a busy concourse of business and pleasure craft. The sounds of oars dipping, rising and slapping, together with other soft sounds from the river, men talking and swans calling, lulled Isabel like a soporific. She had never felt so tired in her life before.

She had been up since five that morning and most mornings in the past three weeks, retching into a bucket in the stables so as not to disturb anyone.

All the queen's gentle ladies she roomed with only knew that she was very devout, rising so early to prayers.

Isabel was worried. Part of her tried to tell herself that she must have eaten something bad and that it would pass soon.

The other half knew the truth of her situation.

It was too traumatic to meditate on and she refused to think about it. When the thought popped up like a duck on water, Isabel pushed it down again.

She had asked to be excused from her duties this afternoon, pleading a headache, which wasn't far wrong. She was waiting to rendezvous with her cousin, Henry Percy.

A missive delivered to her this morning stated the time and place. "At the water steps down from the palace," was his familiar scrawl that she had see slowly mature over the years. She had not seen him since she had arrived back in England and was keenly looking forward it.

Cardinal Wolsey usually visited court on Sundays and with him came Henry who whiled away the hours with the queen and her ladies.

How we both must have changed, Isabel thought—*not children anymore.* She smiled to herself as pictures of the past took her down memory lane: She and Henry sparring in Alnwichs tilt yard, rabbit catching on the other side of River Aln, galloping the moors on their ponies, pulling pranks on the tutor they had both shared for math, music and Latin.

That was all the life she remembered. Apparently her mother was a distant cousin to the Earl of Northumberland and when her parents died, he did the noble thing and brought her into his fold, to the only family she ever knew.

Aunt Catherine, the Countess of Northumberland, had always been very kind. She was always ready with an instructional word and the occasional loving touch. The earl was too distant and busy for a little girl to form a relationship with. He appeared like a king to her. He dressed like one and carried out his authority like one.

She had bonded with Henry as naturally as if he'd been her own sibling. The other children were too small to have much to do with, they being still in the nursery when she had left for France.

Ah, Henry, how I look forward to seeing you, sighed Isabel leaning back on the trunk of a tree.

A waft of earthy mud and rotting waterweeds assaulted her nose as the wind picked up from across the river. Isabel's stomach churned, pushing its contents up into the bottom of her throat. She forced some leftover manchet roll from breakfast into her mouth to still it.

Some children waved to her from a public wherry going down river. She slid around the trunk of the tree, wrapping her cloak around herself. She didn't want to advertise who she was, or where she'd come from. London could be a very unsavoury place for the unwary. Many beggars and people of no fixed abode came and went about the palace. The palace forecourt was always filled with people loitering for food from the kitchens or alms from the wealthy.

Isabel laughed bitterly at herself at that thought. One thought oneself safe in royal residences as guards, armed with halberds and sheathed daggers, stood to attention at just about every door.

It didn't stop what happened to me, thought Isabel, her mood suddenly sullen.

She finished her bread, staring glumly into the river.

The duck of reality rose once again from the water of her depressed consciousness. Too tired to control her mind, Isabel let the truth of her situation wash and eddy where it was most painful.

She was pregnant—by the masked man with the amber eyes.

What was going to happen to her now? She felt totally trapped. There was no way out. She would give birth and be an outcast from society. She would have to give the child up … She would live in an abbey for the rest of her days …

The pain that she would cause the Northumberlands couldn't be borne! A wave of emotional pain washed over her. It was so intense that it felt physical.

There would be no marriage to this Sir Roland Tavistock. No more children, for who would have a ruined woman with no family or dowry?

Tears trembled in her eyes, magnifying the blues and greys in her irises like river stones beneath a natural spring. She felt shame and guilt. It was tempting to fall into its strong currant and let it take her where it will, maybe to the bottom of the

Thames, but a little part of her rose up in furious anger. It wasn't her fault! How dare he? How dare this masked man ruin her life and take no responsibility for it? How dare he?

Isabel shook with anger now. Her hands balled into tight fists. *God help me,* she thought as her face became as hard as iron. *God help me; if he was here, I'd kill him!*

She stopped her internal ravings as a thought dawned on her.

God, I haven't given you much thought over the last little while, have I? Listen to me raging on, committing murder with my thoughts. I have been so consumed with my problems, I haven't even given you a moment's thought. Forgive me, father. Help me, God. Help me in my distress.

Her anger passed; a certain peace settled on Isabel but her thoughts kept running.

Where was this husband of hers? Was he truly her husband? There were no witnesses to the ordeal, were there? Where was he? Did she really want to know? Would he come for her? Did she want him to? Her head spun out with questions that had no answers. It was like looking into the depths of the Thames where shadows beneath could be discerned but nothing was identified.

Her stomach cramped suddenly and intensely. Isabel grabbed her lower abdomen, her whole body tense. After some minutes the pain eased and Isabel began to breathe normally again. She let her body slide down the trunk of the tree, her face very white.

After a while, realising that all was well for the meantime, the temptation to nap couldn't be fought. Isabel let herself drift off.

"Tibby. Tibby? Tibby, are you well?"

Isabel opened her eyes into the face of a grown-up Henry Percy. Handsome, chiselled features had replaced the soft round lines of his face as a boy. But the same compassionate blue eyes bore into hers with concern.

"Oh, Henry. I must have dozed for a moment." She smiled. "I haven't had anybody call me Tibby in years."

Tibby or Tibs was a derivative of Isabel in the North Country.

Everybody at Alnwich had called her Tibby.

"Is the queen so demanding then?" he asked, raising his eyebrows in a mock tease.

Isabel felt an old but familiar response of exasperation rising up in her. She had forgotten how they used to tease each other. She couldn't help but take the bait. "No ... you goose!"

Henry helped Isabel sit up as he knelt down beside her. They gazed appreciatively at each other and then Isabel tried to fix herself up by pushing away a loose strand of hair and wiping the corner of her mouth.

"No drool," smirked Henry.

Isabel playfully hit him. "I see you haven't changed then."

She straightened her pearl-rimmed hood and gave him her hand to help her up. "Let's have a look at you, Lord Percy."

Henry stood with her and profiled left then right and pulled a face.

Isabel laughed a laugh that bubbled up straight from the belly, dispersing her insecurities that lay beneath the surface of her emotions. She forced down her deepest fears and found that she was able to portray a lightness of heart convincingly.

Henry laughed, too.

"I can see you haven't changed a bit, Lord Percy!"

"But you," said Henry lifting his eyebrows at her clothes and deportment. "You are looking quite frenchified. Your English even has a French accent! And you've grown ..." he looked at her breasts, "some extra bits!"

Isabel laughed again, then took his arm and led him along the riverbank. "How like a boy cousin! Let's walk."

Henry obliged. He was now almost a head taller than she and very handsome with it. His blond hair hung almost over his eyes to curl loosely at his neck. He still had his easy smile.

They spoke of old times and of new. Arm in arm, they laughed and reminisced, enjoying the privacy of each other's company. At court, privacy was a luxury. Even the king and queen were constantly in the company of others, night and day.

"So, you are to be married soon, Father says. To old Sir Roland?" said Henry.

"Old? Sir Roland? You know him?"

Henry gave Isabel an apologetic smile. "I'm sorry it couldn't have been somebody our age. You probably won't have to worry about being bedded though. He's far too old for that. Sir Roland Tavistock's land backs our own to the north and you know Father; he's always looking for a way to advance himself."

Isabel tried her best to hide her disappointment and pressed herself to say the right thing.

"Yes. Well, I'm grateful to him. He certainly didn't have to go to all the lengths he has for me: taking me in, making me his ward, sending me to France, finding me a place at court and now, a husband."

"Well, as much as you have benefited, my father will have benefited more. He always has some ulterior motive. As much as we'd love to think the best of him, the truth is, he only cares about himself."

Isabel couldn't ignore the bitterness in his voice. She chose to change the subject. "So, tell me more about my intended."

Henry glanced up at a couple of swallows darting by as he gathered his thoughts.

"Well, his wife died about five years ago and the two daughters from that marriage are older than you. They are well-settled, producing heirs for the families they have married into, but both father and Tavistock hope for a new heir, to benefit them both. It'll be alright Tibs; he's so old, he'll die on you before anything happens like King Louis did to Mary Tudor." Henry patted her arm. "You'll be released within a few months and then marry who you want. Or not if you choose to."

Isabel thought about that. Yes, that wasn't a bad future. Widows had a lot of freedom. And if she was left a wealthy widow she could really enjoy her freedom. She allowed herself to dream, pushing her pregnancy and the uncertain changes it would bring to them all deep down to where it barely made a murmur.

They walked on for a bit in silence, very comfortable in it, despite the years that had past.

"And what about you, Henry? Does 'Henry the Magnificent' have someone in mind for his heir?" asked Isabel lightly, using his father's nickname given to him by others who knew him for his love of pomp and ceremony.

"Yes," said Henry dryly, but not in answer to her question. He wasn't impressed. "Father will no doubt have somebody in mind. He's not one to leave an important issue like that to chance. Well, important issues where he is concerned."

"What do you mean Henry? You don't want to marry?"

"I shall marry," he said with obvious distaste. "That decision is as sure as the river Thames continues to flow to the sea. My station in life requires it. I just hope it is someone I can like.

No, it's not that particularly. It's just that over the years while you have been away, it seems I am unable to please my father, in any way, Tibs. I despair of our relationship."

Isabel furrowed the perfectly winged arches of her brow.

"I don't understand Henry. Has he ill-treated you?"

A hard look glazed over Henry's eyes. "He hates me. That is ill treatment enough. I am nothing to him. His own first-born son! He never listens to me. Whatever I do is not good enough. It can always be done better."

They had both slowed to a halt and gazed at the river, alone with their thoughts. There seemed nothing she could say to ease his heartache. From Isabel's point of view, if it weren't for Henry's father, she wouldn't even be here. He had brought her up as one of his own. True, she didn't know the earl like Henry did, but surely his actions of guidance and provision spoke about love and caring. Isabel decided not to say anything. What Henry was feeling was obviously very real to him.

Eventually she did think of one thing. Picking up his hand and giving it a big squeeze she said. "I do love you, Henry. You're the brother I never had."

Tears shone in Henry's eyes at Isabel's affirmation of him.

Henry kissed her on the cheek, suddenly perky. "And you are a wonderful cousin. I have missed you terribly. Writing letters never quite cut it and I've had to find a new sparring partner, only to be been beaten to a pulp! Don't you dare disappear again or I shall be maimed for life!"

"Oh, Henry!" Isabel cried in affectionate exasperation. She hugged him then grabbed his velvet cap he carried in his hands and tossed it into the wind.

She was rewarded with a look of surprise. Henry gave her a playful shove in return and then ran to retrieve it.

CHAPTER EIGHT

Queen's Presence Chamber, Westminster

"Ah, the young Percys!"

Queen Katherine acknowledged their arrival into her Presence Chamber, despite being in the middle of a card game, her voice still heavy with a Spanish accent even though she had lived in England for more than twenty years.

They stood at the doorway hung with rich tapestry to keep out the damp and chill that pervaded the old castle from the river. Their faces were flushed and their eyes sparkled from the exercise of almost running back up the gardens from the Thames.

"You have been missed, both of you. Come join us for a hand of cards. Do you play cards, Lord Percy?"

Henry led the way, walking between groups of people scattered around the room, to their Sovereign Lady.

Henry bowed over the queen's hand, stiff with jewels

Katherine smiled warmly at Henry. Her once celebrated beauty, Isabel noted, was beginning to look tired. Her golden skin, touched with peach, much expounded upon in her youth, had lost its firmness and there were strands of grey in her auburn hair.

They had both heard that her last pregnancy was not a pregnancy at all, but the onset of the change of life. *The queen must be crushed with disappointment with no male heir to inherit the throne,* thought Isabel, *and now, never likely to be.*

But you'd never tell from her demeanour. Isabel was impressed with the way the queen carried herself. It was like the dignity of a statesman. She had heard from others that her royal bearing never wavered no matter what situation she was presented with, a true princess of the blood.

"Some, Your Majesty," Henry replied. "But I fear I would make a poor partner."

"We shall see," said the queen, not letting him slip away easily and patted at the empty stool beside her. "Come join me."

There were several hands of cards taking place. Indeed, the queen's presence chamber was abuzz with people taking their pleasure at the end of the day with board games, card games, discussing literature and playing music.

The queen focused on Isabel who still stood demurely before her. She gave her a generous smile and suddenly without warning, her eyes misted with love and sentimentality.

"Isabel, I love that name. It was my mother's, you know? Isabella. Woman of that name are destined for great things. Are you better now? The other little maid who came back with you from France, Mistress Anne Boleyn, said you were unwell."

Isabel curtsied low and respectfully to Queen Katherine. "I'm much revived, Your Majesty."

"I'm glad to hear it." The queen's tone had changed and she became the one who must be obeyed. "I hear you rise very early to Mass, Mistress Isabel. We are all devoted to our Lord and Lady, but such devotions that make us ill are of no use to anyone. Do I make myself understood?"

Isabel's mouth went dry with fear at the dismissal. She swallowed the reprimand as best she could and kept her face to the floor so that no one could see it redden with embarrassment.

"Yes, Your Majesty," she whispered, wondering if her secret had been discovered.

Isabel quickly found an empty stool behind Henry's and sat face down, pretending to brush out invisible creases in her intricately embroidered underskirt. Henry reached out his hand behind his seat and gave her knee a comforting squeeze. She grabbed his hand and squeezed it hard in return, grateful that she wasn't alone.

The queen's table was dealt a new hand. With much laughter and bluff calling, the queen won again. "Yes, I see we'll have to hone your card skills, Lord Percy!" the queen crowed with delight.

Another hand was dispensed. Isabel's eyes wandered the room for Anne. She had been very surprised to see Anne at court last week. Apparently, there was not going to be any betrothal with the Butlers. Anne had put on a brave face, saying what would she do in the wilds of Ireland anyway? She had been sent to court to assist her sister Mary. Mary had the king's eye, Anne had said, and probably more besides! She couldn't see Anne or Mary.

Suddenly, a door from behind the queen burst open loudly. All turned to see the ruckus.

Yeomen of the Guard standing to attention at the main entrance to the chamber took a step forward with their gilt halberds at the ready. They abruptly pulled up. It was the king with his boon companions, Charles Brandon, Edward Neville, the Guildford brothers and William Fitzwilliam. They were in good spirits. Noisy and demonstrative, they made their way to the queen's side.

The queen, initially shocked, feigned great surprise at this small unorthodox band making its way towards her.

Isabel had heard that this type of entrance was typical of the King of England. She was even more amazed at the queen who always played up to these so-called surprises. Isabel didn't know if in the same position, she would have had the patience. Why did the King of England want his vanity stroked in this way? He was a man, not a boy. And why did the queen allow it? She didn't understand it, but she knew her place and remained silent.

She had to admit, they were magnificent in their play-acting and everybody was highly amused.

As Isabel looked on with everybody else, she immediately regretted her former thoughts.

Katherine had changed from a queen overseeing her subjects, to a young lover in front of her husband. Katherine's eyes softened and now shone with tears of unshed emotion at this sudden attention from him.

My goodness, thought Isabel. *The queen is in love with her husband as a young maid with a youth. Is that possible?*

It must be, for the evidence was right before her.

Maybe any attention was great attention from her husband because after the doctor's diagnosis of menopause, relations between them had been noticeably strained. Isabel had heard that the physicians said to Henry that his wife's continual fasting had not been good for breeding and had brought on the change of life early. The king, apparently, had left the interview steaming!

Since then, Isabel had noticed more than one moment where the king's eyes had narrowed on Katherine. Blame from him, Isabel was sure, boring into her for lack of living sons.

But now, for this moment, Henry knelt before her in front of everyone.

"My love," he crooned and presented her with a rose and a velvet pouch of coins. "My winnings from tennis. It belongs to you. You so inspired me, that I was victorious! And the first rose of the season for the rose of my life."

He turned and faced everybody with a winning smile, ever the showman. Everybody clapped and cheered. He was their Adonis, their fair Octavus and the embodiment of kingship. Facing Katherine, he rose, also helping her to rise and in front of the whole court kissed her chastely on the lips.

Katherine looked thrilled at her husband's actions, affirming her status in his affections before all, despite all. Isabel saw her closest lady in waiting, Maria Willoughby, nee de Salinas, press a lawn kerchief into her hands for discreet use when the moment was right.

The king then raised his hand, demanding seats, wine and music. As the presence chamber hummed again with excited chatter, Henry and Isabel, delighted not to be the centre of attention, left hand-in-hand, unseen.

CHAPTER NINE

Shrovetide, York Place, London

A few days later during the Shrovetide entertainments, Henry Percy saw her for the first time. She was like no one he'd ever seen before. It was a glimpse of her long, silky, black hair, falling like a veil, as she was lifted in the Italian style of a fast moving lavolta, which caught his eye. It shone like polished onyx.

She was lifted above everybody in the middle of the dance floor. Henry Percy twisted this way and that, to get a better look. He was entranced by her unconscious, sinuous elegance. After the dance had finished, he saw her being escorted back to her seat by a young, very handsome, dark-haired man. They were quite familiar with one another, laughing and touching. He had never seen anybody so mysterious or sophisticated, yet she appeared no older than he. It was the darkness of her colouring and the grace of her person that caught his attention. He felt a stirring in his soul. She was dressed like no other in the room. The cut of her gown was simplicity itself.

It hugged her reed-slim figure and pushed up her dainty breasts. She wore no jewellery except a choker of pearls at her long, very touchable throat. Everybody around her appeared gaudy and frumpy following the queen's Spanish mode of dress, with heavy fabric and square, blunt lines of design.

They had seated themselves next to Mary Carey, who Henry had heard, had become the king's mistress.

Henry leaned over to Isabel, who sat beside him nibbling on sugared violets and marchpane.

"Tibby, who is she?"

"She?" said Isabel, not interested enough to look up from her busy fingers.

"That vision beside the Lady Mary Carey."

Isabel looked up and followed Henry's line of sight. "Oh, that's Anne," she said surprised that she had seen her at last. Unaware of Henry's tight breathing, she rabbited on excitedly. "My Anne. You know, Anne Boleyn who I was with in France. Oh, how wonderful! Come on!"

Isabel shook the excess sugar from her fingers and began to stand up. "Let me introduce you to her. Well, you have both been introduced through our letters for years. I suspect she has been so busy helping to organise the revels tonight that she hasn't had a moment to draw breath. She's very talented in that way. The Duchess of Alençon knew she had a natural talent for these sorts of things and had Anne constantly at her side."

Henry never took his eyes off Anne, remaining seated.

"Anne Boleyn. Yes, but I never … Oh, of course. She sits with her sister Mary Boleyn … ah … Carey."

"Yes, you goose. And that's their brother George." Isabel dipped her sticky fingers in a bowl of rose water on the table, and then shook them dry. "Come, Henry. Let me introduce you to her."

Isabel took Henry's hand. She flashed him an impatient grin. "Come, come."

Henry suddenly baulked in fear. He felt very shy. What was he going to say to this person who appeared to be totally out of his league in sophistication and courtly ways? He had known of Anne through Isabel's correspondence while she was in France but this was different. He knew her and he didn't know her. He dragged his feet trying to gain some time. He felt his mouth go dry and sweat develop on his palms.

Moments later, they stood behind the handsome Boleyn trio. Henry stood behind Isabel dying a thousand deaths.

Isabel rested a few fingers on Anne's shoulder. Anne spun around. Surprise and delight lit up her face. "Isabel!"

Her name came out in her usual French pronunciation of *Isabo*.

Henry broke out in another wave of nervous sweat. *God, how can I speak to her? She's beyond anything I've ever known!*

Henry, Mary and George looked on as Isabel and Anne hugged. Isabel pulled away.

"You must be pleased, Anne. It is all a great success. I must say, it took no time at all for Cardinal Wolsey to invest in your talents."

"My reputation goes before me. What can I say?" said Anne giving a display of total confidence in who she was and her abilities.

Suddenly and crushingly, Isabel spoke.

"Anne. I'd like to introduce my cousin, Lord Henry Percy. Henry, Mistress Anne Boleyn."

Anne looked up as Henry took her hand. His heavy blond bangs swung over his eyes as he bent down to kiss it. He murmured something in French, which he thought might be appropriate. When he raised his head he experienced a slight feeling of intoxication as he fell into the dark, dewy depths of her eyes. Like pools of excitement, they seemed to invite him in. He felt sick and ecstatic at the same time.

Anne smiled; her voice was like dark silk, husky and low with a definite French inflection.

He died another thousand deaths.

"Ah, the infamous Lord Percy. We've known each other for a long time, I think? Almost a decade on parchment and now we finally meet."

Henry looked up shyly through his blond lashes. "Indeed," he said, wishing he could think of something debonair to say.

Sensing Henry's shyness, Isabel interrupted, almost too brightly. "Ah – Henry, this is Mary Carey and George Boleyn. I'm not sure if you know each other."

Henry bowed to both of them, loathe to tear his attention away from Anne. They all had the same dark eyes as their father, but Mary's colouring was like honey. Golden curls framed a cinnamon and cream complexion then fell in a fetching tumble to her waist. He could see the attraction for their king.

A fast-moving galliard had started. George started to tap his feet.

"Come on, Mary," he said, pulling his sister up. "Show us how you beguiled the king!"

Laughing at being pulled onto the floor in such an undignified manner, Mary spun away with her brother.

Isabel was laughing, too, and used the moment to push Henry against Anne to encourage him to act. A quick exchange of looks empowered Henry into action.

Henry bowed again to Anne. "May I?"

"Indeed. Let's," said Anne with a provocative sideways glance at him as she put her cool hand in his.

Utterly amazed at this turns of events, Henry led Anne out onto the floor.

She said yes! She said yes, his soul sung within. The most beautiful woman in the room was dancing with him!

Although on the outside he appeared completely composed, almost aloof, he proceeded cautiously, not wanting any social or personal blunder to colour her perception of him. This was somebody he wanted to impress—or at the very least, not make a fool of himself in front of her.

During the dance, Henry drank her in under the privacy of his lowered lashes. He held her like Venetian glass, feasting on the delicacy of her and of her touch, which was beginning to leave him breathless. Her smile melted his insides. He wanted to dwell there forever. They promised him all his dreams come true.

***

The king was delighted when the next dance found him opposite his lover. He held her close when he could.

"What is it like being Mistress Carey?" Henry's eyes twinkled with innuendo.

Henry spoke of her recent marriage to one of his gentlemen of the chamber, William Carey.

Mary shrugged, exposing her rounded, white shoulders. "Not as exciting as being Mary, the king's partner on the dance floor, Your Grace," and she gave him a saucy grin.

"Ha! I thought not!" laughed Henry out loud, his ego well plumped. Suddenly he became serious. "It's good for your children to have a father and a name, is it not?" He wanted to make sure that any bastard child that she should bear him would be protected in matrimony.

Mary pouted a pretty pout, knowing its effect on Henry.

"You wench!" he grinned, and pinched her bottom, his hand hidden from view in the depths of her skirts.

Anne and Henry passed Mary and the king on the dance floor.

"There goes my sister," offered Mary. "She is back from France after all these years."

"Where?" inquired Henry, looking for a fair young woman like Mary before him.

"There. Black hair. Dancing with Lord Percy."

There was only one woman in the room with flowing sable hair unencumbered by nets or hoods and Henry spied her straight away.

She was nothing the king expected. Mesmerised, his eyes followed her. Dark and willowy, she exuded a sensuality and grace that Henry had not experienced in a woman before. Black, almond-shaped eyes glowed in her creamy oval face. Her lips opened in laughter and, displaying dainty white teeth, were naturally pigmented with the colour of roses. It was like comparing a bubbly, frothy cider in Mary, to a rich red wine, which had velvet depths he couldn't explain, in Anne. Had they come from the same womb?

His older brother, Arthur, came quickly to mind. Yes, siblings could be like chalk and cheese, he reminded himself. Arthur, having their father's dour looks and temperament was quiet, submissive and sickly. Henry and his sisters, Margaret and Mary, had inherited their mother's looks, all red, gold and bonny.

Yes, he reminisced, a stranger would never think that Arthur and I had been brothers.

The dance finished and the king, to his embarrassment, realised that he had been caught staring at Anne. He recovered quickly, by raising both of Mary's hands to his mouth to kiss and returning her to her seat.

Distracted and not knowing why, Henry returned absent-mindedly to his place next to Katherine. His eyes roamed the crowd to get a glimpse …

He was beyond noticing Katherine's white knuckles clenched on the arms of her chair of state. Her usually smiling mouth, even if it was painted on by sheer will, was compressed into a thin white line.

***

Anne Boleyn found herself enjoying Henry Percy's presence as the course of the evening progressed. Towards the end of the evening, she realised that she had totally relaxed with him. He was kind and gentle and had a wonderful sense of humour. She was surprised to find that she had forgotten to apply her beguiling charm with flattering wit and flirtatious glances.

She had really enjoyed herself. It was a feeling of freedom, which was strange because she had never thought of herself as being in any sort of prison.

She pulled herself out of her reverie and tried to ply herself to the conversation that was at her table.

Jane Parker, George's betrothed, had joined them at their table. They sat dissecting the evening's entertainments.

Jane, Mary and Anne had been dancers with Mary Tudor, the king's sister, now the Duchess of Suffolk, hidden in a model castle called Chateau Vert.

The castle had been rolled into the hall after the dining trestles were put aside. Everybody had been surprised as dancers, dressed in white satin and gold thread, snaked their way out of the castle and into their presence.

Jane was bemoaning the clumsy mechanics of the castle's wheels. The train of her gown had gotten caught in the axle. She could have been decapitated if the Duchess's quick thinking hadn't have saved her!

Everybody cast various silent looks at Jane. Nothing more was to be expected from her. She was made from a different mold from the rest of them. Constantly negative and secretive, she was a drain to be around and all hearts sent their silent sympathies to George. Anne shivered; even Jane's smile didn't dismiss the coldness that touched her. Jane was very fair, as she had classic features with sloe eyes, beautiful skin and a mouth turned to perfection but she had a personality that made her ugly.

Anne turned away and used the moment to study Henry as he left the table to source more wine.

Who was this Henry Percy? Just a young man among many, she reasoned to herself. She had met many such young men in Europe. As her eyes lingered on his lean body and unruly blond hair, she felt a warm stirring in her stomach. Just at that moment he turned his head and smiled back at her across the room. His blue eyes conveyed warmth and honesty. They were devoid of the usual lust or courtly adoration that she was used to seeing.

And wasn't he the heir to the great Northumberland fortune? The next Earl of Northumberland? Perhaps he was not just any young man after all. She smiled back at him, a true smile that came from the heart, but if she was honest with herself, also the elated thought of becoming a countess.

Henry returned with a leather flask of hippocras.

Following at his heels was a servant bearing a plate of the traditional wafers that went with the wine. He instructed the serving girl to deposit the plate in front of Isabel.

"She's still hungry, you see," said Henry to the serving girl, his eyes laughing, speaking loud enough for everybody else to hear. They all saw Isabel's embarrassment as a deep blush stained her cheeks, but they laughed with her as she threw a wafer at Henry's chest.

Anne could see that Henry's relationship with Isabel was much like hers with George. A lot of banter and teasing but when it came down to it, somebody you could utterly depend on when you needed it. It comforted her to see it and her estimation of Henry grew.

The small party toasted Anne's success on her first pageant and wished her the success of many more.

The evening came to an unexpected close as the queen suddenly rose to retire. Eyebrows were raised but nothing was said at the early finish to a pleasant evening.

Isabel and Mary rose to take their place in the queen's retinue.

"I'll be right there," said Anne. "I'll only be a moment."

George and Jane also rose, voicing their goodnights to all as they left.

Suddenly it was quiet at the table and Anne found Henry at her side. He proffered his arm. She stood and took it.

"Shall I take you the scenic route?"

"Please," said Anne. Although she was interested in seeing more of this place that sprawled like a palace rather than a private residence, Anne was delighted that he had taken her hint of time alone together.

How was it that a man of the church lived like the king?

Henry answered all of Anne's questions about the redesigning of York Place and its extensive gardens as they walked arm-in-arm through its charming paths lit by flamed torches.

He led her away from the parties of people using the main concourse to the river and walked her through well-tended bowers and manicured hedgerows until the Thames finally came into view.

The water steps were full of people stepping aboard or waiting for their barges. The queen and her ladies could be seen making their way down. People presenting themselves to her constantly interrupted her way bringing her early exit to a crawl.

"Let's sit while we wait. Your presence will not be missed for a bit." Not waiting for an answer, Henry led her aside to a marble bench seat under a blossoming plum tree. Everything was gilded in silver filigree under the light of the full moon. The blossoms above their heads hung like delicate hoarfrost, releasing wafts of heavy scent on the easy currant of the night.

Anne could feel the warmth of Henry's body next to hers. Their arms still lay entwined between them. She looked away, enjoying the proximity of his maleness, trying to be delighted in feasting her eyes on the moon's rays dancing on the ripples of the Thames.

She sighed contentedly.

"Are you well?"

Surprised at the closeness of Henry's voice to her ear, she spun her head around. It met his almost nose-to-nose. She dipped her head quickly, but not quickly enough, for his lips were already laid on hers.

She was taken by surprise and was going to pull back. But his lips were soft and warm. They were unexpectedly gentle and moist. She hadn't expected this bold move from him—he was not a seasoned courtier—but she liked it. His mouth opened to taste more of her and she responded with a shiver of expectancy.

A delicious thrill coursed through her body. She leaned involuntarily towards him taking in his scent. She wanted more. Suddenly Henry pulled away. Anne's head spun out with confusion, her growing desire heavy upon her.

Henry held her hands, his face full of apology.

"Anne. Anne. I'm so sorry. Please forgive me. It is not the behaviour of a gentleman. Please forgive me."

She saw the genuine pleading of his eyes in his handsome face and held a hand up to his cheek. She felt him tremble beneath it.

In that moment, she knew that she wanted to be taken by him. She wanted to be ravished by him as any maid with a man. She was surprised at her own wantonness.

Other women might behave like this, but not her. She was always in control. She had sparred with the best lovers in Europe and remained untouched in heart and body. She had a plan for a good marriage and it was done in controlled steps.

God forbid, was she just like her sister Mary after all? Giving herself to the first man who came along?

"Henry …" she started, unsure of what to say.

Emboldened by Anne's sudden vulnerability, Henry stood decisively and once again offered his arm for her to take.

She stood, knees weak and trembling and looked into his face to gauge his feelings.

"Anne, please forgive me for acting like an oaf. How can any man be contained in your presence?" He gave her a brief helpless smile.

He studied his feet for a bit before he spoke again. "If I may, I would like to visit you when the Cardinal calls in at Court. He visits every Sunday. You are residing at Court?"

"Yes," she said, as if it were a question, still wanting more from him.

"Let me assist you to the landing then and we'll say goodnight. And I'll look forward to seeing you next Sunday."

Anne looked into Henry's eyes and saw the longing that she felt a moment ago. It excited her. *Yes,* she thought, *let this be done properly.* Her estimation of him continued to grow, as she perceived his control over his feelings and protection for her maidenhood. She felt secure and let loose at the same time.

While they strolled, Anne meditated. Should anything come of this newfound acquaintance, her father would also be very happy.

If, perchance, there was marriage, the Howard family would also be pleased. The Howards and the Percys! What a lucrative match that would be! Both were very powerful families in the land. And she brought them together! *Oh, how happy Father will be,* thought Anne. *It will be everything he could desire for me, for himself no doubt. His children will also be very powerful and very rich. Oh yes, this is good!*

Anne took a sideways glance at Henry and felt another thrill course down into her belly; this time it came with the kick of ambition.

They made their way down to the water steps with outward formality, speaking their desire for each other in the pressure of their fingers on their arms.

Both heady with first love, they didn't see the other figure draped in black velvet slide from behind the plum tree that they had just left.

Frustrated in his endeavours, the figure made sure his way was unobserved before gliding silently through the back gardens of York Place like a ghostly apparition searching his quarry.

CHAPTER TEN

City of York

Symus Henshaw awoke with a knife at his throat. The cold steel blade pressed into the skin under his jaw. As his eyelids flew open, he could make out two intruders standing before him swathed in roughly woven fustian. Their eyes glinted as they moved in the pre-dawn light.

They motioned for him to get up, then they pushed him downstairs into his print shop.

Symus turned to face them in silence. He was not easily intimidated. In the printing press business, you learned to accept all kinds of clients.

A scroll was thrust in his face. A short burst of muffled instruction followed.

Barefooted, Symus Henshaw padded around in his nightshirt and lit some tallow candles. He applied himself to setting the blocks for the type.

His face showed no sign of surprise or recognition at the words being created from the irons. He realised that life as he knew it would probably hinge on an expressionless countenance.

As Symus set the press, he was very interested at this turn of events. If he could have chuckled, he would have. He had no great love for the peers of the realm. In fact, he felt sorry for them. They couldn't even fart without somebody making an issue of it. Still, it was profitable for business, if he survived it.

The city of York was just starting to stir as the finished product was presented.

More threats were vocalised as his thoroughness was interpreted as dragging the chain. Symus nodded, it was just as he thought: instant death upon any word of the past hour's activities being leaked.

After some hours had passed, he had the pleasure of biting the gold crown he had just received. He closed the door contemplatively behind his early visitors. Not quite the start to the morning that he would have wished for, but good for business nonetheless.

He hummed a tuneless ditty as he climbed back up the stairs.

CHAPTER ELEVEN

Westminster Palace, London

Isabel could feel the bile rise in her stomach as her consciousness rose from sleep. As quietly and as seemly as she could, in case she was being watched, she passed by Anne's cot and then made a controlled dash out of the bedchamber. Closing the garderobe door, she instantly fell to her knees and vomited up the usual bright green, viscous fluid into a chamber pot. Spots danced before her eyes. She waited for the moment to pass. After a few minutes, she sat up and relieved herself in the same pot.

Thankfully it diluted the bright gobs of colour. She didn't want somebody being curious over its contents. Hopefully nobody had heard the expelling of her stomach. She wouldn't be able to extricate herself out of this situation as the evidence was there for all to see.

Trembling with the exertions, Isabel wiped her mouth with the back of her hand. Her breath smelled sour.

She pulled her nightdress down. As she did so, Isabel noticed some spots of blood on the hem. Upon more investigation, she found smears of watery blood dribbling down her inner thighs. Isabel gazed into space.

What did this mean? Perhaps I'm not pregnant. Perhaps I have some wasting disease! She hadn't had a period for three months now. Perhaps it was a tumour? She'd heard of such things discussed in the French court from the men who had studied dead bodies in Padua, Italy.

Panic gripped Isabel. Tears threatened again. *If only I could confide in someone ... but who?* Confiding in someone could mean banishment court, humiliation for herself and her bene-factors, the Northumberlands. No, she had to bear this on her own. She could not confide in anybody. Her mind went to Henry, her closest confidant.

No, he was so besotted with Anne these days that he wouldn't be able to hear her, as she needed to be heard. *No, I have to do this alone,* she thought.

Isabel steeled her mind and gave herself a good talking to as she rubbed her hands over her face, pushing her hair back to the nape of her neck. *I'm all right. I'm fine. I'm fine. All is well. I can cope with this. God never gives us more than we can bear. God, that's what you said! Those are your words not mine,* she reminded him.

She continued to pray to God in the water closet as the real-ity of her situation caused her to seesaw between fear and faith. It seemed to threaten to push her over sanity's edge. *God be with me! Your word says that you will never leave me nor for-sake me. Show me what I should do!*

Suddenly, again, despite her circumstances, Isabel felt a peace that passed understanding. She couldn't understand it but she had the impression of breaking out of a confined space into an open field. It was like she knew that it was going to be all right despite what she saw with her natural eyes. Out of her mouth leapt praise. It welled up from a sudden spring of joy that had risen from within. *How amazing you are God! Even if I die, I know I go to you. You are my only helper. I give my life to you for your glory!* As she rejoiced with her lips in a barely heard whisper, her tongue tripped up on itself. It was as if it wanted to go in a different direction from what she was telling it to. She stopped for a minute stunned. What was this—had she really lost her mind?

But his word says he gives us a sane mind. She opened her mouth to praise God again and she felt her tongue move, as it wanted to move. She had full control of her mind and her thoughts as she spoke, but all these unusual syllables rolled off her tongue with ease.

God is this you? Instantly a picture of the day of Pentecost came to mind. She saw the apostles in the upper room with the tongues of fire upon their heads. *God? What is this?*

An inner voice spoke back to her directly. "As you have spoken, I will never leave you nor forsake you."

Isabel sat silent and still, not sure whether to move or not to move. She offered no more prayer and heard no more voices. She looked ahead at the panelled wood of the garderobe. It was like she had just been in another place but she was still sitting on her chamber pot.

Outside the closet door, Isabel could hear the queen's waiting women stirring and rising for early morning Mass. She didn't have time to dwell on herself. Feeling like she was floating down from the heights of mountain peaks, she realised that there were chores to be done and she was nowhere near ready.

She washed herself clean with cold water from the bowl on a sideboard and fitted herself with a period cloth should she need it. Hopefully the maids and laundry women weren't keeping a close look on individual's courses.

She needed to keep her secret hidden until she was absolutely sure that she knew what was happening.

CHAPTER TWELVE

Cheapside, London

Silence resounded from the crowd in the baking heat.

Summer had shoved spring out of the way like an avalanche down a mountainside. It slammed onto the landscape, sucking the towns and cities dry of moisture. Wooden houses and structures cricked with complaint in the unrelenting heat. Even the stands holding the populous burned like oven bricks to the touch and warped where they were left unshaded.

The joust was part of the celebrations for the midsummer revels and the king's birthday. All that could be heard was the thundering of hooves as two knights sped toward one another with lances poised. There was a crash as a lance met with solid metal armour. The crowd "oohed" as one.

A knight fell. Instantly there were people at his side.

The winning knight did a victory lap in front of a mass of roaring people celebrating with him. They stood, the seats seeming to undulate as hats and veils waved in the air.

Cheapside, in London Town, had been transformed for the day from a noisy wayfare of merchants into a festive jousting arena. Stands and tents lined the wide street and every spare area had been hung with brightly coloured banners and flags.

Before the next bout, a knight stopped in front of the royal stand. There were many scarves and handkerchiefs at his destrier's feet for him to select and carry close to his heart. Only one bore the entwined K and H insignia embroidered on its corners. He spotted it quickly and with the deftness and agility of a natural-born athlete, he picked it up while still seated. He flourished it in the air then tucked it into his breastplate.

Queen Katherine, flanked side and back with her waiting women, smiled at the knight in the acknowledgement that she was favoured above all. There were cheers of encouragement as this knight and another took their positions. Again, there was now silence as the knights took stock then charged towards one another, lances poised.

The thunder of the horses' hooves was met with a sickening crunch of metal on metal. The fallen knight, foot still in his stirrup was dragged along the ground. He was quickly aided. The crowd cheered as with some help, he stood shakily to his feet.

The victorious knight, hand held high with the chosen scarf, lapping the jousting arena, suddenly pushed back his visor and pulled off his helmet to reveal the king. His short-cropped gold hair glistened with beads of sweat and his cheeks were ruddy with exertions.

The crowd went wild in their delight, throwing their caps and loose garments into the air, waving and cheering. Queen Katherine and her ladies stood to applaud as well. He was showered with roses, flower petals and sweetmeats by them as he made his way back to his tent to take a fresh horse.

Out of the corner of his eye, he caught a glimpse of long, sable hair shining in the sun as Anne Boleyn stood up from where she was seated. The reins relaxed in his hands. His mount ambled to his tent as he feasted on her form. She was seated away from the royal stand and it appeared that she hadn't even looked at him as he won the last bout!

Her hands were on another man's face. They were laughing, totally absorbed with each other. She ran her slender fingers over his open mouth. The blond man caught a finger with his teeth.

Henry felt a wash of anger flow over him. As he continued to watch the pair making love with their hands and eyes, he was amazed to find himself shaking. He tried to look away. He

...

Amanda Hawken

didn't even know her! He nudged his horse on and dismounted the steed at his tent, allowing his grooms and manservants to tend to him. The glow of winning and basking in the admiration of his subjects had been instantly replaced by a sense of gnawing dissatisfaction. He didn't like the feeling. He felt he wanted to bellow at the people attending to him. He wanted to cuff his pages head! He wanted to tear his manservants' fingers from his body as they loosened the straps of his armour!

He found himself glancing Anne's way as he was tended to.

He followed the graceful movements of her arms, the delightfully expressive flourish of her long fingers.

He shivered, imagining them running up and down his own mouth, his hands, his chest, his …

Henry's face grew grim as emotion stormed within him.

Anne flicked her long hair back over her shoulder as she laughed at something the blond man had said. Who was that young man?

"Carey," the king demanded of his lover's husband, a gentleman of his privy chamber. "Who is that with your sister-in-law over there in the uncovered stands?"

William Carey looked up in the direction of the king's toss of his head. Recognition filled his face right away.

"That, Your Majesty, is the Earl of Northumberland's son, Henry. He is a page in Cardinal Wolsey's household."

"Ah, Northumberland's whelp." Henry's voice felt like it belonged to someone else.

"Yes, sire," said Carey continuing his ministrations without hesitation or giving voice to his feelings. Not thinking was the only thing that kept him sane these days; the thought of the hands that he had just de-gloved also caressing his own wife's body last night was too much to be borne. He glanced up at Northumberland. God help the poor man if he ends up in the wake of the king's moral destruction as he had! Greater men than he had forced his hand, and his wife's hand into an impossible situation. They had said God would absolve the sin because it was serving the king whom God had anointed there in the first place. But William knew that that was a lie. His heart bore testament to it daily. The whole situation made him soul sick and he couldn't find a way of recovering, may God forgive him his weakness.

Henry gazed at Anne, as she laughed up into the bleached sky, hazy with summer heat. He followed the sweeping lines of her long white throat with his eyes, over her delicate collarbones and down to her pushed-up breasts. Northumberland was laughing with her. He grabbed Anne's svelte waist and she fell into his lap. Her hair covered their heads like a veil and Henry could almost taste the kisses that were sure to be taking place behind it!

The seed of desire planted in Henry's heart at Wolsey's Shrovetide celebrations, suddenly sprouted, being watered by his lust. Its taproot and growing tip emerged simultaneously. They stretched and curled, the little tendrils looking for a place to spread. In that moment, Henry felt something sliver across his soul. It curled and tightened in his gut like a snake.

Jealousy. Smouldering jealously. Henry could feel it settle, ready to bide its time, but he didn't care. He wanted her and he would get her! Whatever it took!

CHAPTER THIRTEEN

Alnwich Castle, Northumberland

Dressed as a pedlar, pushing his cart of wares before him, he watched the comings and goings of Alnwich Castle.

Making his way up the road to the outer gates he watched the people.

Alnwich Castle coursed like a town within a town.

In his mind he sorted through the citizens of the earl's employ like one might sort through a bushel of apples—looking for the biggest and shiniest, the one most perfect for his needs.

The vibrations of dozens of hooves under his feet made him spin around. He quickly pulled to the side of the road so as not to be trampled. Heron and Turnbull, the earl's right-hand men who delivered the king's justice in the north, rode into the gates of the castle. With them were many of the earl's retainers.

They thundered past the pedlar. Dry, sun-baked sod flicked onto his fustian tunic and his cart, along with the pungent waft of sweat, oiled iron, hot damp horse and warm leather.

He followed their wake into the outer courtyard.

He set up his cart just inside the gate. It wasn't long before the women of the castle surrounded him. His mouth smiled and offered the charming repartee they sought, as they fingered the ribbons and baubles. Under his disguise, his eyes remained focused, roaming the people, searching.

He watched the earl's henchmen dismount.

How typical of the earl to pass on his responsibilities to those puppets, he thought with an inner sneer. *The Earl of Northumberland has no interest in the politics of the region except for his own ends,* he thought with bitterness so deep that it left him shaking. All the earl wanted to do was live like a king, to amass wealth and live in as much pomp and ceremony as he could.

He had made Heron and Turnbull powerful by his abdication of duty in the border country. He was sure that they would only tell the earl what he wanted to know. They probably held their own courts with their own agendas. Of that, he had no doubt.

He had first-hand treatment of their treachery and the treachery of other families in the Border country. Well, hadn't everybody who lived in this region? Even in the Battle of Flodden, Border Clans stripped and pillaged the dying on the field from both sides, rather than declaring support for one political allegiance or another.

It was one of his kinsmen that had tipped the scale for the Flodden war. A Border warden, Robert Kerr, had been murdered and King James IV of Scotland flew south to seek revenge.

And here, it still goes on, almost a decade later, the young pedlar thought.

Suddenly he felt tired, tired of it all. Does revenge take away the pain in the heart? Would it take away the pain that he continually saw in his father's eyes, in his kinsmen's eyes? The death of loved ones, land and goods continually stolen, homes raised and atrocities committed before innocent eyes. These were daily occurrences that they had to deal with.

Tears threatened and he swallowed the weakness down.

He didn't know the answer but he had to go on. And it was all that he knew anyhow. What else was there? It certainly numbed him for the present. It helped him to stay focused for his purpose in life—what he had been born to.

Hatred, black and poisonous started to bubble with intensity again as he watched Heron dismount and give instructions to a groomsman.

Heron was a tall lean man with thin pale hair. Steely grey eyes, hard and unforgiving, stared out of his long gaunt face.

Turnbull was just the opposite. Short, thickset with close-set eyes and red hair sprouting from everywhere, he was a ball of muscular energy. He dismounted his bay gelding in one bound, power and authority springing from every step as he made his way into the great hall of the castle.

As the earl's two henchmen disappeared from the outer courtyard, the atmosphere relaxed. The retainers dismounted with general chatter, some ribbing and the occasional laughter. The horses were led away to their stalls to feed or to the blacksmith, whose hammer on anvil reverberated once again into the warm summer air. The men relaxed onto benches to sharpen or oil their weapons, take a draught of cold water from a barrel or chat up a maid as she hurried past in her duties.

Immediately beside the pedlar, in through the gates, a herd boy directed a gaggle of mischievous geese with difficulty into waiting pens across the courtyard. As the geese settled, the pedlar caught a glimpse of what he sought, a young milkmaid carrying pails.

Her looks were furtive. Her eyes continually darted as she tried to disappear into the walls she walked passed.

He watched her making her way into the buttery. She wasn't like the other maids who flaunted themselves with confidence among the soldiers. Her head hung like a beaten dog.

Her tangly brown hair hung limply about her thin pointed face and her homespun gown appeared unkempt.

He watched her disappear to deposit her pails within the buttery. He couldn't hear what was being said, but he saw meaty forearms blowing cuffs about her head as she left.

The milkmaid slunk away, wiping her eyes roughly as if she had dirt in them.

The pedlar continued to follow her path with his eyes as she went back out to the pasture and he continued to dispense his wares.

There was no sympathy, only calculation.

CHAPTER FOURTEEN

Westminster Palace, Midsummer's Day

"Marry me," he said.

Anne turned her head to look at Henry. Their faces were only inches apart. She could tell by his stance that he had been studying her as they took in the sights below.

They had raced before the others onto one of the highest points of Westminster Palace, most people having been released from their duties to enjoy London's midsummer celebrations.

Her brow furrowed. It was as if he had spoken a foreign language.

"Marry me," he said again.

During the weeks that had passed since he had first met Anne, he had fallen deeper and deeper in love with her.

He felt alive for the first time in his life!

At first, she had entranced him with her sophisticated, witty ways and impeccable style. Now that they had come to know each other more, he had fallen in love with the person she was rather than the façade she liked to wear in front of people.

She had started to encourage him in his dreams. She made him feel that he did have the ability to achieve great things. She had told him that he had awesome gifts and talents. He was amazed! Could anybody learn anything from him? He was a useless good-for-nothing, his father was continually telling him, a hopeless head to rule, no backbone, no head for money, a lazy, good-for-nothing dreamer. These lines were usually delivered with a cuff at the back of the neck or a cold dismissal.

Henry looked at Anne now. In her face, he saw her adoration for him. Was he really worthy to be loved by one such as her? He struggled to believe her words that made him think he had something to offer the world. The words sown into his soul by his father had taken too deep a root to pull out by this recent speech alone.

Anne was speaking to him now. Pulling himself out of his reverie, he heard her words.

"Yes. Yes. Yes."

He was amazed again as he heard her laughter. It was as if he had won the world!

They kissed long and deep, each wanting to remain forever in that state. After a while, they pulled apart, still holding one another, savouring the moment.

"I shall let father know of our betrothal," said Henry.

Anne thought that was very brave of Henry to say that, knowing full well that they would be powerless against any opposition. In retrospect, Anne knew that her father would be very pleased. His daughter would be a countess or a duchess after all! And she had done it all by herself! Mary was a disappointment to him, she knew. Had her advancement into the king's bed got her anything of lasting value for the family? She would be the apple of her father's eye, as she had been trained to be, as she was determined to be.

She had not only been blessed with the love of her life, but with pleasing her family also. She felt fit to burst with her contentment.

Henry pulled a gold ring off his forefinger. It was designed with his family crest. He held Anne's beautiful elegant hand and pushed his ring onto her third finger. It was too big. They laughed together as the heavy encrusted top swung down. They laughed in delight and for their future together.

They held each other's eyes as he spoke: hers smoky black, his vulnerable blue.

"With this ring, I betroth thee, before God as my witness. I take you to my wife for as long as we live."

"… As long as we live," echoed Anne in a whisper.

Anne gazed at the ring. It was heavy, solid gold, with the crest figured in detailed filigree. She saw not only the design but also her future as the Countess of Northumberland, Queen of the North!

Delighted, she offered him her soft moist mouth again. He took it hungrily, the man within him rising. They abandoned themselves to their passions.

If they hadn't been interrupted, they both knew that their vows would have been consummated at that very spot.

At last Isabel Percy, Mary Carey and George Boleyn arrived with Thomas Watt, their neighbour from Kent, Francis Weston and Tom Brereton. They spilled out noisily and energetically from a tiny door onto the Westminster Palace's parapet landing.

They were high above the buildings and town houses of London, giving them an open vista of the city below.

Unnoticed by Anne and Henry, night had spread out across the northern sky like indigo ink running across parchment. The first stars had started to stretch and wink as if waking from a deep sleep. The only remnant of the day was a thin ribbon of cobalt blue glowing on the western horizon.

Everybody found a gap between the parapets.

It was the night of midsummer's eve, the night of the "Marching Watch." It was an annual event for the city of London.

Everybody, from the lowliest servant to the Lord Mayor of London, participated with every street lit and dressed. It was the event in which the constabulary of London were honoured. The watch started at St. Paul's Cathedral and wound its way through Westchepe Street to Aldgate and eventually back through Fenchurch Street. The constabulary were dressed to dazzle. Gold chains rested on scarlet cloaks and guilt harnesses sparkled in the torches, lamplights and bonfires, which lit the way.

Henry and Anne were flung salutations as their friends pushed past to find the best vantage points from which to view the city below.

Exclamations flew like arrows as they surveyed the spectacle below them. The door lintels that they could see were bedecked in green bowers and floral garlands. A procession of various groups paraded below them: the city elders, standard bearers, Morris dancers and minstrels playing. After them, floats depicting all manner of scenes—St. George and his dragon, the Virgin Mary, and Knights on the Crusades— snaked slowly but noisily past.

Merchants and men of substance poured wine into fountains and offered food to the masses, which pressed and jostled together in joyful abandon.

"Come!" yelled George. "I'm going down! Who comes with me?"

"Oh! Let's!" cooed Mary excitedly.

'What is your husband going to say, his wife loose in the city?" inquired Anne with haughtily raised eyebrow, wrapped in Henry's arms.

Before Mary could think of a suitable, witty answer, George interrupted.

"And what are you two going to do?" said George, his handsome face insinuating quite clearly what they would be doing.

Henry guarding Anne's honour said, "We have just become betrothed. Anne has just consented to be my wife so we have lots of celebrating to do."

The party on the roof became instantly still. All eyes were on them both. Henry and Anne could see all of their thoughts as if they had spoken them aloud. There were doubts and questions with the exception of love from Isabel and, unexpectedly, jealousy from Thomas Wyatt.

George broke the stunned silence.

"Well congratulations, I say! May you be better suited than my lot! Nest of vipers that she is."

Everybody knew that he found it hard to even stomach his betrothed, never mind try to love her. Their hearts went out to him. Nobody liked Jane. She seemed to have the knack of being nasty to people, even to those she loved, and even if it was to her own detriment.

Thankful that George had broken the ice, they all came forward. "Yes, congratulations," they all said, patting backs, kissing hands and proffered cheeks.

Isabel hugged Henry tightly, her eyes bright with tears.

"Henry, I'm so happy for you."

She pulled away placing her hand on Anne's arm. "Who would have thought?" She burst out laughing.

Anne laughed with her. "Yes, who would have thought? We'll really be sisters now!"

Francis Weston tugged at Isabel's arm.

"We'll see you two down there," said Isabel disappearing with the rest through the doorway built for a dwarf.

Only Thomas Wyatt held back. When the three of them were alone, he came up to Anne and Henry to offer his congratulations.

Anne offered her hand for him to kiss but Thomas leaned further forward and kissed her full on the mouth.

Her eyes flew open in surprise.

In that moment, Anne became aware of his desire for her. She looked at him with questions in her eyes. She had always known him as their neighbour in Kent ever since she was a little girl. He was now a married man, even though unhappily and it looked likely that they would separate.

But now … now Anne saw him as a man who desired her as a woman, not the neighbour congratulating the girl next door.

Thomas pulled away reluctantly. He looked briefly at Henry. His eyes looked pained and full of sorrow for himself.

"Congratulations, Lord Percy. You've made a very fine haul. Very fine indeed."

He bowed to them, both his eyes lingering on Anne before he left.

Henry was not unaware of what had passed between Anne and Thomas. "He's married," he said bluntly.

Anne looked up at him perplexed. "Yes, I know, but I never knew ..."

Henry spun her around into his arms, his eyes serious.

"Well, you're mine now and he is just going to have to live with it!"

Anne laughed with the headiness of it all.

Glad that the first hurdle was over in setting the course for their future, they paused for a final, exultant kiss, then made their way down to rejoin the others.

***

"Lord Percy!"

Henry swung around in answer to the call.

They were passing through the Great White Hall, which was busy with people making their way into the city's celebrations.

Henry spied the Cardinal vying for his attention across the heads of milling nobles, gentry and the well-to-do. A small party of staff ringed him.

Henry and Anne made their way through the crowd.

"My lord," Henry bowed his head, his arm still holding Anne's hand, resplendent with his ring.

Anne bowed her head and bent her knee slightly in a small curtsey.

"Mistress Boleyn," Wolsey smiled, inclining his head, then fixing his eyes on Henry. "A reminder, Henry, that we leave for Windsor at first light. We have festivities to arrange before the court makes its way out."

"I have not forgotten, my lord," Henry bowed respectfully again. They were about to turn away when Henry's face lit up.

"Oh, my Lord Cardinal! May you be the first to congratulate us? We are betrothed! How fitting it is that you should be the first to hear. God was our first witness!" He turned and smiled a brilliant white smile at Anne.

She smiled back.

"Pray, bless us, sir," Henry continued. "We would be honoured if you would condescend to officiate."

The cardinal raised his eyebrows. "Not so much haste, my boy. I have not heard of this from your father."

"Oh, no indeed, my lord. I have just proposed this very night and she has accepted." Henry squeezed Anne's hand. "I am sure Father will agree."

Skepticism kept Wolsey's eyebrows arched. "Indeed?"

Blind to everything but their love for one another, Henry and Anne excused themselves and blissfully made their way into the midsummer night.

***

Unbeknownst to all below, another pair of eyes bore down upon them from above, in the upper gallery.

The king had been making his way down to the Great White Hall with his very dear friend, Sir Thomas More, when he saw Anne Boleyn leave the hall on the arm of Henry Percy.

She wore a gown of blood red silk that brought out the creamy whiteness of her skin and the ebony blackness of her hair. She appeared to Henry like some sort of sylph, a vision that could be touched. He started to fantasise about who she was and what she may be like.

At the same moment, some courtiers accosted Sir Thomas for some midsummer's night sky predictions. He was well known about court for his astrolabe in the attic of his house and his love of plotting the course of stars across the night sky. Henry had a few moments to himself to observe the crowd below.

He stood transfixed. What was going on?

Northumberland's whelp clung to Anne like a limpet and what was worse she clung to him!

He didn't like it. Not one bit! How dare the young puppy!

Henry barked a command.

Everybody froze at the unexpected outburst. Sir Thomas looked at Henry as if he had gone mad. He was one of Henry's few personal friends who was not afraid to reveal his true feelings in front of him.

Once the king's request was understood, it was acted upon with flustered haste. Everybody bowed low with his or her soul quaking as the king took his leave amongst subdued murmur.

Within minutes, Henry was alone with Wolsey in an antechamber off the upper gallery.

Henry paced. "How is it with Northumberland's son?"

Wolsey was surprised to be summoned in such an ungracious manner. It had not happened before.

Not prepared and unsure of Henry's angle, Wolsey cautiously stumbled out some words.

"Well, Your Majesty … Young Percy is well … ah, is … has integrity in his duties …"

"Yes, yes," said Henry testily, still pacing.

"Ah … he just informs me this minute that he is betrothed to Mistress Anne Boleyn, though I have no notice from Northumberland himself. As far as I was aware young Percy is still betrothed to Lady Mary Talbot."

Wolsey's ramblings were cut dead by Henry's icy fury.

"I forbid it! I forbid it! Do you hear? I forbid it!"

Wolsey was taken back at Henry's rage. He'd seen many faces of Henry Tudor, King of England, but this was something new.

"Your Grace?" Wolsey bowed, keeping his stance low, unsure of what to do next.

Henry managed to get himself under control. He stood stock still, but the purple fusion in his face could not hide his boiling emotions.

"I forbid any marriage between Northumberland's cur and this Anne Boleyn, do you hear? Any marriage!"

Wolsey kept his bowed stance. "Yes, Your Grace. I shall see to it."

"See that you do, my Lord Cardinal. See that you do." His voice was steely hard and just as cold.

Henry strode from the room heavily and slammed the door behind him.

Amanda Hawken

Wolsey felt pricks of uncertainty ripple through his soul.

It was a new sensation for him, he who was viewed as the real ruler of England by the other nations of Europe.

CHAPTER FIFTEEN

Alnwick Castle, Northumberland

The large stones, which gave shape to the great hall, felt cool to the touch. Jennet was glad, because she was beginning to sweat.

She pressed her thin frame against the wall, trying to make herself disappear.

The Northumberland household finally slept after the mid-summers celebrations.

There were only a few hours until dawn, so time was of the essence.

The bodies of Northumberland's retainers were spread all over the hall. An act passed by Henry VII made it against the law for any noble to have liveried retainers. This, of course, prevented any one peerage growing stronger in arms than the king himself. The Earl of Northumberland did just enough to please the ruling sovereign. He kept retainers but they wore their own armour. It was easy to keep support behind him, as most northern families had no time for the laws that percolated up from the south.

Some family and friends had long left for home, but others with their personal servants had to find their own space. Every available corner and crevice that offered support or shelter was occupied by a body and not necessarily human. Jennet saw many dogs lying with their masters.

She'd have to run like a wraith not to disturb them.

Nervousness, together with her natural overbite, caused her to unconsciously suck her bottom lip.

She studied a route to where she needed to go.

A resounding clink of metal on stone brought her out in a fresh wave of nervous sweat. She swallowed, her eyes as wide as the gold plate that hung on the walls.

A few hounds lifted up their heads and pricked their ears, waited, then lay down again.

The noise clanked again and she froze with fear. Her knees just about gave way as she realised that it was herself. It was the gold crown that she had sown into the hem of her under-garment.

She pulled herself and her skirts gingerly away from the wall.

She'd never owned any sort of money like that and it was the only way she knew to keep it safe and away from prying eyes.

And cook was very prying! The thought of cook's piggy eyes made Jennet shiver with intimidation.

The man had come to her as she churned the butter alone in the dairy. He was very nice and very handsome! He lingered at the buttery door before he came in and sat down beside her. She had been very nervous of his intentions, having been abused by every young male that had ever crossed her path. But this man was different. He just wanted her to help him. He said that he couldn't do this task without her. Would she help him with the payment of some silky blue ribbons for her pretty brown hair? When she hesitated, he brought out a gold crown from his pocket. She wanted to tell him that she had only hesitated because she was trying to get used to the idea of some-body being kind to her, treating her like a normal person. He told her to be very quiet about it or they might both get into trouble. He was really nice to her. He treated her like Hugh from the stables treated Maisry from the laundry. They were sweet on each other.

He had kissed her on the cheek before he left, promising to meet her by the River Aln tomorrow. Jennet touched the spot that he had kissed and relived that perfect moment. He didn't need to give her the money. She would have done it for his simple kindness. She had been cuffed many times dreaming of romantic love instead of putting her back into her chores. Now it was here! Her own young man! Her very own!

But she mustn't tell anyone and she mustn't let him down, he said.

Before taking the path that she had mentally mapped, Jennet sought for the scroll that he had given her hidden in the depths of her apron pocket. She was slightly dismayed as she felt its edges sticky with gravy. She wiped it clean as best she could. The blue ribbons were also in her pocket. She loosened one out, shaking off the crumbs, to tie it around the scroll. Hopefully it would disguise the worst of the soiling.

She was to lay the scroll on the earl's writing table where he did lots of reading and spoke to important people. She was to "lay it in such a way as to make sure he might find it," were his glorious words.

She ventured out, her delusional notions of romantic love fortifying her.

CHAPTER SIXTEEN

Windsor Park Palace

It was during the archery when Isabel first felt it, a period cramp.

As the day wore on, she realised that her tummy cramped every hour on the hour. It wasn't that uncomfortable. She tried to ignore it. There were plenty of diversions happening to take her mind off it. Wolsey had taken it on himself to be the entertainments director at Windsor. The whole court was praising his great skill and talent for this type of thing. He had excelled himself this time, Isabel heard over and over. She was sure that Anne had a hand in its artistic direction. There was to be a feast that night in honour of the king. The king had praised Wolsey for his organization before a small group of intimates. Wolsey was seen to have breathed a heavy sigh, as he moped his brow in what he assumed was a private moment. Everybody thought it was expressing relief upon delivering an acceptable display of entertainment.

Nobody would know that it was a sign for Wolsey of reinstatement back into Henry's affections that caused him to wear his heart on his sleeve for a brief moment in time.

Today there had been hawking in the morning, archery at noon and a play held at an outdoor theatre just before twilight. After the play, everybody ambled back into the castle to gather in the queen's presence chamber before the honouring banquet.

Isabel stopped on the brow of a mound to let another cramp peak then dissipate. She pretended to take in the view to the north. Being at Windsor was like a breath of fresh air after the closeness of London. The park grounds spread out from the castle like a green sea of tranquillity. It was dotted with islands of grand old oaks, ashes and birches. Then beyond, the dark green forests of Windsor Great Park misted blue and mauve to the horizon.

George Boleyn drew up beside her and offered his arm to escort her into the queen's chambers. Isabel was grateful of the support.

"So," he ventured as they walked. "We are to be brother and sister?"

"It appears that way and I couldn't be happier for them both. Love in marriage, it's a rare thing."

"Rare indeed."

George's bitter tone caused Isabel to look sharply at him.

"Oh, George. I'm so sorry."

He smiled his disarmingly handsome smile and squeezed her arm. "As you say, marriage and love together is a rare thing. Jane will bring me other things no doubt. What about you? I can't imagine the great Earl of Northumberland not making good on his investment."

"I don't see it that way. I am grateful for whomever he chooses for me. He didn't have to make me his ward. But yes, you are right. He has made good on his investment as you say. I am to marry one Sir Roland Tavistock whose lands are adjoined to his own."

"Love do you think?"

Isabel let out a laugh. "No, I don't think so. His children are older than me."

"Oh, Isabel. I'm sorry."

"Well, I'm not,"

"Yes you are."

"Well, maybe a little bit, if I'm honest," she offered giving him a rueful side-glance.

"Always looking at the best in people and situations— that's a rare gift, Isabel."

George stopped and pulled her around to face him. Other couples and groups meandered by. He kept his voice low in a conspirator's whisper. "I know, let's run away and elope; then we can both be sure of not marrying into tragedy."

Isabel laughed and smacked him playfully on his arm.

"George, you are a delight and if I thought that you were half serious, I'd scare you and take you up on the offer."

As they continued to stroll in silence, Isabel snatched a glance at George's profile. It was heavy with the weight of his thoughts. Isabel clutched his arm tighter, understanding him. *Life is so full of promise, yet here we are struggling with duty, and ourselves, weighed down with cares rather than enjoying the moment we have.* Aware of her gaze upon him, George turned and as they locked looks, each saw the others mutual concern. It comforted them to a degree but they both knew they had futures to face that they would rather not. Both sighing, they continued in silence up to the castle.

Upon entering the queen's chamber George deposited Isabel next to Anne, who sat as close as convention would allow, next to Henry Percy.

Isabel thought that they both looked radiant in their love for one another.

How wonderful, true love, she mused. *Will it ever come to me?*

She felt another cramp come on. They were getting more frequent but not gaining in intensity. She wriggled in her seat, as if to try and make it go away. George returned with a goblet of wine for her and Anne.

Isabel took it greedily, downing half of it in one go. Suddenly she felt angry, wishing the nagging pains would go away.

Why did he do this to me? The blackguard! I should be enjoying my life! He stole my future from me. Tears almost threatened again and she swigged down the other half of the wine emptying her goblet.

"Whoa, there Bessie!" exclaimed George.

Isabel reddened in the realisation that she had been observed, but composed herself quickly. "My goodness, I didn't realise how thirsty I was."

George raised a disbelieving eyebrow but decided to leave it.

Cardinal Wolsey entered the queen's presence chamber.

As he did, everybody clapped him in recognition of the honour given to him by the king with the banquet to follow. He made his way to the queen, who congratulated him also.

She was very cool about it, but most people knew that Katherine was not fond of Wolsey.

He had a habit of promoting Henry's illegitimate son, Henry Fitzroy, above Mary, their legitimate daughter, whenever he could. It was obvious that he was devious in his friendship with her. She eyed him warily, as she would a serpent.

He bowed low and remained to converse, as well as she would allow.

The general chatter returned to normal.

Wolsey then made his way slowly around the room, accepting compliments and words of affirmation. Some of his critics wondered if the Cardinal thought himself to be king as he paraded before the court, giving himself great airs.

He paused as he passed the Percys and Boleyns. Appearing to act on an afterthought, Wolsey took two steps back and entered their circle.

His intrusion into their midst had to be acknowledged. They all stood and bowed with light felicitations on their lips.

Wolsey nodded and smiled in return, but the tone of his voice was decidedly severe, the volume rose for all to hear.

"My Lord Percy, I marvel greatly that you consider marriage to such a one as this," he flicked an unsavoury glance at Anne as if she were a leper.

People couldn't believe what they just saw.

The cardinal folded his puffy hands on his great pouch of a stomach.

"Yes, I marvel that you would be such a fool to consider marriage with a knight's daughter. You, my lord, who, after your father's death, are likely to inherit one of the greatest Earldoms in this kingdom!"

Henry's face bloomed scarlet with embarrassment. He had never been publicly humiliated before. If it weren't for his love for Anne, he would have suffered in silence, his determination to stand, wilting like cut grass under the midday sun. However, bolstered by their affections for each other, Henry was not about to let Wolsey bully him. Anne meant more to him than life itself.

A few people in the now silent room coughed nervously and shuffled their feet to cover up the very uncomfortable moment.

"My Lord Cardinal," Henry's voice rang loud and true with equal strength. "Need I remind you that Anne's mother is the daughter of the Earl of Surrey, whose lineage is not to be disputed; and if it were, you would be standing on treasonous ground!"

Several gasps were heard around the room. He continued.

"Anne's lineage and character are beyond reproach, sir! And her years spent in the most royal households of Europe, stand her in goodly stead to be by my side as a peer of England!"

Every muscle in Henry's body was taut enough to snap. Only his face twitched as he clenched and unclenched his jaw.

Wolsey was surprised. He most certainly didn't expect confrontation from his page like this. He was usually a most compliant young man.

Wolsey passed another withering look at Anne, who stood defiant with Henry.

Bewitched, thought Wolsey.

Realizing that he had made a scene in front of the queen, the Cardinal backed down. "I'll speak to you both later."

He bowed to the queen, making his apologies.

All heads in the room followed his exit as his red robes swirled in his wake.

Livid in her humiliation, Anne trembled with anger she'd never felt possible.

Her eyes smouldered darkly as they witnessed Wolsey's exit. Those around her heard her controlled voice. "If it ever lies in my power, I will work the Cardinal as much displeasure as he has done me!'

Nobody believed a word of it.

***

Isabel was concerned.

She tore a strip of roast beef from its bone. It was beautifully done. The meat just melted in her mouth.

The cooks had made a fine show of the venison hunted locally at Windsor Park. Hung until it was falling from its hooks, it had been roasted, boiled or salted. Some had been cooked to shreds with cinnamon and buried in great coffin-like pies.

Isabel eyed some platters of snipe and woodcock, but she thought twice about it. The cramps were coming about every five minutes now.

Isabel made a decision and felt better for it. She motioned for a servant behind her to fetch the last of her red wine from the sideboard behind her. She emptied it in one swallow, handed the glass back to the servant and stood up.

On her right, George Boleyn looked reproachful and captured her hand.

"Not to bed early again?"

"I'm sorry, George …"

"Isabel. Where do you go?" Anne questioned her from her left.

"I have a dreadful headache, Anne. I'm going to retire early."

"Well, if you're sure … I'll look in on you later. I'll talk to old Mistress Luke to see if she has a tisane for your headaches you are getting."

Isabel murmured her thanks and hurried out of the banqueting hall.

That was the last thing she wanted, the king's old nurse finding out what was really going on—just in case it was a pregnancy. She'd be able to tell just by looking at her no doubt.

Lavish entertainments had been programmed for the evening, so Isabel knew she'd have some quiet time alone.

She made her way back to the queen's women's apartments unhindered. Perhaps a good night's sleep and some rest was all she needed.

The cramps continued as she undressed and snuggled down into her cot. She pulled up her down-filled counterpane, more for comfort than for warmth, and instantly fell to sleep.

Isabel woke about two hours later. She knew she had come to the moment that she had been denying to herself.

She was glad it was now here … here to face.

She was also terrified that it was here to face.

It was another uterine cramp that had awoken Isabel, but this time it came with a burst of liquid between her legs.

She had relieved herself before coming to bed, she reasoned to herself, but it didn't feel like a bladder release.

Gingerly, Isabel rose from her bed to look at what happened. She lit a wall sconce and a rack of candles. Tucking her long blonde hair behind her ear, she looked down at her nightgown, which clung to her legs like unwrung laundry. The hem dripped in rivulets, pooling amniotic fluid onto the flagstone floor. Her bed had a sodden patch in the middle. Isabel knelt and used her counterpane to try to soak up the mess, which had disappeared into her mattress.

Having second thoughts, she ripped off her sheets and made up her cot fresh. She hoped the wet mattress wouldn't soak through. She wiped up the mess on the floor with the sheets and tucked the wet linen under her nightgown.

She looked back. The bed looked untouched.

The next cramp that came tore a gasp from Isabel's throat. It was intensely dragging and squeezing. A cold clammy sweat beaded instantly on her forehead. Isabel felt suddenly nauseous and faint. She put a hand to the wall to steady herself.

She had to do this. She had to. Fight the nausea, she told herself. She had to get out. For somebody to find her like this would be the end of life as she knew it.

I'll find a place in the stables. I'll be like Our Lady Mary giving birth to Jesus, she mused light-heartedly to herself, but she found no comfort in the thought.

After the cramp faded, she quickly threw on a full-length cloak with a hood, to cover her face and started to make her way barefooted into the corridor. She checked herself and went back for her evening slippers. A barefooted lady would definitely draw attention.

Feeling a bit better and more in control, Isabel pulled up her hood and made her way carefully to the stables and other outlying buildings that might offer her privacy and sanctuary.

Oh, Lord! It was coming again. Another cramp.

She looked wild-eyed, trying not to panic, for somewhere to lean. She had arrived at the entrance hall in the palace.

It was almost empty, with most people present at the banquet.

She hid behind a pillar, hoping nobody would come the way she was facing. The cramp proved to be stronger than the last. The dragging sensation within her belly almost pulled her to the floor.

She had to find solitude quickly.

A gaze to her left showed her a way out through a side door. She took it quickly. Once outside, she tried to make sense of the type of outbuildings she was looking at. Panic started to rise again. Another gush of water trickled down the inside of her thighs. A whimper escaped her lips.

She went forward, not knowing which way to go. Isabel tried the door of the first building, her hands shaking.

It was locked!

Snatching a quick look around to make sure that she was alone, she tried the door of a smaller building next to it.

The door swung open. Relieved, she slid into its blackness.

***

His lips split into a slow smile like a sharp knife piercing swollen flesh.

He saw her profile as her hood slipped back slightly from her face. He couldn't believe it. He had found her at last. He had beaten them to her. The legacy was going to be all his! It was his right as the first born!

And she was alone!

He must be quick. There could be no more lost time. He followed her stealthily as she left the pillar.

***

Something cold slapped Isabel's face. It took her breath away. She cried out as she stepped backward and was slapped in the back. She spun around in terror, holding up her hands in self-defence.

The blackness was complete. Isabel couldn't tell where her attacker was coming from. She couldn't even see where she was.

This couldn't be happening again! How did they find her from France?

There were no sounds other than her breath coming in short, sharp, erratic bursts. She put her hands out gingerly into the dark. They were met by more slaps of gritty, dry flesh. Lots of them!

Her relief was immense.

She was in the curing house! She let out a weak, hysterical laugh.

Salted fish, probably sturgeon for their size, salted pork and beef hung about her head and shoulders. She reached out and touched the meat hanging about her to reassure herself that she was correct.

Yes, a leg of pork here, fillets of fish to the side.

Isabel could feel another cramp coming on. She hunched over to avoid being hit by the salted meat and searched for a comfortable place to sit. Hands outstretched and eyes wide in the dark, she shuffled forward until her palms met a wall. She followed it down to a corner.

The cramp forced her onto her knees. Her body belonged to the gripping force of the pain. She couldn't relieve it in any way. No position, no rubbing would make it go away. She couldn't believe there was such pain to be endured and still live. As the wrenching subsided, a sobering thought hit her like another slap in the face.

Perhaps that was it. She had just answered her question. She was dying.

Isabel turned cumbersomely into a sitting position, wedged in between a barrel of salt and the wall.

Her eyes slowly acclimatised to the dark. She could see a crack of light outlining the door that she had just entered.

Isabel crouched on her haunches as she unrolled the wet bed sheets that she had tucked under her nightgown. She put them under her to keep herself from the hard bricks of the floor.

No sooner had she settled when another cramp came on.

Isabel moaned. As much as she tried to keep quiet, it slipped out before she could hold it back. As the pain rose she felt like she was being torn in two.

She felt like pushing. She rose up on her haunches again, clenched her teeth and balled her fists. She could feel her stomach being wrenched from her body.

She felt it slide out from in between her legs. It sloshed onto the hem of her nightgown.

Oh, thank God, the pain was gone. Only a dull ache remained.

Drained and somewhat dazed, Isabel looked down at what had arrived between her feet. Yellow light, emanating light from wall sconces outside the curing house, found their soft hues touching the curves of her stillborn baby boy, no bigger than that span of her hand. He seemed to lie in a bed of chopped liver.

"Jesu, have mercy", she whimpered helplessly.

She had been pregnant after all!

Isabel tentatively put her finger to the still warm flesh—her flesh!—and touched her dead son.

Isabel felt stunned. She couldn't comprehend what had just happened.

As the minutes ticked past, grief gradually hit her. First the tears rolled unnoticed down her face. Then her voice found itself and a quiet keening grew into great, heaving sobs. Through her tears, she picked up her baby boy. He was perfectly formed.

She wiped him clean with her tears, tore off the hood from her cloak and wrapped him up. She held him to her chest and sobbed and sobbed.

She cried for the injustice done to her, for having to bear the shame of it alone. She cried for the death of her son and probably her future.

After a time, she laid her son aside and she cleaned herself up, her chest rising and falling with dry heaves.

Wrapped only in her cloak, she stuffed the bloodied sheets and nightgown behind the barrel of salt.

She held her dead baby once again and looked into his tiny face. A love and compassion that she didn't know she had flooded her heart.

"I name you Henry after your uncle, my beautiful sweet Henry. Fly into the arms of God, little one. He waits for you there. You may not have asked to be born into this world but you will always be loved."

Feeling dizzy and wooden with tiredness, Isabel lay Henry down beside her; she barely had the strength to hold him now. She would have a little sleep then decide what to do. She was so tired. *Yes,* she thought, *I'll sleep a little, and then get up when the palace is quiet. Perhaps I'll bury my little Henry in the orchards somewhere, early in the morning.*

Even as she thought those thoughts, sleep took her.

***

Isabel felt that she had just closed her eyes when she was forced to wake up again.

It was too soon! Go away!

She tried to snuggle down into unconsciousness again.

A hand clasped over her mouth.

Her eyes flew open in terror.

110

Awake now, but still tired and drained beyond belief, Isabel tried to focus on what was happening. She felt disoriented.

What was going on? Her body was being moved but she couldn't muster the energy to clear her brain of its fog.

She felt like she was being rolled, then heaved. The dark night had disappeared into total blackness. Opening her eyes wider made no difference.

Perhaps she had died after all and this was hell.

The faceless beings of that place had come to take her away into their home of deeper darkness.

***

As the evenings activities in Windsor had came to a close, Anne and Henry lingered together in an alcove while Wolsey's party gathered to leave for York Place.

Their kisses were devouring of each other. They pressed their bodies together trying to become one as much as they could with clothing between them.

Henry pulled away gently. His body shaking with con-trolled passion.

"Anne, Anne, Anne," he closed his eyes to minimise the temptation of kissing her again. "Till next Sunday, my love."

"Next Sunday …" whispered Anne, drowsy with desire.

Henry extracted himself reluctantly and ran swiftly, with a quick wave, to join the Cardinal with his secretary and other pages at the water steps. As he waited to board Wolsey's barge, he turned his head to see Anne's back disappearing into the night. The sight of her left him with a warm glow of happiness inside and a hardening, which he tried to disguise by hugging his cloak to himself.

Gentle banter and light-hearted ribbing about the night's events between the pages whiled away the short time back down river. So it was with complete surprise, as they entered the hall at York Place, to be pulled up with a sharp command barked from the Cardinal.

"Lord Percy!"

Henry turned in his tracks from where he had just begun to mount the stairs. Wolsey stood still, his podgy hands resting on his great stomach, tapping in agitation, in the middle of the hall.

His tone drew everybody's attention. They all slowed to a stop as they headed to their chambers for the night and looked back and forth between Henry and their master.

Henry stepped down from the stairs and took a few uncertain steps towards the Cardinal. Everybody waited to see what would happen. The Cardinal didn't discourage them.

"As you know," started Wolsey slowly, with a heavy sigh, as if he was explaining a simple fact to a dimwit. "No marriage of a peer of the realm can be contracted without the king's permission. Do you not understand this Lord Percy?"

Wolsey continued not giving Henry any time to reply. "You have offended your father and your sovereign ..."

Henry interrupted. "With all respect, I am old enough to choose for myself, my lord! Anne's noble parentage is equivalent to mine ..."

"Enough!" roared Wolsey. "Think you that the king and I don't know what to do in such weighty matters as these?"

"My lord," interjected Henry with another nervous swallow but still standing strong. "Our betrothal has been announced before witnesses. I cannot extricate myself from this engagement without offending my conscience."

Wolsey gave Henry a weary look, dropping his hands to his side. "You wilful, wilful boy. Shall I make it plain? His Majesty has already an intended for the mistress in question!"

Henry was stunned into silence. Had he heard correctly?

"Yes, Lord Percy, even though she does not know it yet herself."

Henry looked nonplussed. He shook his head. It couldn't be true!

"You are betrothed to another lady. A Lady Mary Talbot, I believe?"

Henry felt like he was sinking. He shook his head. "No, no, no, my lord ..."

"Lord Percy, you leave me no option but to write to your father this minute. As of now, you will never see or contact Mistress Anne Boleyn again. Do I make myself understood? You will stay, under guard if necessary, here at York Place until your father is informed. Mr. Melton!" Wolsey barked again, motioning to another page standing by. "Take Lord Percy to his room. Remain with him there, until I release you."

James Melton, looking almost as downcast as Henry, led his friend slowly up the staircase.

Stunned, Henry followed in silence.

Within his room, now his prison, Henry went straight to his desk and proceeded to write furiously. James laid a hand on Henry's shoulder.

"Henry, whatever are you doing?"

Henry spoke as he wrote, his quill scratching and leaving blotches of ink in his haste to write. "Take this letter to Anne, as soon as you are able."

James leaned over Henry's shoulder and read a line. "Don't allow yourself to marry another man. Remember our promise, which only God can loose …"

James stood up, his face full of concern. "Henry, I have come to love you like a brother, but for the love of God, you can't go against the king's wishes. You'll end up in the tower … or worse!"

Knowing it was true, Henry cried out in anguish. He lashed out at the writing material in frustration, wiping it to the floor. Ink splattered and paper flew. James jumped back to avoid ink on his hose.

As everything settled, Henry laid his head in his arms and sobbed as if the world had ended.

***

Anne awoke the next morning with something irritating her in the back of her mind.

As she slowly woke up, she kept still, not wanting to wake Mary sleeping next to her.

She had made her way to Isabel's chamber after leaving Henry last night. She was nowhere to be found. Her bed was untouched. It was very odd and disturbing. Nobody had seen her.

Anne snuggled into her blankets. Perhaps she had met a man? Perhaps she had been held up in an alcove as she had been. Yes, that was probably it. She was sailing close to the wind, though, leaving it that late to get to bed. She would be getting a reprimand from the queen, that much Anne knew for sure.

The queen was a kind and compassionate woman but she would not stand for dilly-dallying among her ladies.

Mary stirred beside her as a pounding sounded at the door. Anne rose reluctantly, shuffling as she threw a shawl about her shoulders. She opened the door.

It was their brother, George.

Anne frowned, wiping the sleep from her eyes. "George, do you have to be so loud?"

She left the door for him to close and jumped back into bed.

George closed the door and plopped himself with great gusto onto the edge of the four-poster.

Mary dragged herself up from under the covers, still half asleep. "Hello, you," she purred affectionately. George pulled one of her tussled locks in a return greeting.

"Worn you out has he, our randy lord and master?"

"George!" scolded Mary with a half smile, which told both Anne and him she enjoyed every minute of the king's rutting.

He put on a serious face for Anne. "You, Mistress, have an audience with Wolsey, our Uncle Howard, and Father, right this minute."

Anne frowned again, pulling the blankets under her chin. "Why?" she pouted.

That was the last thing she felt like doing.

"Come on Anna, times-a-wasting!"

"Are you serious? Right now?"

"I'm deadly serious, *mon cher*. I mean it. Father does not look happy."

Anne reluctantly left the bed. "Oh, what now? Is Mary needed?"

"No. Only you."

"Do you know what it's about?"

"No. I only know you should have been there five minutes ago."

Anne muttered under her breath as she began to dress, flustered and awkward without the help she was used to.

A few moments later, they left Mary to her slumbering and made their way to a room off the chapel. George opened the door and gently guided Anne into the gloom with his hand at the small of her back. She snapped her head back as George closed the door behind her, his presence remaining without.

Unable to see that well in the gloom of the cavernous room, she took a few careful steps forward. As her eyes adjusted to the light, she could see her Father, Wolsey and Norfolk seated like judges behind a long table.

"Come," she heard one of them say.

She walked forward some more and stood in a weak pool of sunlight spilling down from a casement high above. She could feel its warmth seeping into her bones. It felt good. She relaxed, clasped her hands behind her back and focused on the panel of men before her.

"Father?"

Her father ignored her and deferred to Wolsey with a nod of the head.

"Come here, you silly girl," said Wolsey coldly.

Suppressing hurt from her father's lack of support, she squared her shoulders and faced the Cardinal.

She'd never thought of anybody as an enemy before, but before God, she felt it now. Enmity threaded through her like a vine creeping up from beneath the flagstones and winding its tendrils around her limbs. They climbed, finding their way into her chest and there twined their barbs into her heart. Her eyes glittered like flint.

"Sir?" she challenged.

"This matter between you and Lord Percy has come to an end."

There was a deathly pause.

Anne felt like she'd been slapped in the face. Emotions rose but she quelled them quickly. She would not let Wolsey see that he had got the better of her.

"Lord Percy has already been precontracted to Lady Mary Talbot for some years now and the wedding will take place in the next few months." Wolsey did not know this for sure, but his suggestions were as good as done. He was sure the Earl of Northumberland would readily agree, having caused his sovereign grief through his disobedient son.

"You will never have contact with Lord Percy again. You are dismissed from court until further notice. Have I made myself clear?"

Anne fumed. Her hatred of Wolsey fell into depths that could not be voiced.

Rigid with anger and pain and wounded pride, she spun on her heels and slammed the door behind her with all the strength she could muster.

Sir Thomas Boleyn rose and bowed stiffly to Wolsey and Norfolk as he made his way out to escort his daughter home.

Would things never go right? Damn Wolsey's meddling; it could have been a good match. Damn Anne for not watching where she placed her affections without his say so.

The ride home to Hever was bound by tension and heavy silence as both father and daughter, so very alike, sunk into worlds of their own.

CHAPTER SEVENTEEN

Suffolk Countryside

Isabel was jerked awake.

The English countryside flew by her. Dawn had broken about an hour before and the day held the promise of a late summer, sun-kissed day. The cloudless, pewter sky, which had given way to pale violet was now giving way to a brilliant azure hue as the sun's rays touched the infinite dome like an artist's brush on canvas.

It was a few moments before she realised she was riding pillion on a large stallion.

Isabel didn't recognise any landmarks. Strange, gently rolling hills, dotted with wattle and daub hamlets, passed by. The occasional head looked up from a scythe and animals stopped their grazing to stare at the fast moving intrusion.

By the positioning of the sun, she could tell they were travelling north. The rider guided his large black stallion over another jump. She went to use her arms and legs to balance herself, but it was not necessary. Her captor had a firm arm around her waist. A gush of blood and sharp pain flared from her pelvic floor as the horse landed.

Feeling movement in his charge, the rider spoke into her hair as his chin rested on her head.

"Awake now, are we?"

She felt the warmth of his breath on her head and stiffened.

It was the voice of that man, the one with the faint French inflection, the voice of her husband.

CHAPTER EIGHTEEN

Alnwich Castle

The Earl of Northumberland, an early riser, entered his study with his favourite wolfhounds, having seen the sun rise on the rocky moors as he exercised his falcon.

The smell of freshly baked bread drifted to him from the main hall as Alnwick Castle reluctantly stirred itself into the day's activities.

A young page stood by to receive the earl of his cloak and gauntlets. He bowed silently and left the earl to begin his day's activities.

Two scrolled parchments caught Henry's eye as he passed by his writing table to the window. Scratching the heads of his dogs with absentminded affection, he picked up one scroll and undid the blue ribbon.

His attention focused as he came across the wax seal. His brows furrowed.

It was sealed with the crest of an old deceased family.

He knew that the family was deceased because he was made aware of it almost twenty years ago.

As he read, his face hardened.

After a moment, he grabbed the other rolled missive, broke its blank seal and shook it open.

He couldn't believe it. He looked from one letter to the other. What was really going on? Were these enemy factions working together or was it just fate that the two requests from decided enemies should end up in his hands at the same time?

He turned both parchments slowly in his fingers as if that action might release their true motive. Whatever it was, he was going to have to be above everybody's game if he and those dear to him were going to survive. And one of them would pay! Yes, one of them would pay for their trumped up insolence! How dare they threaten him! He who held the greatest earldom in the realm! They had risen too high in their own eyes. It was up to him to cut them down.

He paced his study as he mentally ticked things off for a plan of action. But no plan would form. There was only irritation. The forgotten memories and dark thoughts of a particular time of his past flooded back into his consciousness.

One of the messages was done in type, very unusual. There would be no way to track such a letter. There were print shops in just about every established town.

The seal was something different. He knew that that belonged to a family that dwelt in the border country.

Not a man to sit back and wait, he quickly made a decision to find Heron and Turnull.

"My lord?"

The earl spun around to face his wife, Catherine, who stood in the arched stone lintel.

He smiled kindly on his wife. She had served him well over the years. She had stood beside him and supported him in all his endeavours.

Theirs was not a love match. They were like chalk and cheese on many different issues, but they had long made a decision to stand as one where their family and future were concerned. In this, they were totally unified.

Behind the curtains of their bed, they discussed their business, planning and plotting their way forward, as well as sating their healthy physical appetites.

All but for this one issue, a burden that he alone had carried and one that he'd thought was dead and buried.

He stuffed the troubling pieces of parchment into his doublet.

To sidetrack his discerning wife, he took her hand and pressed it to his lips, he flicked his tongue on the back of her hand.

"My lord," she demurred uncomfortably. "The servants ..."

He held her eyes with a compelling look as he raised his voice. "If I want to take my wife to bed in the middle of the day, it is nobody else's business but my own. I am the master of this house and nobody is going to gainsay it."

Catherine blushed furiously. Before she could question or berate his actions, he drew an arm around her waist and planted a kiss on her mouth as they walked back into the hall.

"Harrumph."

The sound of their house steward pulled them both apart as he made his way towards them with downcast eyes, the back of his hand at his mouth.

He bowed a stiff bow, as much as his arthritis would allow.

"My lord, a messenger. A messenger from London."

They both raised their eyes to a travel weary figure who came a few paces behind the steward. He presented himself with a deep bow from the waist.

"My Lord Earl, my lady, I have urgent correspondence from my master, Cardinal Wolsey."

The messenger drew forth a slim parchment with Wolsey's seal from his doublet and presented it to the earl with a bow.

The earl dismissed the messenger to the kitchens for refreshments.

Back in his study, the earl broke the seal and read silently. After a while, the hand holding the letter dropped to his side. His face seemed to instantly drop and line. Catherine had come in quietly behind him and stood with her back to the closed door. She waited patiently. He was oblivious to the curiosity that coursed within her. She couldn't hold back any longer.

"Henry?"

The earl shook his head in disbelief. When he eventually found his tongue, it was forged with fury.

"That impudent puppy!"

"My lord?"

The earl swung around and shook the letter at her. Rage suddenly animated his face. "Our son has just had the audacity to offend his majesty, the King of England!"

Catherine's hands flew to her blanching face. "Oh, God save us! What has he done? What has he done?"

She groped for a chair and slumped into it, her legs suddenly unable to bear their weight.

"He has chosen to have an affair with one Mistress Anne Boleyn, one of the queen's waiting women, and announced his betrothal to her. All the while, the king has another intended for her! And he already betrothed to Mary Talbot! By God's blood, it is not to be borne! I must be away to London immediately! We cannot be in a position of offending another king!"

Husband and wife looked at each other in alarm as an eerie feeling of doom settled over them.

Many years ago, the earl had offended Henry's father, King Henry VII. They had been fined ten thousand pounds. They had only paid a tenth of the fine when it had been suspended, but they both knew that his son could call it in at any time.

They both swallowed the feeling of escalating fear and potential disaster. When it came to personal survival, they would always do what had to be done.

They lived like their own monarchy in the north but if self-preservation required some bowing and scraping, by God, that's what they would do.

Damn that boy! I'll have his hide whipped until there is nothing left! Useless good for nothing! The earl didn't voice his thoughts to his wife as satisfying as it would be to vent his anger. Nothing would be gained by adding to her pain.

Henry knelt beside his wife and took her hands within his. She searched his eyes, looking for comfort.

"All will be well, Cat, my love. All will be well." He applied his voice to her like a salve. To himself, he added, *I may kill him, but all will be well.*

Then another thought dropped into his mind, one no less weighty than the last.

Isabel.

He hoped that she was all right. Were the seeds from his youth harvesting before his eyes? How could they? He had thought they had been dealt with at conception. It was treachery. That's what it was. It came from a source that had been close at his side for more than thirty or forty years.

He didn't voice that thought either.

He patted his wife's knee as he stood up.

In a moment, he was gone, leaving her to stare at the fading indentations of his fingers on hers.

CHAPTER NINETEEN

Colchester, Suffolk

He had planned on sleeping under the stars as they travelled north, so as not to attract attention, but as he pulled his horse to and set to alight against a rocky incline, he realised that Isabel was unconscious. No amount of verbal ribbing or gentle shaking was bringing her around. It was only then that he noticed the stain of blood seeping ominously through the woollen cloak he had wrapped her in.

With a grimace, he hooked his chin over her shoulder and peeled away the sodden patch of cloak. He felt slightly stunned as he viewed her lap saturated in fresh blood.

He felt for a wound, but nothing was obvious.

With a sudden start and a warm rush to his cheeks, embarrassed, he wondered if he was looking at woman with her monthly course, but surely not with this much blood?

A doctor. He needed a doctor. He wrapped Isabel up again. Her head hung like a limp rag doll, her face deathly white.

The nearest town that they had just skirted was the old Roman founded town of Colchester. It lay just a few miles south. He turned his stallion around and headed back the way they had come.

Darkness had well settled as they entered the ancient town. Parts of Roman dwellings still existed, even the castle, though much diminished from what it used to be. They passed a few inns and taverns, but the rider with his pillion chose the busiest one, so as to melt into the crowd. The brightly coloured sign, declaring the establishment of The Ox and Plough, was bathed in a warm golden light as patrons came and went. The mouth-watering smell of roast meat wafted on the air along with bursts of laughter and convivial chatter.

Isabel's captor turned his steed into the inn's stable court-yard behind the main building. A cocky young stable lad swanked out of the gloom. He munched on an apple as he confidently took the horse's bit.

"M'lor'?"

"Can you water and feed him, boy?"

The cocky youth chucked his chin into the air in affirmation, swallowing his mouthful. "Of course, m'lor'," he said in his broad Suffolk accent, noting the quality of horseflesh that stood before him and the well made travelling clothes of its rider.

"Wha' a beauty you are then!" He stood back to admire the horse's confirmation then drew in and fed it the last of his apple.

"May I help you with the missus, m'lor'?"

"My wife has taken ill. Is there a doctor here about? We need to have a room."

"Yes to both m'lor. Doc Fines be just up the way. I'll git him meself after I sees to 'is nibs 'ere. Sees em light from yonder door? Mistress Simcock be runnin' about. She be the propriertess of this 'ere inn. She'll find you yon' room."

The rider, with his bundle, slithered down the side of the horse.

"Through there, m'lor'," encouraged the stable hand with the tilt of his head towards the light emanating from the back door.

"Thank you, lad. I'll see you right in the morning."

"Pleasure, m'lor', pleasure," said the stable hand, delighting in looking after so fine a specimen of horseflesh.

To the left of the back entrance, the kitchens were bustling with energy of serving the evening meal. Hot, moist air wrapped suffocatingly around the tall, young man with his wife in his arms.

A large, well-upholstered woman was making her way towards him from the dining room, empty trenchers stacked in her large, capable hands. Her face glowed with perspiration causing her grey hair to curl in damp tendrils about her cap. Her face lit up as she saw him; her cheeks shone like rosy red apples.

"Well, sir! Good evening to you! How may I be of assistance?"

"Are you mistress Simcock?"

"Aye. That be me, my good sir."

"Your stable lad directed me this way. My wife is ill. I need a room and a doctor."

The proprietor turned her head and bellowed back down the hallway. Within seconds, a young serving girl came running and bobbing simultaneously.

"Mary, take these trenchers and refill them for the table next the window by the fire. Be quick smart about it girl! I have to see to this gentleman's needs."

Mary obliged without a word. Mistress Simcock wiped her hands on her abundant apron.

"Come this way, sir."

He followed the large woman, her skirts swaying from her hips like a ship rocking in a sheltered harbour.

Wall sconces lit the way with a muted light. It appeared to be a quality establishment with the wood polished and gleaming.

Mistress Simcock opened a door at last. Her hips made it through with no room to spare. The room was of a medium size, laid with fresh rushes on the floor. It smelled clean. The one bed, big enough to lay five people side by side, was made up with fresh quality linen with a cot at its foot and a table with two chairs stood under a window facing north.

"Here, lay the poor lamb down," Mistress Simcock patted the bed. "I'll just light the fire—Oh, my lord! She's losing blood!"

Mistress Simcock caught a glimpse of his wife's garment under the cloak.

"Yes, can you tell the doctor to hurry?"

"She don't need no doctor, she needs a midwife. How many weeks gone is she?"

Weeks gone? What was she talking about?

Mistress Simcock gently drew aside the cloak. "She ain't shown' yet, maybe, twenty weeks at the most." She patted the cloak back in place to keep her warm.

"Poor luvey," she clucked sympathetically. "Is it your first?"

His face was blank. "First what?"

"Why, your first child o' course?"

Isabel's captor paced in front of the fire, with a cup of spiced wine in his hands while Mistress Simcock went in search for the local midwife. This was a situation that he hadn't counted on. He wasn't sure how to take things from here. He wished Jacincka were here. She would know what to do.

The inn grew quiet after a while. The kitchens had finished their work and patrons had found their way into their rented beds or back home.

Both doctor and midwife had seen to Isabel. She had not been losing the baby, but had indeed lost it some hours ago.

By the lack of distensions of stomach and breasts, the diagnosis was a stillborn at about twenty or so weeks.

She had lost a lot of blood, hence the unconsciousness. The flow had been staunched and nettle tea was at the bedside ready for ingestion when Isabel came around. The doctor gave strict instructions that she was not to be moved under any circumstances and he would make morning calls until matters improved.

He wondered where the body of the dead baby had been put, since the event must have happened just before he found her.

He rubbed his brow and looked at her now. Clean, padded up and resting quietly, she looked very pale and fragile.

He frowned as his thoughts led him on into anger.

His anger grew until he didn't know how to vent it without destroying something, and that would only draw unnecessary attention. So he maintained his self control by pacing.

The words now came back to him, words that had been thrown to him in delighted spite before they had left France for England—words that he'd taken to be empty.

"She belongs to Gavyn, Richard. You may have been my first-born but I disown you. This legacy belongs to me and mine. I won't forget what you've done. I'll never forgive you. Do you hear me, Richard! I'll never forgive you!"

Richard's face glowered as he remembered his father's words spoken only a few months ago. Rage had overtaken him. It was a symptom of a deeper issue: abandonment. Rage had so overcome him that he had taken his father's life.

He was not a murderer. He mourned deeply for the loss of his father, of the relationship that he would now never have, but his father deserved it. How dare he abandon him, his first-born son!

In the last few months, he had wallowed between self-righteousness and despair. But now he had risen up and he was going to take what was his!

Isabel's unexpected infirmity had momentarily floundered him. He knew that Gavyn had beaten him to it. *But it doesn't matter,* he thought to himself. In fact, the more he thought about it, the better it was for him. He could turn this whole situation around to his advantage.

As Richard swallowed another mouthful of wine, his mood lightened with every step he paced.

Yes, he thought, nodding his head to himself, *yes. Being a childless couple won't be my fault. Her womb will have been damaged by this unfortunate event. I must find the doctor's price. Everybody has his or her price. Most times they just don't know it.*

He almost laughed out loud with delight and his pacing was interrupted with a little skip.

His pacing lost its energy in the darkest hour before dawn. He pulled out the pallet bed from against the wall and sunk into a dreamless sleep.

He awoke groggily into a sun-filled room. For a few moments he couldn't remember where he was but as his eyes fell on Isabel, his mind became instantly alert.

Isabel hadn't moved at all but with relief, he saw her chest continuing to rise and fall.

He made a decision to put all his energies into nurturing a relationship with her. His plans for her were all that mattered right now. If he didn't have her, he didn't have anything. So nursing her back to health was his main agenda.

He rose and washed in cold water with the pitcher and bowl provided on the side table. He decided that subterfuge might be best in the circumstances; she would find out soon enough.

A knock at the door produced breakfast from Mistress Simcock herself, with lengthy instructions on how to ladle the thin, beefy broth into the invalid. Laying the tray aside, he sat at Isabel's bedside and tried to rouse her.

He smoothed her thick blonde hair away from her face. She had refined features. He stared, appreciating her beauty. He loved beauty in all its forms. He loved art and architecture, scenery with all its lines and forms, music and poetry.

He had never known about these things in his childhood. He had been torn away from his family by a border skirmish. After being lost at sea, he was found again, only to be worked like an ox in the field. It was only a few years ago that his lover had opened his eyes to the beauty that existed in the world. His amber eyes glazed over, as he seemed to go into a trance. His mind travelled into his past, as it often did, into places of pain so deep that even his conscious mind didn't know that it was there. It seemed to him that he just blanked out sometimes. When he was brought back to the present, he assumed that he had been daydreaming.

When he came to, he focused on Isabel again.

He paused to admire her delicate features. Dark lashes, blonde at the tips, a straight nose and a mouth that curved naturally and cutely at the corners. Even in repose, it looked like she was smiling, a smile devoid of colour maybe, but delightful to behold anyway.

He stroked the side of her face and called her name.

There was no response.

He rose and wrung out a lawn cloth from the ablutions bowl and then wiped her brow. Isabel moaned and slowly turned her head away from him.

Her eyes gradually fluttered open.

Grey-blue irises, flecked with rust and ringed with dark blue stared dully back at him.

"Good morning, Mistress Percy," he ventured with gentleness.

Isabel could only manage a moan. She tried to move. Seeing her difficulty, he reached around under her arms and pulled her up into a sitting position.

"I feel like I'm made of wood," she said trying to focus on the man who woke her. Her head spun out and she waited with eyes closed until the dizziness disappeared.

"The doctor says that you have lost a lot of blood, which he says is not so bad as it will get rid of the bad humours that made you loose your baby. But you have to eat and drink to regain your strength again." He stopped to see that she was taking in his words.

"Isabel? Do you understand me?"

She nodded ever so slightly and slowly opened her eyes.

"Good. Good girl. Do you feel up to taking some broth?"

She groaned an assent.

He walked to the table and picked up the steaming broth from a tray. He turned to see recognition, with fear and apprehension in her eyes.

He stopped in his tracks.

What was going on in her head? He remembered his mission, to get to know her and gain her confidence. *She had to be terrified at being abducted. Wasn't I?*

"Would you like some beef broth?" he offered again, holding the bowl up with raised eyebrows.

She nodded again, but her distrust of him was still evident.

He didn't take offence and he resigned himself to the thought that she might never trust him, but he would do what he had to do.

He carefully poured a spoonful of the nutritious meaty mixture into her mouth.

She closed her eyes, trying to conserve energy as she swallowed.

"I'm sorry for the loss of your baby."

His words of sympathy made her eyes open. She looked directly at him. Was this the same man that raped her? He looked the same but he could have been a totally different person.

"Our baby, I'll have you know," she whispered in anger. She looked up. "But how do you know?"

He concentrated on feeding her as he spoke. "A doctor and a midwife have been here. I'm sorry for your loss."

Her glare at him was as dark as death but she still took from the offered spoon.

He ignored her look and after she had finished the broth, he pulled the blankets up under her chin.

"Sleep now," he encouraged. "You need to rest. Here, have a sip of nettle tea." He put the cup to her lips.

She grimaced at its bitterness.

"The midwife said it's good for your humours. I'll be here when you wake. When you're feeling better, we'll talk. You'll have a few questions, no doubt?"

She looked at him blankly then closed her eyes as her body took the rest it needed.

CHAPTER TWENTY

Hever Castle, Kent

Anne stared vacantly at the brocade tester above her bed.

She had spent most of her time here since being banished to Hever in disgrace.

The stress of everything had brought on massive headaches and only lying in a dark room would alleviate them.

The only sign on her face, bearing witness to the torrents of tears shed over the last week, were the whites of her eyes. They were slightly red. The skin on her face had never changed colour. There were no blotchy red spots or swollen puffy eyes. Her skin remained as cool and creamy and as dew fresh as a crocus in the spring.

She barely touched her food. When she was coaxed into a spoonful of something from the kitchen, she found herself choking on it, the smells bringing on waves of nausea.

Her grief over the loss of Henry and the loss of dreams of a future with him seemed to threaten the very life that was in her.

Her slight frame had reduced even more, to where her ribs had begun to show in her chest and her hip bones jutted through her underskirts.

Her father had not spoken to her since delivering her to Hever. Her mother, home from court from attendance to the queen, had not spoken much either. When she did speak, her berating of Anne was full of her own personal frustrations, about the disappointment that she had been to them, especially after all that they had done for her and Mary. Giving them an education overseas in royal houses and this is how she thanked them? Playing the whore? That comment really hurt Anne. That her own Mother chose to believe Wolsey's words over her own was the ultimate in betrayal. The lack of support from her parents left her spiralling down further into despair.

Fresh, hot tears slipped silently down her temples and into the strands of hair lying dankly on the pillowcase.

Isabel, Isabel, how I wish you were with me! I need a friend! Perhaps I'll write to you. Invite you to visit, if I'm allowed visitors.

Henry, Henry why don't you fight for me? Anne felt herself getting angry with Henry. *Stand up and be my knight in shining armour! Fight for my honour that has been besmirched by Wolsey! Why won't you come? Are you such a boy that you won't stand up for me?*

Come and get me that we may run away together. Don't you know that I would love you for the rest of my days!

We could live far away from those who have hurt us. We would love and grow old together. Henry ... Henry ... Henry ...

Salty tears continued to flow as she thought of his caresses and kisses that she would know no more. She could dwell for eternity in one of his kisses. His kisses peeled open her soul, like a flower beneath the sun, petal by petal.

I will never flourish again, she thought mournfully. *My soul will dwell in a continual winter, dormant until it dies. How can I live without him? How? How?*

But if he is not man enough to come for me, how shall I live with that?

More tears flowed.

Something woke Anne up. She felt slightly surprised; she hadn't even realised that she had drifted off to sleep.

There were people in the courtyard below.

The casements of her leadlight windows were open and the sounds of gay banter, laughter, horses' hooves on cobblestones and the jangling of bits in horses' mouths drifted up to her. It was a light, happy sound, borne on the swirl of a sultry afternoon breeze.

Anne felt hot and sticky. She rose and walked to the window.

A warm breeze dried the sweat on her skin as it caressed her body. She blinked her eyes because she couldn't believe who stood talking to her father.

It was the king!

As she put her hands on the window ledge and gripped the sill for a closer look, her shift fell off her left shoulder, baring the most part of a pert breast. In that same instant, the king looked up catching the movement in the periphery of his vision.

She instantly moved back into the shadows of her room, but not before Henry caught a glimpse of his heart's desire.

Seeing her thus only confirmed his actions for finding himself here. A thrill of lust and passion rippled through him.

It was her! Oh, and how exotic she looked! Dark hair spilling over her shoulders and her gown barely covering her modesty! It had been worth the deception of making his way here, of telling his company, and indeed himself, that the hunting down this way was excellent at the moment.

Oh, and what did you know? Hever Castle! Well, it wouldn't be neighbourly not to call in on his dear friend, Sir Thomas!

Henry shoved aside any feelings of guilt in his heart of dabbling in adultery. In fact, it barely registered at all, so strong were his feelings storming within him.

The visit was all in fun and totally unplanned; if things came of it, so what?

Sir Thomas Boleyn followed the king's gaze to Anne's window.

The movement at the lead casement came and went in an instant, but the look in the king's eyes lingered a moment longer, just enough for a seed of discernment to sprout within Sir Thomas. It quickly took root, like fire running along a trail of gunpowder; it then blossomed into revelation that filled him with a burst of unexpected euphoria.

His mind raced around. My God! My God! Could this situation that his family found itself in, be orchestrated by the king himself?

Could it be, that the person disgraced, was to be their saviour? Why else should they be favoured by this unexpected visit? The king had never gone out of his way to visit here before, even though they were only one hour's ride out of London. Yes, there was more to this than met the eye: first Mary, now Anne. Opportunity, how best to play the opportunity?

Sir Thomas veiled his thoughts to the king as he invited him and his small party into the cool depths of his house for refreshments.

Hever Castle was quickly shaken from its oppressive moodiness and into a fever of heightened activity.

The best of provisions were dug out, dusted off and whipped up for the royal party.

Anne was momentarily forgotten as a light meal was brought forth and washed down with the best wine Hever had to offer. For the first time in days, Hever Castle resounded with the light-hearted sounds of good-natured ribbing, stimulating conversation and abundant laughter.

It was a passing comment thrown down to Sir Thomas as Henry mounted his horse to depart, that the real reason for his visit surfaced.

How was it that they had not been served by his daughter Anne? Was she not well?

Sir Thomas informed Henry that Anne had indeed been indisposed these last few days to which explained her lack of presence. Henry voiced his disappointment at not being able to see her and promised to send her something from the palace hot house that would revive her spirits.

As the king and his small hunting band made their way back to London, Sir Thomas walked thoughtfully back to find his wife. The euphoria at being reinstated into the king's favour was beginning to dissipate. He knew that favour would only be maintained under the king's terms, spoken or unspoken. The king would take and they would be left with spoilt goods. Spoilt goods never fetched a good price.

He found his wife overseeing the washing and polishing of the silver plate used for the refreshments. He felt a moment of pleasure watching her. God had blessed him with a woman who was indeed virtuous, her price far above rubies, as she was fond of telling him. She was capable and she knew her duty. She supported him in his plans and used her Howard name to their advantage whenever she could.

With no warning, she had stirred the sullen servants into producing succulent food and provided a delightful atmosphere of welcoming warmth with her intuitive ways.

She turned her head and smiled at him as he entered the room. He was always amazed that not a hair was out of place despite the demands put on her in these last few hours. She had always been like that.

"My dear, may I talk with you a moment?"

The servant's ears were itching for gossip after the king's impromptu visit. They were disappointed as Sir Thomas led the Lady Elizabeth away.

Across the moat, arm in arm, they appeared to the casual passer-by to be taking the air, relaxing in each other's company.

"Thomas?" inquired Elizabeth when they were at a safe distance from flapping ears.

Sir Thomas took a deep breath before unravelling his thoughts before his wife. After he had emptied himself of his theories, his wife looked at him with incredulity. She opened her mouth to say something then shut it.

They stood standing, still arm in arm, under a large walnut tree staring at the horizon in silence, both staring into their own versions of the future.

Cows lowed from across the meadows dotted with buttercups and daisies. A few clouds appeared from the west, heralding the close of a flawless autumn day.

Lady Elizabeth was the first to speak. Thomas could see that she felt as torn as he was for their daughters. He had always imagined them to have good marriages, which would bring honour and strength to the name of Boleyn, especially in Court circles. They had worked hard to set a right course for their daughters, from hiring a French governess when they were small to an education with Queen Claude, the most pious woman in Europe, as young ladies.

Where had they gone wrong? Mary had been used and cast aside, by a king no less, but still cast aside and although married to a gentleman of the king's chamber, it was without affect. There was no increase for the family by way of money, lands or titles. Mary's husband, William Carey, only had a small farm to his name.

Now Anne. Was she to suffer the same fate? To be ruined of a good marriage? What could they do? To push Anne in front of the king would lead to a second-rate marriage like Mary, but what were the options? Withholding Anne from the king's affections could well mean loss of favour, which equalled life as they knew it, or worse, imprisonment for the slightest offence.

He had seen it happen many times with royalty ever since he had been a page in Henry VII's court. He had seen favourites come and go, the jealousies of some poisoning those who held close confidences to the throne. Then came the enquiries and the inevitable trials, which of course would come to nothing, then imprisonment or the loss of a head.

He felt for Anne; he felt for himself. It wasn't fair. He and Elizabeth had done everything they could to position themselves and their family to prosper.

A marriage with the Percy family would have been a great advantage to them all. He could imagine the Earl of Northumberland would have found ties to the infamous Howard family just as advantageous as he had found them.

Damn Henry for not keeping his eyes to his own wife!

Thomas felt his anger rise and quickly tried to diffuse it. Venting his anger would be a waste of energy. He must use that energy to focus on what was best for them all.

He knew that nothing could be gained by letting your heart rule your head. Anne would have to realise that too and if she had any sense, she would recognise that this was a good opportunity to practise that.

He also realised that Anne had her first taste of calf love. That sort of love, he remembered from experience, was the most painful, but the sooner she understood how life was really played out, the better off they'd all be.

Thomas could see his wife accepting the inevitable.

She tried to smile as she swallowed her bitterness. Unfortunately, it only contorted her mouth into an ugly twist.

It was a look that mirrored his own thoughts. He squeezed her hands with affection. He had prayed for advancement and here it was, but at what cost? He shook his head to himself. He didn't want to think about it.

"We had better encourage her to eat some dinner tonight," said Elizabeth, still gazing across the fields. "We can't have a scrawny mistress for our sovereign."

CHAPTER TWENTY-ONE

York Place, London

Henry the Magnificent thundered down to London, with unaccustomed frugality for the sake of haste, to find that his son had aged ten years.

Unlike Anne, who slept away her days in a stupor of depression and anxiety, Henry's inner turmoil kept him from sleep. He'd drift off at night only to wake an hour later. There, he would toss and turn until dawn, or more often, he would rise and wander the vacant hallways or the gardens of York Place by moonlight.

He, like Anne, had also lost his appetite. Rather than endure being spoken to or spoken about, Henry just disappeared at meal times. He put his hand to his duties during the day but there had been no heart in it. Wolsey could not fault him in obedience but he could see that Henry had withdrawn into himself where no person could go and he was glad to release him into his father's hands.

Northumberland and Wolsey arrived at York Place from a private audience with the king. After showing the earl to his own private writing chamber, Wolsey despatched James Melton to alert Henry of his father's presence; he then left to give father and son some privacy.

James found Henry sitting on a marble bench under a plum tree. He was gazing blankly out to the River Thames, a book of

Greek Myths in Greek and his own book of transcriptions, closed in his lap.

Henry looked totally unkempt. His blond hair was in disarray. Dark shadows circled his eyes and a gaunt pallor haunted his face.

Henry followed James like a lamb to the slaughter. He went silently and uncaring of the next moment.

The earl was alarmed at his son's physical condition. It made him angrier than ever that the boy didn't have a strong mental attitude to handle disappointment. Life was full of disappointments. He would have to learn fast if he was going to amount to anything.

God's blood! Why was he straddled with such an addlepated jax for his first-born!

As James closed the door behind him, Henry stood as one condemned, waiting for the expected barrage of words to come.

Sickened at the sight of his insipid son, the earl released the torrent that was expected. He slammed his fist onto the corner of Wolsey's desk from where he stood, barely able to contain himself.

"I have just come from the king's presence. He has very magnanimously accepted our apologies for disturbing his peace! My son! Disturbing the king's peace!" He broke off and tried to control himself. He took a deep breath and continued with controlled calm.

"He wishes you well in your up and coming marriage to Lady Talbot, which has been arranged for the spring. You don't know how blessed you are, boy; it could have so easily gone the other way. Do you understand?"

Henry kept his eyes on his father. "And what of Anne's father? Did you hear anything? Who is the intended the king has for her?"

As Henry spoke the last few words, his voice started to break on the verge of tears. The earl was amazed to see his son's face crumble, giving into a sob then suddenly change into unadulterated rage.

His chin trembled with loathing and spittle spotted his mouth as he spoke like one possessed, his hands clenching at his sides.

"Who is the murdering son of a whore? She's promised to me! Me! We said our vows before God! If he touches her, by the …"

"Henry!" his father bellowed, cutting him off.

The earl was surprised at the ferocity coming from his son. He didn't know he had it in him. It pricked a little pride in his son; perhaps he had balls after all. It just took something he believed in to bring it out, but it was all misguided and rebellious. He would have to show a strong hand to keep him in line.

"If you persist in this I will cut you off! I will have no choice! You shall be no son of mine! Nothing will come of your infatuation with Mistress Boleyn! Nothing! She is lost to you! Don't you understand? She is lost to you! You must make a choice. Marry Lady Talbot and live a life of honour before God and your king or be cast away from me and mine? Which is it to be?"

Henry knew that he didn't have the strength to live life cut off from everything that he knew. His father's last words sounded as a death knell to him.

The earl watched his son's anger instantly evaporate.

His shoulders seemed to slump as the fire in his eyes died, like a dampened a candle.

"We also have another matter to discuss."

His son looked at him blankly.

"Where is Isabel?"

The blank look was still there.

"Isabel, man! When was the last time you saw Isabel?"

The earl could see his son trying to put coherent thought together. Eventually, words made their way out of his mouth.

"Ah, we last saw each other at Windsor Park. Ah, a few days ago now. The whole court was there for some festivities that the Cardinal had set up."

"Was she well?"

"Ah, yes. She'd been having a few headaches … but other than that, she was well."

"Was she seeing anybody?"

The earl received a questioning look.

"Anybody that you didn't know?"

"Why?"

"She's gone missing."

The earl left his son with instructions that they would be heading north as soon as Isabel had been found. He was to be packed and ready when that moment came.

CHAPTER TWENTY-TWO

Colchester, Suffolk

The minute Isabel opened her eyes, she knew she was on her way to recovery. It was the first morning that she didn't feel like closing her eyes again and snuggling down into sweet oblivion. She felt ready to face the day. She stretched languidly, thrilled at the feeling of energy coursing through her body. She hadn't felt like this for quite a while, not since before her pregnancy and she joyed in the feeling of it.

Now that she was on the way to improved health, Isabel thought about escape for the first time.

She would have to devise a way to get back to London. Surely, they would be looking for her now. Anne and Henry must be aware of her plight.

All in good time, she encouraged herself silently. *I'll wait until I regain my strength and look for opportunities to escape.*

Her husband, suddenly aware of being watched, turned and lifted his head to look at her.

She was taken aback by his handsome features. It was like she was seeing him for the first time. Curly, dark brown hair framed a chiselled face with a strong nose and defined cheekbones. He had shaved already and his darkly fringed amber eyes held no animosity as they had in France. Indeed, he smiled at her calmly and confidently, looking pleased to see her awake.

She frowned at herself for finding her captor attractive, then frowned again at her judgement of him. Over these last days, even through the haze from loss of blood, she could only remember kindness from his words and gentleness from his hands. His company had been very easy to be in.

Isabel could only concede that she was very confused now. He seemed like two different people. That can only mean she must be on her guard. If he was a tyrant once, he could be again.

Isabel gave him a quick, contained smile as she pulled herself up to sitting position.

It was a smile that didn't reach her eyes, he noted as he came to her aid fluffing up her pillows.

"I see God has answered my prayers. You appear much improved."

Isabel murmured a thank you, blushing suddenly, feeling embarrassed at being in a nightshift in the presence of a man she barely knew, although he had known her intimately.

Instantly discerning her discomfort, he tried to ease it with information that would help.

"Mistress Simcock saw to all your needs while you required assistance. Even the nightgown you wear belongs to one of her daughters. Let me assure you that all propriety was adhered to in your distress."

Isabel shot him a quick look. "Th … thank you. Mr… . er, Mr… ."

"Yes, now would be a good time for introductions."

He pulled up a chair beside her bed, took her hand in his and bowed over it.

"Richard Kerr of Kinwelach and Van der Veldt at your service."

Isabel looked surprised. So surprised that she looked him full in the face with wide eyes and her mouth forming a perfect *o*.

"Kinwelach, you mean Kinwelach Castle of Kinwelach Heads?"

Richard laughed. "Yes to both questions. May I ask why the surprise?"

Isabel remembered to close her mouth.

"Well, I know the name from geography lessons and because it was not so far from where I was born. A few days ride. We could have been neighbours perhaps? I thought it had long been razed to the ground though."

"It had been, but my father has since rebuilt it."

Isabel became quiet. "My home was razed to the ground also, I heard."

"Well, not quite."

Isabel flashed Richard a burning look full of questions. "Not quite? Do you know my home?" she asked incredulously.

Richard reached for her hand to stay her heated curiosity.

She flicked it off, her eyes not loosing contact with his.

When he didn't answer straight away, a dim dawning took shape in her mind, but not sharp enough to make any sense.

"What is this about, Richard? Is this why you have taken me?"

Richard smiled, not giving anything away. "All in good time. It's time to eat. We can't be ruining all the good work we've achieved over these last few days or so ..."

As if on cue, there was a knock at the door and Mistress Simcock swept in with a tray laden with food, enough to feed a family of ten. Mouth-watering aromas wafted and curled their way around the room as she laid the tray on the table.

Mistress Simcock dusted her floury hands on her abundant white apron, then stood with her hands on her hips.

"My, my! Just look at you! What a sight for sore eyes, eh Mr Kerr? You look wonderful my dear! Just wonderful! Well, don't stop now. You still need to eat to regain that strength of yours. We can't have you breeding more bairns looking waif like, can we Mr. Kerr?"

She winked at Richard.

"Absolutely not," Richard agreed, passing a conspiratorial grin at Isabel, with his eyes rolling to the heavens as he closed the door behind the large woman.

Isabel smiled despite herself.

Silence ensued for the next while as they both tucked into the breakfast fare.

At last, Isabel sunk back against her pillows, sated, hugging a mulled wine to her chest. A comfortable silence was broken as Isabel voiced her most desperate question.

"So why did you rape me?"

Richard looked up from wiping his knife, surprised at the suddenness and bluntness of the accusation.

Feeling afraid but determined to get an answer from him, Isabel bore her eyes into his.

He put his knife down and sighed. He moved his chair around to face her and leaned on his forearms over crossed knees. He meticulously picked a fallen crumb from off his hose.

"My dear, although we were created man and wife in a chapel in France, it wasn't me that deflowered you. I don't do random women."

Isabel felt stunned. She had expected an apology, if not an explanation. Now she was struggling with two new lots of information. It was taking its time to sink in, but there was no time for that either, for right at that moment the door burst open.

Isabel was certain that she was on the road to recovery, but now she was seeing double. The man who stood at the open door was also the man who sat beside her!

Isabel looked from the man to Richard, then from Richard to the man. She frowned and blinked her eyes as if to clear her vision.

They were exactly the same!

Blessed virgin, twins?

"My dear brother!" said the man mockingly. He swaggered into the room as if he owned the place. Pulling off his gloves, he sketched a courtly bow at Richard. He turned and offered the same to Isabel. "Oh, and my lovely wife. Whoring are you my dear?"

The intruder spoke with a welcoming tone, but the intent was menacing. He came in after closing the door and perched on the end of Isabel's bed.

Isabel squirmed back into her pillows.

The intruder continued as if he had not a care in the world. He twirled his cap in his fingers, fingers that were identical to his brother's. Isabel found it hard to believe what she was seeing.

Richard stood up to confront him. "You have made a whore of her, not me! And through that, you have killed her opportunity to bear another child! She lies here in childbed after losing your stillborn, not through my lack of propriety! Through your interference, she will never carry another child again! You have just wrecked everything!"

Isabel felt like she'd been slapped in the face with that unexpected piece of news: *never to bear children again?* The thought stunned her.

The fist came from the right. Even Isabel didn't see it coming. It knocked Gavyn to the floor. Even before he could pick himself up, Richard was dragging his twin brother to the door.

"Stand up, you swine," Richard grunted angrily as he pulled his brother up. "How dare you intervene? How dare you take from me what is mine! We'll talk in the tap room."

Gavyn stood unevenly, wiping away the fresh blood that oozed from his split lip. Richard shoved him out of the room into the hall and closed the door behind him.

Isabel listened to their footsteps as they faded away down the hall.

The quiet resounded in her ears as she stared blankly into space trying to process this new information. Her mind spun out. *Twins? No hope of having children again? What was this all about? They must have the wrong person. Who am I to them? They must be mistaken. Why me? What have I done to them? God? God, what do I do?*

Isabel's prayer tumbled from the English that she knew into the tongues that she didn't.

She continued to pray as she shook her head as if to clear it from her tangled thoughts. *Calm down,* she told herself, *let's calm down.*

After a time, Isabel realised that this was the moment she had been waiting for. It had arrived sooner that expected and she had a moment of doubt. Would she be able to stand without weakness? Walk without stumbling?

As a plan formed in her head, she prayed for God's strength to do what he was showing her to do.

With determined focus, she pushed aside her bed covers and swung her legs to the floor.

Isabel swallowed the last of her wine and stood up from the bed. Her head spun a bit and she held the corner of the table until it came right.

She looked around for some clothes. Realising that she had none, she stepped into Richard's castoffs, which lay over the back of the chair. She pulled his doublet on over her nightshift and rolled up the sleeves. A pair of leggings went on with boots that slid up to her mid thighs. She quickly knotted her long hair and pushed it under his cap, which she then pulled down to cover her ears and eyebrows. Half her face was hidden in shadow.

She grabbed the leftover breakfast and stuffed it into every pocket and lining she could find. Without wasting time, with fluid motion, she opened the door and slipped out into the hallway.

She closed the door and made her way silently down the stairs. Head down, she reached the corridor. The general chatter from the dinning room and taproom grew louder. She could hear Richard's voice. They must have just been around the corner. Not hesitating, Isabel headed out the back towards the stables.

The bright glare of the day hurt her eyes. She flattened herself against the wall until the initial pain in her eyes receded and adjusted to full daylight.

The day was bright and gusty. A cold wind bullied storm clouds across the sky and buffeted the birds as they tried to make their way. The yard was bustling with all manner of activity. People stood in small groups, passing the time of day with luggage at their feet. Horses were being saddled and stable hands went about their work with pails or pitchforks in hand.

Isabel walked unnoticed and unhindered across the straw-strewn cobbles into the stable. Although she had felt full of energy upon waking, Isabel now felt the full force of her true state of health. She leaned against an inside wall as a dizzy spell threatened to bring her to her knees. She could feel the blood leave her face. She knew it would have that grey look. Isabel felt utterly drained. A wave of nausea washed over her. She fought it. She would need every ounce of breakfast ingested for energy and who knows when she would next eat?

Even as she leaned, she scoured the stable for Richard's stallion through black spots swimming before her eyes. She shook her head and squinted, absolutely determined not to give in to her weakness. She spied the stallion easily. He was hands high above most of the other hacks in the stalls.

She looked for the tack room.

Forcing herself away from the wall, she made her way towards it. Just then, stable hands came out of the tack room carrying a saddle and bridle, heading directly towards her. Her heart leapt out of her chest and into her mouth. She felt herself freeze in fear of being discovered, but the stable lads walked past, and just nodded their heads at her with a bright and cheery, "Morning m'lor'."

Knees feeling like jelly and stomach doing flip-flops, Isabel slid into the tack room. She broke out into a cold, clammy sweat, perspiration beading instantly on her forehead. With shaky hands and fumbling fingers, she selected a saddle and bridle. Her feet slipped and slid in Richard's boots, a couple of sizes too big for her, but she continued on, making every movement count so that no time was wasted.

Thankful of an upbringing in the country, Isabel remembered how to saddle and bridle a horse. She didn't allow herself to think thoughts about how large the stallion was or if he would be too much to handle. She knew that she couldn't go there in her mind if she was to get away successfully.

Girth finally tightened, Isabel led the stallion out into the daylight, her head down. She led him around the bustle of activity and out onto the road that stretched from the north to the south. Without stopping, totally focused, Isabel mounted and turned the great black stallion south. With continuing fluid motion, she dug her heels into the animal's sides. His hooves bit the road, spraying turf and stones in an arch behind them.

Grim faced, Isabel hunkered down to avoid the drag of air and stared steadfast towards the south.

Richard was so consumed with anger towards his brother that he didn't notice the five other men in the room who had casually surrounded them. He didn't see as three of those men closed together as a wall at his shoulder.

He did see a quick blur, as someone's fist suddenly aimed for under his jaw. It was far too late to react. He dropped like a stone.

Apologising to guests and servitors about their legless friend who had imbibed too much ale, especially at this hour of the morning, the group of five carried Richard out to waiting horses. They were away to the coast within seconds.

Minutes later, Gavyn appeared at the inn entrance. Puzzled, he looked to the left then to the right of the step. Not seeing what he desired, he made another search of the inn as nonchalantly as possible in his anxious state.

His brows lifted as a thought crossed his mind. He made his way out to the stables. His search came up with nothing. Taking his gelding and mare from a stable hand, he asked the boy very casually if he'd seen a great black stallion. "Oh, yes," replied the lad. "What a beaut! Looked after right royally we did!"

"Did you see where he went?"

"Is he gone, mi Lord? I never saw 'm go. What a fine piece of horse flesh, eh, mi lor'!"

Slightly frustrated but realising that he need only to be patient, Gavyn mounted his own, less elegant piece of northern horseflesh, with the other, empty in tow, and headed on his long journey north.

CHAPTER TWENTY-THREE

Hever Castle, Kent

Anne watched as the house steward returned to the castle from where she stood in the herb garden. A basket of late, hothouse strawberries with a letter bearing the royal seal had been perched for her atop a tree stump.

She surveyed the gift from where she stood with chilling distain. The head of lavender rolling between her slender fingertips was suddenly squeezed, releasing its sharp, aromatic scent.

Unbeknown to Anne, her mother watched her from a casement above. Dressed in dark damask, only the pale oval of her face appeared at the leadlight glass.

Anne had still not moved. Suddenly she lifted her head to see the king's courier as he clattered out from under the portcullis, over the moat bridge, then on into open fields as he made his way back to London.

A few days after the king's unexpected visit, she had been summoned into her father's study. Her mother stood behind him like a frozen pillar.

Anne raised her eyebrows in question to her but was met with an indifferent facade that refused to be engaged.

Not even invited to sit, Anne listened as her father began to tell her of his suspicions. It would now seem that the King of England might have a secret interest in her. If this proved to be true, the family must rally together in strategic support for any gains that may be made. It was probably the king that had put an end to her affair with Henry Percy, and Wolsey was nothing more than the messenger boy. Her father expressed his sorrow at the end of such a promising match with the Northumberlands.

This comment surprised her after his continually cold reception of her since coming home to Hever. But nevertheless, he went on to say, "we must proceed with any advantage given to us as a family."

"You will play the game of the virtuous young maid. You will keep the king interested as long as you are able, for all of our sakes. Hopefully there will be dividends at the end and a marriage when it is all over. We cannot have bastards sired in this family. But the king has been aware of that with Mary, so will be equally attentive of you—one would hope. Your job is to push forward a match that will be advantageous to us all. Don't be like Mary, accepting whatever comes your way with no pension.

"You have to think of your future and your children's future. It's unfortunate that your husband will have you … ah … spoiled, so to speak, but that is the way in matters such as this.

"This was not our plan for you Anne, and we grieve with you over the loss of what could have been. But the king has rolled the dice in this game. We have no come back but to play as he wishes. Choosing not to do so could create dire consequences for our family. We expect your obedience in this, Anne. Is this understood?"

Anne laughed bitterly to herself. What else could she do? She could walk away from her family and life as she knew it, but where would she go and what would she do?

She kept her own counsel and said nothing. She only nodded in acceptance and was promptly dismissed.

As she escaped to the orchard after the interview, the enormity of the situation started to sink in. What an incredible state of affairs!

The King of England was interested in her? She could scarcely believe it. She had no interest in playing the whore like her sister. *Just let him try to play with me. Just let him try! He'll have nothing of me. Nothing!* She swore to herself.

Now, as the basket sat waiting for her, she could see that it had begun, just as it had for Mary.

Up above, Elizabeth Boleyn, full of nervous tension, pressed a thumbnail to her lips as she continued to watch her daughter.

Anne, long wrung out by spent emotions, could feel the familiar rise of white hot anger towards Wolsey, and now, the king. As it rose, she realised that she didn't even want to go there. She was tired of feeling strung out by it all. Her present numbness was helping her get through the days and she wanted to keep it that way.

Elizabeth saw her daughter pick up a rock from at her feet and place it upon the unopened letter and basket. Clearing her skirts from the lavender bushes, Anne, then made her way to the moat that surrounded Hever Castle. Holding the gift at arms length, she dropped it into its inky black depths. A few white swans turned their heads, but the ripples in the water hardly signified.

As slender and elegant as a reed with its head bowed in the wind, Anne walked away.

No words came to Elizabeth Boleyn as she turned away from the window like a passing spectre, just a spreading feeling of ice growing in her belly.

CHAPTER TWENTY-FOUR

York Place, London

After two day's gruelling ride and one bitterly cold night out in the open, Isabel finally arrived at her destination: York Place stables in London.

It had been hard—hard beyond belief. It had only been absolute determination of will that kept her going. Isabel had pushed the capable stallion as hard as she was able. The first night was spent on the edge of a forest where a small stream trickled its way through from the hill behind to the valley below. Beards of lichen trailed from the branches of the ancient trees and the smell of moss and dampness pervaded the woodland floor.

Isabel barely had the energy to brush the lathered animal down. She walked him until he cooled, then tethered him to a tree with enough free rein to crop the lush grass.

With her mount settled, the temptation to sleep without food was huge, but Isabel steeled herself and forced the drying, crumbling leftover breakfast from the inn into her mouth.

After cupping a few mouthfuls of the sweet stream water into her mouth, she curled up into a ball against a giant tree root, oblivious to the cold and damp and fell instantly asleep.

Isabel woke late, stiff and chilled to the bone. Through the tree canopy, she could see that the sun was high in the sky. A groan escaped from her lips as she tried to stir herself. She desperately wanted to escape back into sleep.

Come on, get up, she scolded herself inwardly. She cast a look across the stream to make sure that the horse hadn't wandered off in the night. To her relief, her glossy, black ride was where she had left him. He was happily munching away. Isabel snorted softly in wry humour. It was probably the best fresh feed he'd had in a while. He had the look of a spoiled, dry fed mount.

Isabel checked her bleeding while she relieved herself. It was still quite heavy, but looked like a normal monthly. She buried the old rags and ripped up some new ones from the hem of her nightshift. She washed in the icy stream. Her skin smarted, immediately taking offence, goosing a bright red.

Feeling somewhat more alive, Isabel downed the last of yesterday's breakfast, mounted her reluctant steed, which snatched a last mouthful of juicy pasture, and rode carefully into the open sunlight.

Isabel was relieved; there were no cottages or grazing stock to be seen. After getting her bearings, she encouraged the stallion into a comfortable canter. She eventually found the road south that she had left last night and then squeezed his sides in to full gallop.

She only stopped twice to relieve herself. Her strength was waning but she didn't give in to it. The sun almost did a full sweep of the sky before London came into view. She slowed. People and houses began to crowd the landscape. Pulling her cap down, she tried to keep from drawing any attention to herself. After a few wrong turns, she eventually found herself at York Place.

Passing herself off as a messenger boy, she waited in an anteroom for Henry Percy.

Isabel sank onto a bench, which jutted out from an ornately carved wall. Grimy and dirty, she felt that she was almost at the end of her strength. The constant pushing of herself to reach this goal had almost emptied her of all physical and mental reserves that she had rebuilt in Colchester.

The door opened in a sudden rush with the head of an expectant Henry Percy looking around it. Isabel saw his expression of hopefulness change to puzzlement as he laid his eyes upon her.

When Henry saw a tired, scruffy urchin, he frowned.

With much effort, Isabel drew off her cap. Her long blonde hair cascaded silkily to her waist. In the white grubby face were some eyes that he recognised.

"Isabel?"

"Henry." Isabel's voice sounded like wheels on gravel.

"My God, Isabel! You are alive!" Henry dropped to the bench beside her and took her thin, cold hands in his. "We had all thought you to be dead! What happened? Are you all right? You feel so cold. Come to my room, I'll have a fire lit."

He drew her to her feet and put an arm around her waist. "Father is here in London. I'll get word to him. I'll get James to ready the guest room."

Isabel could only nod. As she allowed her body and mind to relax, exhaustion set in. It crept through her body quickly.

She was glad of Henry's arms. They were the only things holding her up.

Wolsey came into view as they reached the landing. Surprise and puzzlement crossed his bloated features at the unusual sight before him. As tired as she was, Isabel could tell that he was at the ready to pull Henry up for some perceived misdemeanour or other, but uncertainty held him back.

"Cardinal, Isabel has been found," said Henry. "Please inform my father. I'll have James to prepare a guest room."

Wolsey surveyed the dusty figure in Henry's arms and was taken back to see Isabel's familiar face amid men's attire. His severe, distant presence changed in an instance. He bowed, becoming most gentle and attentive.

"Mistress Isabel! Welcome home! Is there anything I can do for you?" said Wolsey extending a warm touch to her arm.

Isabel looked up wearily but managed a smile. "Thank you, Cardinal. Something to drink …"

"Right away. Right away. Henry, get her warm by the fire. I'll get it up forthwith."

Wolsey was already halfway down the stairs as his last words flew out. He barked some orders to some passing pages, which sent them scurrying in two different directions.

He cast a quick look back before he turned from view and saw two people both whipped by life.

He knew instantly that one would survive and the other would not.

CHAPTER TWENTY-FIVE

Derbyshire, Midlands

The Northumberland party, together with the Shrewsburys, made their way north from London under a cold, leaden, mid-December sky.

Wrapped in wool and furs, the party surveyed the passing winter landscape with hooded eyes. Their expelled breath froze in the air and billowed like little clouds to trail behind them. Every now and then, the sky would release the season's first light flurry of snow. The delicate flakes danced like dust motes in an airless barn to land gently, then to melt away as if they had never been.

The youngest member of the party suddenly broke away from the group.

She was full of youthful vitality and satisfaction of having her heart's desire. She laughed out loud with hands raised to the air. Her laughter sounded like the sharp tinkle of icicles as they fell from eaves to splinter on the ground below.

It set Henry Percy's teeth on edge. He scowled at his new wife to be as she pranced on her palfrey like a child.

He was beginning to hate her. It was bad enough to be married to someone other than Anne, but to be bound to an irritation such as Mary Talbot was almost beyond measure.

"Henry! Henry! Look! Aren't they delightful?" Mary squealed with enthusiasm, the tip of her nose bright red with the cold.

Henry looked away, embarrassed at being tied to this person lacking in grace and decorum.

After Isabel had been found, preparations to travel north were quickly assembled. He knew his father had despatched messengers to the Earl and Countess of Shrewsbury who were also in London and of course to his mother at Alnwich to advise them of the king's wishes. Also, he overheard his father sending a letter to Sir Roland Tavistock. He had passed that information onto Isabel. Maybe his father was thinking of getting them both married in the spring.

On the first leg of the journey, they travelled with the Shrewsburys back to their midland home. Both earls made use of the time discussing the business end of the alliance. The countess and Mary talked endlessly of the decorative side of the wedding arrangements, material for the gown and the jewels she might get to wear. Mary had trotted tirelessly between her stepmother and Henry filling him in on all the decisions they had made and asking his approval. He was amazed that she wasn't offended or felt rebuffed at his silence or terse answers. Was she a simpleton? He felt exasperated at her lack of perception of his feelings for her.

A gloved hand touched his forearm.

He knew it was Isabel. They had travelled side by side since they left London. Her eyes communicated understanding and agreement with his thoughts.

Tears swam in his eyes.

If Anne couldn't be his wife, it should have been Isabel. She understood him as no other person could.

He grabbed her hand and squeezed it in appreciation, blinking his tears away. Isabel pulled out a folded, sealed note from her glove and slipped it into Henry's.

He looked at her with a question in his eyes. She motioned silently to him, so as not to draw attention, to read the contents. Isabel was going to leave it until they had arrived at their night's destination, but seeing the pain in his face, weakened her resolve.

Henry took the note, broke the seal and read the contents as discreetly as he could with his hand resting on the pommel of his saddle.

"My darling," he read, "keep this note close to your heart when you want to think of me. Know that at this time, I am also thinking of you.

"You are never far from my thoughts. Indeed, there are moments when I am consumed with thoughts of you. Remember that although we are separated in body, my heart is always with you continually and will be forever. It may be treason to be with you in this life, but know this, that we shall be together in the next.

"Forever yours, your true wife before God, Anne."

Warm tears now flowed freely to freeze on his face as a northerly wind picked up. He slid the note into his doublet and thought back to the last day he'd spent in London. His face took on a faraway look, a smile played about his mouth.

***

He had felt ridiculous.

Henry had peered out at the Kentish countryside from underneath a black veil, a woman's veil.

It had been Isabel's idea.

She had always been the leader of the two of them, even when they were little. It was always Isabel who had taken him by the hand to encourage him to do this or that. Since she had arrived back from France, he could see that she had grown even more in confidence, and even in what he perceived as rashness!

She had asked his father's permission to visit Anne Boleyn before leaving for home. She had produced a letter of invitation from Anne for her company while she was at Hever. The earl had denied permission of a long stay—she must travel north for her own nuptials—but he would allow a day visit with a handful of his retainers for her safety.

She was to be back in London before eventide.

On the said day, Isabel arranged for Henry to be laid low in bed with one of his maladies, which now struck him on a regular basis, since his enforced breakup with Anne. A servant's silence had been bought to keep Henry's room locked and to make sure he received no visitors.

Isabel took with her an old gentlewoman who was "veiled for disfigurement from a bout of the sweat."

They had left very early in the morning, just as the house was rising. The swirls of early morning mist were slowly lifting as the sun made its presence known and Isabel and her escort were quickly swallowed up like sugar in a melting pot into the stirring streets of London.

Once out of London, they covered the countryside quickly. The day, though cold, was fine and Hever Castle loomed clear and welcoming before them at mid-morning.

In the inner courtyard, they were met with joyful greetings. Anne and Isabel enveloped each other with cries of delight. Various house staff with Lady Elizabeth Boleyn fussed around the newly arrived guests organising them into the hall.

Lady Howard, Anne's grandmother, freshly arrived from Norfolk to mind Anne at Christmas while her parents went back to court, stood aside like a bristly black crow, disapproving of everything.

The escort was taken to the kitchen for refreshments. Hopefully, with the right amount of pie and ale applied, it would produce some interesting gossip from London, especially the king's court.

Isabel was quick to introduce her afflicted companion, Mistress Waltham, and then just as quick to turn the attention elsewhere. Nobody gave the tall, rather ungainly woman another thought.

Henry almost missed catching Isabel's gloves as she tossed them carelessly into his hands.

Waltham? Where did that come from? Henry fumbled with the gloves, but managed to keep his mouth closed as he tried to keep in character.

Henry had followed the chatty group into the welcoming rooms of Hever. Grandmother Howard shuffled after, rubbing her wizened, papery hands together.

Henry felt a wave of nervous sweat break out over his body as he imagined the old lady's discerning black beady eyes seeing right through their charade.

Choosing her private salon overlooking the park, the Lady Elizabeth drew them all upstairs from the great hall into a cosy setting around a large fire, Henry sitting behind Isabel, as was the expected station.

Through the veil, he gazed longingly at Anne, drinking in all the detail of her as a man parched.

Her black, glossy hair was held in a golden net. She wore a plain gown of such a deep burgundy, it appeared black in its folds. His eyes caressed the deep cream of her skin. He stared at her beautiful fingers, cupped in her lap. They played with a gold girdle, which hung at her waist. With a thrill, he saw the ring that he had given her at their betrothal threaded through the chain. How he wanted to hold her hands, feel them on his skin. The very thought of it stirred his soul to anxiousness. He shifted uncomfortably in his seat.

"We are returning to the north tomorrow. My marriage to Sir Roland Tavistock takes place in the spring so there is much to do," said Isabel, in answer to Elizabeth Boleyn's question.

"Hence, the rather quick visit. Are you enjoying Christmas at Hever this year Lady Boleyn?"

"No. I am recalled to court, but Anne will celebrate here, with my mother, Lady Howard."

Lady Howard was as brown and as wrinkled as a walnut. Severely dressed in black, her dark eyes glittered as she inclined her head towards Isabel, her back remaining ramrod straight.

Not a woman to be trifled with, noted Henry. Anne was in for as dismal a Christmas as he.

"Isabel, do tell us of your new husband. Where will you be living?" Elizabeth Boleyn asked.

Everybody leaned forward in anticipation, not wanting to miss a word. At that moment warmed ale and sweetmeats arrived. A serving girl stood to Isabel's side and offered her ale upon a silver platter.

It was a wide swing of an elbow that did it. Pretending that she hadn't seen the proffered tray. Isabel swung around to speak to Anne making sure her elbow connected with the liquid refreshment.

The ale flew from a pewter goblet in a perfect arch. Isabel was very proud of it. It landed very heavily upon Mistress Waltham's lap. The gasp wrenched from Henry's throat was real, as were the flying arms, and his chair flying backwards. Everybody rose, but Isabel reacted first, being well rehearsed in her mind's eye.

"Oh, my goodness! Please excuse my clumsiness!" She patted Henry's lap, but to no significant avail with a thin lace kerchief. "Anne, may I please prevail upon you to take us somewhere where we may dry out Mistress Waltham?"

Not waiting for any direction from her hosts, she took an arm each of Anne and Henry's and led them away, turning her head back as she did so.

"Please excuse us, Lady Elizabeth, Lady Howard. I shall be back directly."

True to her word, barely a minute passed before she returned as they were still restoring order before the fire. With much enthusiasm and before any questions could be asked, Isabel drew their attention away from Anne and Mistress Waltham and captured their imaginations with married life, as she perceived it, in the wilds of the North Country.

"Anne."

A click sounded as a key turned in its lock.

Anne knew that voice.

She froze in her actions of shaking out a towel.

But how could it be?

She didn't look up, too scared that it might not be true. How could it be? She didn't want to break the spell.

Am I so lost in him, that I hear his voice in another's?

"Anne."

There it was again. It wasn't her imagination.

She turned her head quickly.

Henry had dragged off the cap and veil.

He stood before her, his blond hair tousled and adorable, his beautiful blue eyes radiating love.

Anne almost couldn't believe it. Her love stood before her – in a woman's dress!

"Henry?" Anne's eyes looked him up and down quizzically.

He came to her quickly. They stood only inches apart.

"Yes, Anne, it's me."

Her beautiful hands cupped his face.

"Henry. I thought … I hardly dared …"

"I had to."

"It's treason."

He whispered, "I know."

"How?"

With each word, they drew a breath closer to each other.

They both closed their eyes, one inhaling the proximity of the other. It made them almost giddy with longing.

Their lips came together as a feather touch, but it was like they had both been seared by a branding iron. They both drew back sharply and trembled as a thrill of desire pulsed through their bodies. They looked into each other's eyes. There they both saw love, heartache, belonging, homecoming, acceptance and terror of loss. They came together and loved. They loved each other as if it was their last day on earth. Indeed, they both knew that it might as well have been.

***

Henry's smile disappeared as his memories faded and the real world came back into view.

He opened his doublet and shirt under his cloak, exposing his chest to the bitter cold. He did so with furtive glances. He did not want to draw any attention, especially from Isabel, who had taken it upon herself to play mother to him.

He loved Isabel, but he would not be deterred from his course of action.

The freezing air instantly stung his skin then numbed his chest.

Good.

The daylight hours became shorter with every day that passed and the weather finally succumbed to the power of winter. Henry breathed in deep breaths of sleet-driven air over the miles, allowing his body to become thoroughly chilled.

During their comfort stops, Henry made sure that he was always right next to a fire. If that were not possible, he kept his cloak on until he sweated. He managed to hide his deteriorating condition until they reached Sheffield Manor.

The manor was very modern, only over a decade old and the yellow bricks, which still appeared freshly hewn, looked warm and inviting.

It stood on a hill overlooking the surrounding forests. It had a beautiful vista, even with the lowered cloud and everybody stopped to admire it as they took a breather before dismounting.

Sheffield Manor staff appeared at the doors of its steps and came forth to help the party into the house.

Henry was thrilled that he felt like he was burning up and that his head pounded so hard that it might split. It now hurt to breathe. His chest had become so painful, it felt like his back had been stuck through with a dagger.

Anne, I go on ahead. I will be waiting for you.

Henry let go of his determination to stay seated on his mount. The damage was done. It was sheer bliss to lose himself in unconsciousness.

Henry didn't even feel himself sprawl on the freshly raked pebbles as he dismounted, but everybody heard the sharp crack as his head hit the edge of the steps leading into the house.

Mary screamed.

CHAPTER TWENTY-SIX

Sheffield Manor, Sheffield

There was nothing much to do.

Isabel looked out at the serene winter landscape through a crack in the heavy drapes and blinked at its brightness. Snow was banked high against anything that stood vertical. There was no distinction of grazing land to forest. It was just one blanket of crystal white carpet. The sky had opened up to reveal a measureless blue without a smear of cloud and the sun appeared almost brazen in its tawdry brilliance, setting the snow alight like diamond dust.

The drapes had to remain drawn to keep out any bad humours that may come in through the draughts.

Isabel felt oppressively hot in the airless room and took her sense of refreshing from the whiteout before her.

The severe storm, which had swept down from the north on their first night at Sheffield Manor, had finally subsided. Travel had been impossible. That also meant travel was impossible for others, too. She looked for movement in the countryside. Where were Richard and Gavyn Kerr now? Would they come for her again? Yes, they probably would. If they had the audacity to take her from such a public place as court, they would certainly find it no problem to pick her off in the country. They hadn't forgotten her after she left France. They came after her. It would make sense that they would do the same again in the future. It unsettled her immensely. Another thought that came repeatedly back to her was the body of her little Henry. Was he still wrapped in her cloak hood in the curing house? Hopefully somebody good had found him and given him a burial. Isabel swung between anger, verging on rage at what Richard had done, from taking her from her baby's body, to inconsolable grief at her loss.

She tried to act normal but everybody could see that she was off her food. Isabel had covered it up by admitting worry for Henry. This brought a whole flurry of well-meaning concern, which she had to take with good grace to cover her own secret life.

The earl was another matter. She could see him watching her sometimes when he perceived she was unaware of it. What was he thinking? Why was he watching her?

When she had been well enough to receive visitors at York Place, the earl was her first. He hugged her as a father might but it was delivered with a stiff reserve, not because he was angry with her, she perceived, but it was just his way. He was rarely a man to show outward emotion of an affectionate kind, unless it served his purposes.

He had stepped back to admire the beautiful young woman she had become. It was such a change, he had explained, from the little girl they had left behind on the windy shores of Dover as a child pf honour in Mary Tudor's bridal retinue.

He had then started to talk about the dangers of giving to the poor. It should always be done through the proper channels such as churches and abbeys. If she had such a heart for the less fortunate, he would see that her heart's desires would be seen to, but only through him, where she would have his protection.

Isabel remembered looking at him as if he'd gone mad. What was he talking about? Then it dawned on her and she changed her facial expression quickly lest he should see her confusion. Wolsey had obviously filled him in on the story she had fed Henry and James as they fussed around her when she had first arrived at York Place.

She was unsure about shedding light on the truth. So, to give herself time, she spun a story, God forgive her. She had taken her life into her own hands she realised, rather than obeying God and telling the truth.

It was a decision made in fear rather than faith, she realised, but now the dye had been set and how could she unset it? She had been accosted while exiting a side door at Windsor, she lied. It had been a door close to the kitchens where many hopefuls lingered. She had innocently handed over a few low value coins to make her way through the crowd. The people grew desperate and she became a victim of her own kindness when fighting ensued. She remembered waking up and not knowing where she was. Apparently somebody had carried her to a place of recovery within Windsor Castle, but she had been too unwell to travel onto Greenwich when the court had moved on.

Isabel tried not to be too specific after that and hoped not too many probing questions would be asked. They weren't. Crowds of beggars and the like at court were always a problem. A burden had slipped from her shoulders at that moment.

She remembered the awesome feeling of being free! Outwardly she was still the marriageable girl she had always been. She had brought no shame on the family!

What a relief!

She had been more than willing to listen to the earl's arrangements for her marriage. Marriage to a stable, older man was just what she needed. Protection, security and quiet life in the country had never looked more appealing.

She could see that he was very pleased with her attitude and had left her with a satisfied pat on her shoulder as he left.

With a sigh, Isabel looked back at Henry lying white and inert on the large bed in front of her.

He was still unwell from his fall. The doctors didn't know if he would live or die but it was a good sign that he had recovered consciousness after the initial fall. In his lucid moments, he would call for Isabel. She held good hope that he would be fully restored. She prayed quietly under her breath for Henry but she knew God was returning her mind to the wrong turn she had made in not telling the truth.

The click of the door latch alerted her to someone entering the room. It was Mary. She had brought with her some needle-work.

She obviously meant to stay for a while.

Mary greeted Isabel with a sour look that said, what are you doing here again? To the nurse at Henry's bedside she gave a quick smile.

Isabel was aware of Mary's growing hostility towards her. She knew it was jealousy due to Henry asking for her rather than Mary when he was awake. Isabel had tried to talk to Mary in a roundabout way that her jealousy was unfounded but Mary was too young and insecure to hear it.

The cheery, rotund nurse at Henry's bedside reciprocated Mary's smile.

"I'll leave him to you young ladies," she said, heaving her-self up, as she rose to leave, brushing her hands on her apron to make it smooth. "Perhaps you can get him to sup something when he awakes. Make sure the fire stays stoked. Doctor says there's still an excess of black bile within him. He's been purged and bled, so we just wait for the best now. At least he's cooler and he doesn't toss and turn so much."

"Thank you," returned Isabel as she closed the drape.

As the old nurse huffed and puffed her way out of the room, Isabel came and closed the door quietly behind her.

Isabel could feel Mary's malevolent glare on her back. Coming in the opposite spirit to return peace to the room, Isabel suggested that Mary sit beside Henry and wipe his brow.

Mary didn't say anything but after an uncertain look, did take the chair at his bedside.

"You'll make a wonderful wife," said Isabel, trying to en-courage but knew she was lying through her teeth. No amount of good motives on her part was going to make this up and coming marriage a good one. She could just see it. Henry loved someone else.

Isabel picked up a book on the stool by the fire, resigning herself to a morning of prickly silence.

At noon, the nurse returned to relieve them both so they could partake of dinner in the main hall below.

As the two women descended the stairs side-by-side, Mary, eyes still focused ahead of her, casually tossed a question to Isabel.

"So, what is she like?"

Isabel took a sharp look at Mary. She knew whom she was talking about and the stiffness in Mary's carriage belied her careless attitude. It was obviously a question she had been sitting on for quite some time.

"Who?" she said nonetheless, very politely.

"Anne Boleyn."

"Ah," said Isabel at length, not making it easy for Mary. "What do you want to know?"

Mary kept looking forward as they walked. "Some say that she is sallow and not beautiful at all. Some say that there is nobody like her, that she is very talented, witty and becoming."

"She is all of that, Mary."

Mary shot Isabel a frown, totally frustrated with the answer. It was not what she wanted to hear. She wanted it black or white. She wanted a valid reason to hate Anne other than just being her opposition. "You spent time with her in France, I believe?"

"That's correct."

Silence, just the whisper of velvet and damask as their skirts brushed the polished wooden floors.

A different tone directed Mary's voice. "Did ... did they love each other?"

Isabel kept her head straight ahead, too, and answered knowing it would be like a dagger to Mary's heart. She didn't flinch at thrusting it. "Yes."

Isabel could hear Mary trying to swallow a sob in her throat and immediately regretted her emotions getting the better of her. *God forgive me, again. Will I ever be free of myself?*

"Well," said Mary, jutting out her chin in defiance of what she had heard and she grabbed Isabel's forearm making her look into her challenging, over bright eyes. "Henry is going to love me now!"

Isabel looked tiredly at Mary, not wanting to argue, sick of herself and Mary's immaturity. "You will be husband and wife, Mary."

Isabel walked away from Mary, knowing that those words should have meant the world to her and also knowing that her tone stated the opposite.

***

Mary dressed well this morning. She had pinched and slapped her personal maid into tears as she demanded her toilette to be just so. She even yelled at her stepmother's maid demanding attention for this and that.

As she stood before the beaten silver mirror, her eyes shimmered with her own tears. She felt ashamed at having behaved so badly but she needed to be beautiful for Henry.

He just had to kiss her goodbye today! They wouldn't see each other until the wedding.

The Northumberlands were leaving within the hour and she had to make some sort of impression on Henry. She realised that he had been recovering from a bad fall and that the black bile of his chest took all of his energy to get well again, but he hadn't even smiled at her once! He had not spoken two words to her from London to now. He had called for Isabel, though. If he called for her, then he could just as easily call for her. Why didn't he?

I have to make him say goodbye to me today, please God, make him desire me. Let him love me! Let him kiss me!

Her watery eyes cleared and she was able to see her reflection. Her mousy coloured hair was worn loose. It had been brushed so much that it clung to her scalp. At the base of her neck, it trailed thinly down her back. *It does have some wave in it, which carried some merit,* she thought.

She turned sideways to get a better glimpse of her eyes. Pale blue irises stared back at her through lashes so blond that you couldn't even see them.

Her mouth did a downturn, all those ministrations for nothing. She still looked as pasty as ever. She did the usual and bit her lips then pinched her cheeks. Colour bloomed instantly but she didn't feel she looked any better for it.

Her eyes travelled to her cleavage. Her rich red velvet gown was worn low over her breasts with a square cut bodice. She had her maid pull the laces on her chemise underneath as tight as it could go, to create the effect of an ample bust, but that too was a disappointment. She still looked as flat as ever.

Mary threw her mirror to the floor with disgust. It clanged and clattered across the polished floorboards.

She paced her room in agitation, torn from behaving like a young woman with decorum to screaming her head off like a desperate shrew.

What was happening to her?

She'd never felt like this before.

Mary became angry as her thoughts focused all the more on Henry. *How dare he do this to me! The least he should be is cordial! I would give him my love willingly if only he would accept it! He has done this to me! Isabel has done this to me! That Anne Boleyn, who I have never even seen, has done this to me!*

Her stepmother, who arrived at her chamber door, interrupted her pacing; Mary gave her a sullen glance. She always managed to look beautiful, never a hair out of place! Everybody else was always something she was not! She started to hate herself.

"Mary," exclaimed her stepmother, holding out her arms to her and gave her a light hug. "How lovely you look dear but I won't have you bringing our maids to tears." She took Mary's arm and tapped it with reprimanding fingers. "Well, never mind that now. Henry is making his way down to the hall. Come down and say your goodbyes."

She led Mary downstairs to the hall, where everybody milled saying their goodbyes, and led her out to the steps. She would be the last line to farewell their guests.

Her stepmother gave her an encouraging squeeze of the arm, then took her place by her husband, the Earl of Shrewsbury.

The Earl of Northumberland looked resplendent in white fox fur as he made his way to his host. Jovial and in excellent spirits, pleased that long-awaited negotiations were now at last settled, he clapped George Talbot on his back.

"Well, George, I want to thank you for your hospitality. You have been a most gracious host and I shall reciprocate in the spring! I shall have my lawyers draw up the necessary documents for what we have been discussing for the marriage." He turned his head to see where Henry was.

Mary followed his eyes to his son who had just finished pulling on his gloves. He had been up for three days now. He was painfully thin and his skin looked unnaturally stretched over his bones. He was left with a hacking cough, which left him clutching his middle to contain the pain. Mary so wanted to be close to him, to tell him that she would make it all right but his icy reception of her kept her at bay. He spoke to her only under duress.

The earl turned back to Elizabeth and bowed over her hand.

"A pleasure indeed, Madam. Thank you for your provision, especially regarding Henry and your invitation for Christmas, but we must press forward in this clement weather or Catherine will never forgive me. Thank you once again, dear lady."

Mary received a peck on the forehead from the earl. He towered over her in his height and strength. He pulled back and chucked her little chin. "Well, daughter-in-law, we shall see you in the spring. You'll adorn Alnwich well!"

Mary basked in his affirmation. Her smile followed him out to his retainers and waiting horses.

"Goodbye, Mary. Red suits you"

It was Isabel. She was dressed in blue velvet, slashed to reveal embroidered primroses on yellow silk. It matched her hair, netted for the journey. *She looks beautiful,* Mary thought. *How can I compete with that?*

Unbeknown to Isabel, giving birth and surviving hardship had changed her from a young girl with rounded, wholesome features into a svelte woman of underlying strength beneath physical delicacy.

"Goodbye, Isabel."

They both gave each other weak smiles of truce for appearance's sake.

Then he was there, tall and pale, but he still made her heart flutter. She had hardly opened her mouth to say goodbye when he was gone. A curt nod was all she had received from him. Mary looked at his back in utter disbelief and dismay as he was helped onto his horse by a manservant. She had thought that he would relent some, especially since the next time that they would see each other would be at a chapel altar. She was too full of shock to feel depressed.

She gathered with all the rest of the household on the Manor steps to wave farewell.

Henry never looked back.

CHAPTER TWENTY-SEVEN

Falconrood Hall, Northumberland

The next day, two day's ride directly north of Sheffield Manor, before the first rays of the sun had begun to creep upon the winter scape, Falconrood Hall started to stir into life.

Despite its name, Falconrood was neither majestic nor notable any more. It had been reduced to a little, untidy affair, which wore its neglect with subdued dignity.

In its day, many years ago, it had been a place of renown, a hive of the wool industry, which had catapulted the north of England into new wealth.

The extensive grounds that had been well cultivated under the guiding hands of the lady of the house, now passed away, were back in the hands of unruly nature. Just as dust and cobwebs had reclaimed the great barns and weaving rooms, weeds now dominated the roses and lavender, which hedged the hall.

The blanket of snow had softened the worn look of Falconrood and the servants within were looking forward to some changes. Their old master was going to marry again.

Perhaps the new bride would bring life back to the old hall even if the prosperity of latter days was never to be repeated.

The depleted staff of worn-out faithfuls gathered in the kitchen and huddled around the ovens.

The first chore of the day was to rekindle the ashes in the kitchen hearth for the first meal of the day.

It was tradition for Falconrood staff to start their winter mornings with a meal of freshly baked bread with beef and ale, something they never did in the summer. The idea of working in the freezing conditions outside was made all the more palatable as they enjoyed the treat of warm food and a warm fire to sit by before they started the day's work.

Good-natured banter was tossed about the room as the cook, almost as old as the hall itself, put together a tray for the master's room.

She wiped her hands on her not so clean apron and called the housemaid away from the hearth.

"Margery! Come get his Lordship's tray and be quick about it! You know he likes to be up with sparra's!"

Margery rose from her stool and hurriedly poked some bread and beef into her mouth while she straightened her cap.

"Yes, Ma'am!" she mumbled with her mouth full. She ducked as the cook took a swipe at her for speaking with her mouth full.

"Mind your manners now, girl! You won't be here long if you don't keep your manners!"

The maid rolled her eyes; she was still considered new staff, even though she'd been at Falconrood for ten years.

The cook piled her own breakfast trencher full to overflowing as Margery left the warmth of the kitchen to take the tray to the master of the house.

Falconrood Hall was not large and the maid quickly navigated the dark staircase to the master's rooms. Setting the tray aside on an oak sideboard under a fluttering wall sconce, she knocked on his door.

The expected "enter" didn't happen immediately. She shivered in her thin wool fustian while she waited. She used the moment to use her tongue to try and probe out some beef that had stuck between her teeth.

After a minute of silence, she knocked again. The cold of the house was really getting into her bones now. She did a little jiggle, hopping from one foot to another and rubbing her arms to get warm.

This was odd. The master always bid her enter on the first knock. She was a bit unsure of what to do. Should she enter unbidden? She could get scolded. Should she go back to the kitchen for advice? No, definitely not. A scolding and blows were sure to come forth from the cook.

Margery started wringing her hands as she began to fret. She shook it off, straightened her shoulders and knocked again.

Still nothing.

Deciding to be brave and take the lesser of the two evils, she took a deep breath, laid her hand to the door latch and slowly started to lift.

The door swung open easily.

Their master was still slumbering. Should she wake him? No, she would just leave the tray on his writing desk.

Creeping quietly, so as not to awaken him, Margery tiptoed to the table beside his bed.

It had been her intention not to look at him, in what seemed to her, his uncovered state.

She never moved her head but couldn't help her eyes from darting to the left as she started to set down the tray.

Her ear piercing screams tore through the house. They were so loud that the tray, which was totally abandoned from her hands, didn't appear to make a sound as it crashed from the desk to the floor, splattering its contents all over the herb-scented rushes.

CHAPTER TWENTY-EIGHT

Alnwich Castle, Northumberland

The weather started to close in on them.

Isabel looked up at the sky. The brooding clouds had lowered and with it the temperature and the early afternoon light had become tinged with blue.

The slushy mud underfoot was now being silently carpeted by thick snow falling in fat, puffy flakes. It started slowly and intermittently, and then turned relentless within an hour.

"We'll push on," said Northumberland, speaking to everybody's unvoiced opinion of finding shelter or continuing forward.

The Earl of Northumberland's voice sounded dull and flat, as the snow absorbed the sound. Snow settled on his cap and shoulders like another cloak. "It's not long now. Do you see that knoll up yonder, between the trees? The River Aln is just beyond and then you'll have your first glimpse of Alnwick."

Everybody looked with interest in the direction where the earl pointed his gloved hand.

The thought of warm food, mulled wine and a warm hearth woke everybody up from survival mode of one foot in front of the other into an animated interest in their surroundings. "Look!"

One of the earl's retainers held his arm up pointing to the north.

They all pulled their mounts to a halt. Two riders came bar-relling up and over the knoll that had been pointed out to them by the earl. Snow billowed up behind them as if a storm were chasing them.

The party kept their stances uneasily as the horses shied and fidgeted, sensing uncertainty and fear from their riders.

Silently, Northumberland's retainers took their positions of defence in front of the earl and his family, hands on hilts, ready for any action that may be needed.

As the figures drew closer, their details became clearer. Hollering could now be heard with vigorous arm waving.

Another cough racked through Henry as he tried to steady his gelding. He held his snow-encrusted sleeve to his mouth. Isabel's look of concern turned to alarm when Henry let his arm down. The snow on his sleeve was speckled with fresh blood!

The yelling could now be interpreted as whoops of delight.

"It's Lords Thomas and Algernon, sire!" exclaimed one the earl's men.

"What the ...?" The earl nudged his mount forward.

Everybody followed warily until they themselves could make out the familiar faces.

Thomas and Algernon reined in sharply at speed, causing a spray of snow to fan out behind them.

They were breathless with their laughter.

"I won!" shouted Algernon, the younger of the two. His honey blond hair, matted with snow, stuck out in all directions.

"Never!" argued Thomas, a head taller than his younger brother, his dark hair sensibly under a velvet cap.

He looked at his father.

"Father, who was first? Was it me? I know it was!" Thomas reached out to give Algernon a playful shove. His brother side-stepped him easily, laughing.

The earl was not to be drawn by their play. He frowned.

"What are you doing out here? You should be at home pro-tecting your mother!"

The boys looked at each other. It never crossed their minds that their mother might need protecting. She had a whole castle full of men at her fingertips.

Thomas looked back at his father. "We just came to out to greet you, Father. A scout let us know that you were coming …"

"And we've been stuck inside for weeks with our lessons." Algernon tried not to sound like his whining younger sisters and knew that he was failing.

"There are no excuses! Roaming the countryside in winter without an escort and leaving your mother unaided is unacceptable."

The boys looked at each other, trying not to pull faces, which if seen, might receive a cuff.

Without another word, the earl pulled away leaving everybody to follow him. The retainers fell into their protective formation to the sides of the family.

"Henry! How was London?" called Thomas, all eager to hear about its amazing sights, as he stepped in beside his older brother.

Before Henry could reply, another cough spasm took hold of his body. It left him white-faced and trembling.

"If that's what you get visiting London, I'd rather stay here," ventured Algernon stoically.

Everybody smiled; even Henry managed a brief one.

Isabel saw the look of shock on Thomas's face, as he looked at his brother. She decided to draw his attention away from Henry, to give them both some time.

"Hello, Thomas."

Thomas spun his head around to Isabel who rode on his other side.

"Well," blinked Thomas in surprise and some self-consciousness at being in the presence of a beautiful young woman, not an everyday occurrence for him.

He swallowed before continuing, "And you must be Isabel."

"Yes, Tom," she smiled. "How are you? You probably don't remember me. You were still in the nursery when I set sail for France."

Thomas pulled himself up in his saddle to make himself appear taller. He shrugged his shoulders trying to appear worldly wise.

"That was a long time ago," he said casually. "I train in the tilt yard with the men now."

Isabel smiled inwardly at his attempts to impress her.

"I'm sure you do," she said gracefully. "When a man, do as a man."

"Exactly," agreed Thomas, puffing out his chest.

Algernon had raced out ahead of everybody. His mount almost reared as he pulled it to a sudden stop on top of the knoll.

"Alnwick!" he yelled and took off like lightening.

Isabel felt an excitement jangle in her veins. She hadn't seen her home for more than ten years. Would it still look the same?

Would people remember her? Would she be received as one of the family again? Would Catherine Percy welcome her into her arms as a mother? Or had she and Henry caused the family too much disappointment?

The excitement turned quickly into nervousness. On the knoll, she saw Alnwich. Her heart lurched within her. It looked smaller than she remembered but regal nonetheless with its rambling outer bailey and distinctive seven semi-circular towers. It was very welcoming, with golden glows emanated from the windows ever brighter as darkness started to fall.

Tears pricked her eyes as she followed everybody on the last leg home.

Isabel's worries were unfounded.

Welcoming arms embraced her, one after the other. First Catherine, Countess of Northumberland, then other members of the household, nursery maids and tutors and staff who knew her as a young girl. They fussed and patted over her as they drew her into the main hall.

Catherine has not aged much, Isabel thought. A few more lines around the mouth but her eyes still sparkled with the passion and life that she remembered and the warmth of her heart was transmitted through her hug.

Henry was also made a fuss of. The women especially clucked about him, making sure that he was in need of nothing. Nobody made mention of how terrible he looked, but Isabel could see Catherine looking at him with concern. Nothing was mentioned about Anne Boleyn and nothing was said about Isabel's missing days. It was as if that part of their lives never happened.

The main hall was decorated for Christmas. Holly and mistletoe hung in thick ropes around the grey stone walls and large apple bowers, and stumps crackled away in the great hearth releasing a tangy scent.

Thomas took it upon himself to act as personal host to Isabel after she was led to have a brief refresh and clothing change. She could tell that he was sweet on her. She liked him, too. He had a very charming, masculine way about him.

He presented her to his young sisters Margaret and Maud. Behind them stood their governess. In her mid-thirties, she held herself stiffly, the air around her seeming to crackle with self-efficiency and discipline.

Isabel smiled at her then turned her focus to the two little girls that the governess had pinned in front of her with a firm hand on each shoulder.

"Well, how wonderful to meet you at last," said Isabel smiling down at them.

Margaret and Maud made little curtseys to her. They were dressed for the occasion looking like little-adult versions of their mother with their square, Spanish style hoods and stiff bodices encrusted with seed pearls.

Margaret had the blonde looks of Henry, and Maud, slightly darker, took her looks after Thomas.

Margaret, the older and more serious of the two, well-trained in etiquette, was the first to speak.

"Thank you very much for your letters from France."

"You are very welcome, Margaret. I see you are doing very well in your French lessons from your replies to me."

Margaret beamed at the compliment and nudged Maud in the side to say something.

Maud rolled her eyes comically up to her older sister and tried to keep a straight face as she tried to cope with being the centre of attention. She reminded Isabel of Henry in his lighter moments.

Margaret gave her a stern look as if to say, "Say something!"

Maud suddenly flashed her dark eyes back at Isabel.

"We can have dinner with you in the hall tonight, instead of the nursery!" She piped up brightly, jumping up and down with excitement, as much as she could, under her governess's firm hand.

"And what a treat we are in for," said Isabel turning around to see great platters and trenchers of steaming food being placed on the covered trestle tables.

The gold and silver plates accompanied by Venetian glass goblets were a setting that would have been acceptable in any royal residence across Europe.

At that moment, the aging house steward creaked forward into their midst and announced that dinner was served.

Isabel grabbed Henry's hand as she passed by him and gave it a squeeze. She could tell that he was finding it hard—hard to breath without coughing, hard facing life without Anne.

He gave her a wan smile.

Henry and Isabel sat as guests of honour at the top of the horseshoe dining arrangement with the Earl and Countess of Northumberland. On the other side of Henry sat some of the earl's right-hand men, Heron and Turnbull. She was introduced to these men and their wives before she sat.

The women gushed their appreciation at being invited for the twelve days of Christmas at Alnwick. Isabel was glad to be interrupted by Catherine who directed her to her place of honour.

Unlike celebratory dinners at court, this one was opened with the Alnwick chaplain delivering a small sermon from the huge, gem-encrusted bible and a drawn out blessing in Latin over the food. The largely Catholic assembly bowed their heads as they crossed themselves in a synchronised "amen."

It reminded her of the faith of most northern people, whose spiritual hearts belonged to Rome. The English court bowed to Anglo-Catholicism, but her own leanings, she was beginning to understand, leaned towards death—death of her own wants and desires to follow God and definitely physical death if anybody got wind of her faith in action. Isabel understood why Jesus has been born in a manger. A manger was a receptacle for food. Jesus was food for human souls and now he was creating her to be the same. Isabel smiled wryly to herself. Poor Mary would have tasted nothing but bitterness from her during her stay in Sheffield. Ah well, God was the author and finisher of her faith. She would taste better to Mary in the days to come as she continued her walk of faith.

Isabel enjoyed the dinner, although she was aware of being constantly gazed upon by Heron. His steely blue gaze unsettled her. Whenever her eyes met his, he turned away.

At the end of the meal as the dishes were being cleared away, the earl stood up and all became quiet as he motioned that he wanted to speak.

"I am pleased to announce that there will be two Percy weddings in the spring, Henry, of course, to Mary Talbot, and Isabel to Sir Roland Tavistock." The earl rose his glass and saluted both Henry and Isabel. Everybody stood with him and toasted the health, wealth and success of Henry and Isabel in their newfound happiness.

Everybody then spoke at once, very excited about planning the preparations of two weddings. After dinner, the trestle tables were eventually folded away and people began to organise themselves on stools, benches and the occasional chair for the evening's entertainment. First was a recital, which had obviously been well-rehearsed by Margaret and Maud for this occasion.

Maud sat very carefully on a low stool and began to pluck a lute. Margaret took her place slightly behind her and started to sing a ballad in a very sweet voice.

Isabel could see their music teacher, a Mr. Follows, whom she had met very briefly, encouraging them through the recital, to the side, in the shadow of the holly.

Halfway through, Isabel noticed the house steward come in and stand behind the earl. He then bent down and whispered something into his ear. The earl rose silently and left the hall with his house steward, his daughter's sweet voice continuing to rise and fall with the lyrics of the ballad.

The earl entered back into the hall as claps of appreciation resounded at the end of the recital. Margaret and Maud plied their little stiff curtseys to everybody and were quickly encouraged away by their governess to their beds.

Isabel looked over at Henry who sat beside the hearth. He was looking quite ill now. *He needs his bed, too,* Isabel thought. She rose to go and suggest it to him.

Catherine intercepted her and pulled her quickly down onto a bench to the side of a wall.

Catherine looked grim.

Nonplussed, Isabel looked at her.

"Isabel, I'm sorry. We have just received some terrible news. I wanted you to know right away."

Isabel frowned. What could be so terrible? She was home, safe in the arms of Henry and Catherine Percy, within the impenetrable walls of Alnwick castle.

"What?" she ventured, frowning.

"It's your betrothed, Sir Roland Tavistock. He … " she swallowed. "He has been found dead. I'm so sorry, Isabel."

"Dead?" said Isabel, puzzled. "Did he die of illness?" she asked, remembering that he was old enough to be her grandfather.

Catherine's face looked very grim now. Her eyes seemed to look right through her as she crossed herself. "Murdered," she whispered.

"Murdered?" Isabel sucked her breath in, her heart pounding.

"His throat was cut in his bed," she crossed herself again as if protecting herself from such a gruesome end. "Mother of mercy, protect us from these wild northerners."

Isabel felt like she had been doused in cold water. The feeling of security that had been built up throughout the evening started to trickle away from her like water from a leaky bucket.

***

Isabel raced Henry and Thomas back to Alnwich.

Spring had arrived with days of sunshine, warmth and puffy clouds. The fells and dales sped past them in a blur of soft colours in various hues of violet, brown and yellow on the wind-blighted hilltops, down to the vivid green of spring pasture, dotted with buttercups and dandelions surrounding Alnwich. New growth of bulrushes and water reeds grew thickly along the river Aln, bowing gently before the warm spring breeze.

Thomas passed Isabel with a whoop and a yell. Isabel laughed but the wind whipped away her voice before she could be heard. She looked back to see how far Henry was behind her. He was way back across the valley, having just picked his way down out of a rocky outcrop that dropped to the valley floor from a flat ridge. It looked like he had stopped with a groom at his side.

A fit of coughing, no doubt, thought Isabel. Henry had gathered strength after Christmas and into the spring, but the cruel, hacking cough had still remained.

He missed Anne terribly, Isabel knew. She had seen him weeping when he thought himself to be alone.

What wasn't helping was the earl's attitude toward his oldest son. Isabel felt for Henry as he continually wore his father's rebuffs of "useless, hopeless" and comments of "having no backbone."

Isabel nudged her heels into her mount to catch up to Thomas. She caught him just before they entered the outer gates of Alnwich.

They laughed together, invigorated by physical exercise and appreciation of each other's company and walked their horses into the stable yard. They were surprised to see that a small party of newcomers had arrived. Groomsmen and stable hands were busy tethering the saddled mounts into empty stalls.

"Whom do these belong to, Simon?" asked Thomas of a passing groom while he helped Isabel dismount.

Isabel smiled a wry grin to herself as she felt Thomas grip her around the waist and not let go when she reached the ground. He seemed to push the boundaries of what was acceptable when it came to being with her, but she was sure that he knew that.

As much as she loved the attention from this rash but lovable young man, she gently removed his hands.

"I'm not sure, Milord," replied the young groom. "I haven't seen him before, but these be northern ponies, of that I'm sure."

"Shall we?" Thomas offered Isabel his arm to walk her into the castle. His blue eyes sparkled with mischief, displaying a little of the hothead he was, but underneath, she knew he was falling in love with her.

It was an immature love, she perceived, and it would always be about him. It would be a lucky girl who captured his heart when he matured. She hoped one day that she would know the love of a man—a man that she could respect, one who would love her and share the same passions as she did. Did that sort of love develop from a marriage contract? Was it a dream?

She quickly brushed the thought aside. It was only a dream for Anne and Henry and it certainly was for her now that Sir Roland lay in his grave. Henry and Mary's wedding was not even a month away. Who knew what the future held for her now that Sir Roland was dead? Best not to think too much. If she did, she might end up like Henry who seemed to live his life like the living dead. Life held no joy for him. He had lost hope without Anne.

A movement out of the corner of her eye caught her attention.

"Is that little Jennet Poll?"

Thomas stopped and looked in Isabel's direction.

The girl from the buttery slunk past a stable wall.

"Yes, it is," said Thomas, wondering why Isabel would bother to notice a lowly servant girl, especially an unkempt one.

"I remember her as a toddler. A sweet girl; simple though, wasn't she? The head laundress's daughter, as I remember."

"Yes, let's go in," said Thomas impatient to see who was visiting.

"You go. I'll just say hello."

Thomas looked at her as if she'd grown two heads.

Isabel sighed. "It's all right for you. You have had family around you all your life. I am just being reacquainted. You go. I'll only be a minute."

Thomas gave her a "whatever you want" type of shrug and ran into the depths of Alnwich.

Isabel followed Jennet and quickly caught up. She caught Jennet by the arm.

"Hello. Jennet isn't it?"

The thin, pale slip of a girl looked frightened. She had the look of a hunted fox with her dark brown eyes darting to and fro.

"It's all right, Jennet. Do you remember me? Isabel. I've been in France for a long time."

The girl looked up at Isabel without recognition. Her face was smudged with some sort of grime and her hair hung limp and stringy under her cotton cap.

Isabel vaguely remembered some horror surrounding her birth; she was too small to remember the details. She did remember a feeling of being shoved aside for an emergency, of hearing women speaking in hushed tones and intermittent screams that were muffled through walls.

"How are you, Jennet?"

"I'm all right," she said hesitantly in the monotone voice of the simple.

"Well, I'm glad," said Isabel.

There was some uncomfortable silence as Jennet was unsure how to act. She stared at her fingers as she fidgeted with her apron.

"Well, I'll be off, Jennet. It was lovely to see you again."

"Yes, madam," said Jennet, bobbing her head with relief and she sidled off toward the buttery.

Isabel looked back at the sorrowful figure and feeling slightly annoyed and dissatisfied for no reason, peeled off her gloves and walked back into the entrance of Alnwick Castle.

A housemaid ran to her assistance and helped divest her of hat, gloves and cape.

"They are waiting for you in the hall, Mistress Isabel."

Isabel gave the maid a sharp look, her beautiful wing-shaped brows coming together in a frown. "Who?"

"The earl and countess with the visitor, mistress."

"Visitor?"

"Yes, mistress, you'd better not keep them waiting. They told me to tell you directly."

Isabel tried to smile away a sense of foreboding that was rising. "Thank you, Elspeth," said Isabel touching her forearm kindly. "I had better go directly, then."

Elspeth dipped a small curtsy and carried Isabel's belongings up the wide staircase.

Isabel made her way into the great hall still warmed by a fire despite the ambience of spring now upon them. She saw the earl and countess standing beside a man in dark clothing. Thomas stood by the hearth looking into the flames that crackled up the chimney. He appeared sullen and moody as he leaned his elbow against the stone.

Everybody but Thomas looked up at her entrance. A healthy glow flushed her face and wisps of white gold hair that had escaped her snood while riding, hung in loose ringlets about her face. She made an effort to look tidier and lifted her hand to brush her wayward hair back into its place.

The earl came forward and took her left hand. He led her to their visitor. "My dear, may I present to you Sir Willem Van der Veldt, wool merchant, from Brussels."

Isabel looked into the amber eyes fringed with dark lashes that had haunted her nightmares for so long.

Isabel felt stunned. He had found her, just as she had feared he would. She felt like a trapped bird, suddenly feeling sick.

He smiled a smile that would melt any other heart and raised his left hand, dropped it suddenly, then raised his right hand to bow over hers.

Isabel was too traumatised to take any notice of the quick change of hands. The earl and countess, also, were too interested in their own agenda for the meeting to notice.

"Enchanted, Mistress."

Isabel saw his eyes dance, as they appeared to mock her. The sick feeling gave way to intense anger. She didn't know whether to grab her hand back and wipe it or to slap the amusement from his face. She did neither as the fear resumed, making her legs feel weak.

The earl, marvellously attired as usual, standing head and shoulders above his ward, interrupted her inner turmoil and patted her hand. "Sir Willem has asked for your hand in marriage."

Isabel blanched even more.

"He tells me he met you while you were in France. Is this true?"

Isabel gave a stiff nod.

"Well, that's wonderful, isn't it Catherine?" Husband and wife smiled at each other. "I have accepted his hand of marriage on your behalf. I'm sure you are well over the shock of the death of Sir Roland. It is now time to move on.

"Sir Willem is a very successful wool merchant. He not only owns land in the border country but also down in Norfolk.

He shall keep you very well, I should think." He faced Sir Willem. "You also live in the Lowlands I believe?"

"Yes, the business is there but I also have family on my mother's side on the French Belgium border. We grow the wool in England but we spin, dye and weave in the Lowlands."

Catherine, looking pleased, clapped her hands together. "Well, Isabel, a double marriage ceremony after all?"

Isabel hardly heard Catherine as she looked at Sir Willem with confusion. Didn't she know him as Richard Kerr?

Horror filled her again. Or was it Gavyn Kerr? Which twin was it? They both had that strange accent of soft border burr with a French lilt.

Sir Willem pulled his velvet collar aside as if the inner cambric lace was scratching his neck.

From the angle of the light coming in from the upper casements, she saw the raised white flesh of a scar that had healed over between his collarbones—the wound that she had put there many months ago in France!

Her world spun out and darkness took over.

Henry entered the hall, having arrived back from what was a torturous ride across the moors, just in time to see Isabel fall gracefully to the floor in a puddle of silk and damask.

***

The earl paced the inner courtyard with his wolfhounds and mastiffs to think. Sir Willem had just left to go north. He didn't give any thought to Isabel recovering in her room.

Women were the weaker vessel, as God had made plain; these things were to be expected. What she needed was a husband at her side.

But he was disappointed.

He was disappointed in having to settle for a merchant husband for her. Not for her, but for himself. He had invested in Isabel, in sending her overseas to live in various European courts, hoping to capitalise on a large return, of aligning himself with another peer of the realm, a royal house on the continent.

Relationships made one stronger and he needed them for influence.

Damn Henry! It was entirely his fault! How could his own son, his first-born, be such a disappointment!

He shook his head from side to side in disbelief. Thomas was more of a man than Henry would ever be. He was a bit rash and unwise at times but that could be corrected. Henry's mooning was something he found hard to stomach.

Well, he would be wed soon, he comforted himself; perhaps that will make him forget this Anne Boleyn.

Overall, the fact remained that Henry had put him in the position of being on the back foot. Even though the king had been magnanimous about his son's flirtation with this mistress Boleyn, he was not likely to forget it and any further favours, like a marriage into nobility for Isabel might be seen very dimly.

The earl kicked a stone to release some of his rising anger. It hit one of his dogs and it yelped in pain. The earl rubbed the hound's ears to ease its misery. The other dogs snapped and snarled at each other's snouts with jealousy in their master's sudden affection toward one of them.

He yelled at them in a tone that would have made one of his pages water his breaches in fear. They whined with their tails between their legs in submission.

Isabel had been an unexpected bonus in his life, the payment of an owed debt, but so much more. Although unexpected, like everything else, he wanted to make the most of what was in his hand.

He had planned out Isabel's life for his own advantage and now it was mostly lost. Isabel had a good dowry, which had come with her. It hadn't cost him a cent.

The spoils of war, and not even his own!

He stroked his well-trimmed beard, wishing that all business opportunities were so easily come by.

Sir Nicholas Heron interrupted his pacing.

Heron and Northumberland appeared to greet and then play with the dogs as they spoke. No prying eye or flapping ear would discern the secrets that they shared, secrets that their own wives weren't even party to.

They threw dry, sun-bleached bones for the dogs to fetch. Between their laughing and rough housing, their voices were low, focused and steady.

"They still don't know," said Heron.

"God's blood," Northumberland swore, hissing through his teeth. "Save me from these barbarians!"

"We will find who murdered Tavistock. The marshal and his men are following trails as we speak. They're weak but it's something."

"Good. In the meantime, I have to make second best on my spoils."

Heron shrugged. "Ah, well," he said sagely. "A bird in the hand is worth two in the bush."

"Just so," said Northumberland, with a faraway look in his eyes. "Just so."

Heron bowed and left. If he had turned around, he would have been surprised to be confronted with a gaze of pure hatred coming from the earl.

Henry was amazed that he had managed to veil it from Heron as they spoke. It seemed that even the greatest peer in the realm was no less vulnerable than anybody else in the North Country defending himself against border warfare.

CHAPTER TWENTY-NINE

Norfolk Coast

Some miles down the coast, the same blustery winds that hounded the battlements of Alnwick castle slammed a merchant caravel against English docks.

Richard Kerr stepped off the gangway with purpose. The smell of brine and rotting fish assailed his senses despite the wind. It was mixed with old straw and dung from the passing of wagoned drays. The noise of people selling wares, seagulls screeching above, and the shouts of sailors swinging from rigging as they loaded produce filled the air.

Without hesitation, he stepped into the pressing cacophony.

His fury at finding himself back in the Low Countries with a cracked jaw, he was sure, only served to make him more determined.

As the first-born twin, the family inheritance belonged to him! Isabel belonged to him. Now that his father was dead, it would be easy to step in and claim what was his. His father had been the patriarch of the Kerr clan. Nobody, not even his uncles if they were still alive, had the charisma and leadership skills of his father.

There was nobody who had the ability to take over clan strategies, he believed. So it was going to be very easy to take back what belonged to him. He loved and admired his father even though he had never been loved back. He never once thought his thinking was warped in murdering his father. He loved him even in death and that was all that mattered. He understood why his father had hated him. He had murdered his mother.

A hand grabbed his arm. He spun around, ready to confront, fight if he had to.

A face that he loved but had totally forgotten as he abandoned himself to his obsession, smiled broadly in front of him.

Doubt and uncertainty rippled through Richard as he looked upon his lover. Should he have brought her to England? Probably not, but he had a weakness for her. Almost twice his age and probably considered rather plain, she was his soul mate, always a calm harbour for his stormy soul.

Oh well, what was done was done, he thought, brushing off the negativity. That sort of thinking would only drag upon him like a weight. He had to focus on his plan. He would be successful. In fact, gripping his lover's hand as he laughed out loud, it would be easy.

CHAPTER THIRTY

Alnwich Castle, Northumberland

Henry stood at the window embrasure. From the back, he looked like an old man as he wrapped himself up in wolf furs against the chill.

His soul was as miserable as the day outside.

The pasture was richly verdant as the spring had set in but soft grey clouds had come down so low that they caressed the hills and treetops, blocking out the sun with their fine, misty drizzle.

Henry rubbed his chest trying to rub away the dull ache that this sort of weather seemed to bring. He was finding it hard to break through the fog in his mind. He wanted to lie down and sleep forever.

The creak of his chamber door opening slowly made him turn around. It was Isabel, his little flicker of light in the perpetual darkness of his life. She was looking furtive.

Had she gotten thinner? Not surprising. Their double wedding was to be held next week after his father returned from London. His presence had been required for the creation of the king's bastard son, Henry Fitzroy, into the Duke of Richmond.

They both waited for the event as if it were doomsday.

He couldn't quite understand Isabel's reaction to her new suitor. Her betrothed was young, successful and very amenable, from all accounts, but any mention of him and she seemed to act as if he were the devil himself. She would go pale and quiet and back away from any conversation. He had to be better than old Tavistock surely?

Maybe it was just a case of fear of the unknown.

He smiled at her now as she entered his chamber. She smiled back a real smile, a cheeky smile, which produced that adorable dimple in her cheek. His interest was piqued.

"Isabel?"

"I have something that may make your day," she said.

"Yes?" he said after some prolonged silence, knowing that she was teasing him.

She pulled out a folded piece of parchment with an unbroken seal from inside of her silk lined sleeve.

She took a covert look around the room to make sure nobody was there and led Henry to the window seat. The cold emanating from the stone made Henry pull his furs even more tightly about himself.

Isabel dipped her head as she leant towards him and whispered. "It's a letter from Anne."

Life flooded into Henry as hope and expectancy filled his heart. His emotions were so full to bursting that he couldn't even speak.

"Shall I read?" Isabel whispered.

"How?" he managed a choked whisper back.

"Enclosed in a letter with a wedding gift from old Lady Hartleford. I recognise Anne's hand. Lady Hartleford is a close confident of old Lady Howard, Anne's grandmother. She resides at court keeping us young fillies, as she would say, in order, with a big stick—her acerbic tongue!"

Henry's face became alive with anticipation. He smiled a rueful smile. "Good old Lady Hartleford!"

"Who would have thought she had some good points?"

Henry nudged Isabel impatiently. "Come on."

Isabel rose and latched Henry's bedchamber door, then made herself comfortable beside him. With pale slender fingers she broke the seal and pried open the stiff parchment.

Henry also now recognised the stylised slant of Anne's handwriting. The ink was thin and blotched in some places. It had been written in haste.

"Dearest Isabel, Should you be reading this I will have been successful in my endeavours, to which I thank God for. Please burn this missive after sharing it with my love, if that is possible, as my actions of writing and sending this letter could be seen as treasonous. Give my love to Henry whose love I carry daily in my heart.

"What an injustice done to us both! I have since found that Wolsey was only a messenger ordered by the king himself to separate Henry and me.

"I have learned that the king wants me for himself, just as he had my sister, Mary ..."

Isabel broke off, stunned at this piece of information. She looked up at Henry to gauge his reaction.

"The king?" Henry squeaked. He felt like he had suffered a blow to his stomach. Sweet Mother of Mercy, no wonder he had been dispatched north in such haste; no wonder his arguments had never held. It wouldn't have mattered how suited he and Anne were as a couple, politically or otherwise; the king had spoken.

The king ... Henry let the thought sink in. The greatest in the land desired his Anne! The king could have anybody!

Why did he have to choose his love? It was so unfair! He felt like screaming, tearing the place apart. He wanted to vent this utter rage and hopelessness with no care for the consequences, but he did none of that. He was weak and he hated himself for it; he knew he did care for the consequences, even if it meant living a shadow of a life. If he did decide to come against the king, his life would be abruptly cut short: a few weeks of heaven then death by being hung, drawn and quartered, the end of all traitors.

Henry gripped Isabel's hand, tears brimming in his eyes, his thoughts once again spiralling down into blackness and despair. "There is truly no hope is there? How can anybody fight the king?"

Isabel's chin trembled as she felt Henry's pain. With her own troubles barely contained under the surface, she was finding it hard to be strong for Henry. She sniffed in a deep breath to help control her emotions and squeezed his hand.

Isabel continued. "I remain at Hever still. I will resist his attentions, never fear. I swear before God that I will never end up like Mary. It is against God's law for a maid to live thus. I pray that the good Lord will speak to the king's sensibilities and let propriety have its way.

"I must finish quickly, Lady Hartleford is leaving and I have to get this letter stowed away with her. Henry, if your ears or eyes are party to this missive, then know that my love is with you always. It will never change. Remember our vows we made together on the battlements of Westminster Castle. They remain true before God.

"Isabel, God's blessing on your up-and-coming nuptials. I hope your life will not be so ill-fated as my own. Love and prayers, your dearest friend, Anne.

"Postscript: Write to me when you can. I would like to know where you would be residing, so I may write again."

Isabel folded the parchment and held it in her lap. "That's all."

"The king," said Henry, his troubled eyes seemed to search the floor at his feet. "The king … No wonder my father thundered down to London to collect me. He could well have kept my head on my shoulders … kept his head on his shoulders."

They sat in silence.

Henry looked at Isabel, his blue eyes wrenched in pain. "Why couldn't his eyes have fallen on somebody else? It could so easily have been someone else."

Tears rolled silently down his cheeks.

Isabel didn't answer as she rose and stood at the hearth in which a fire had been lit upon his mother's orders. Her mood had turned as gloomy as his.

He watched her place the letter into the flames. He felt like yelling *no* as he watched the flames lick the paper yellow and turn it black. Anne's very fingers had touched that paper.

He could see them in his mind's eye, very slender, delicate, and graceful, brushing away the blotting sand. Could they have held some of her perfume?

Too late now, her touch and her scent were in ashes, glowing red and orange then turning black and grey in the grate, as dead and devoid of life as his own.

***

The day of the double wedding dawned bright and clear. As the sun rose, its golden rays gilded everything they touched and the colours of the landscape developed into deep rich hues. But for Gavyn William Kerr, alias Willem Van der Veldt—his dead mother's maiden name—the world was getting decidedly dimmer. All the colours he viewed through his own eyes were turning grey.

A garrotte was tightening around his neck. Lack of breath was now causing black spots to appear before his eyes. He never expected his death to come like this. Just before it went totally black he felt a brief moment of incredible pain as something solid impacted him on the side of his head. Every thought and struggle for life was let go as he slumped into oblivion. His body crumpled to the cold flagstones on the floor of Alnwick Castle vestry.

Richard dragged his brother's body to a large oak chest. He opened the heavy lid and tossed out the vestments within. Priest's robes and richly embroidered altar cloths were lumped into an untidy heap on the floor. He quickly dragged Gavyn's body into the empty chest, folding his limbs so that the lid would close properly.

He peeked outside the internal door into the family chapel. The priest was making final adjustments to the candelabras and one or two house servants were finishing the final polishing of the extra pews, which had been pulled out of storage. Satisfied that he had not disturbed anyone, he silently closed the door.

A door that could not be closed into the vestry, one that always remained open, and one that was not easily discerned was a peephole that had been created many years before by bored pages waiting to perform their Sunday duties as choirboys. In their boredom, they had worried a knot in a plank of wood so much that it had fallen out creating a nice eyepiece for anybody behind the wall to view from. It was at hip height and in the shadow of an oak sideboard.

With the pages long since gone, only one other person now knew of its existence, one other person whose only real participation in life was to watch other people's lives.

The knot in the wood winked as the eye behind it shifted position.

***

John Turnbull paced the gates of Alnwich Castle, his sharp, piercing eyes ever watchful under his bushy brows, mindful of its comings and goings, especially with the wedding celebrations today. His short stocky body exuded authority as he strode. People made way for him, bowing respectfully to one of the earl's right-hand men.

The wedding was not a big affair, the heir apparent being held in disgrace by his father and the king, no less! *And,* he mused, *his ward being quickly bundled up to some wealthy merchant with Sir Roland not yet cold in his grave!*

John Turnbull shook his head to himself. He wasn't as close to the earl as he had once been and he wasn't always party to his plans these days. Maybe that was because they didn't spend a lot of time together anymore. He was always sorting disputes north in the border country and the earl himself always seemed to be in London for something or other. *Self-preservation more than likely,* he thought to himself grimly.

He stepped aside, allowing a cart of green produce to pass. Another cart of fresh fish followed. The baskets in it overflowed with salmon, whiting, eel, and pike. Nothing was ever done by halves where the earl was concerned. They would dine very well at midday. Well, that was one thing that hadn't changed, he supposed.

The earl still liked to live like a king!

His thoughts turned serious again as he turned and followed the carts up to the castle kitchens.

He walked, not for surveillance—he had his own men to walk and guard the walls—but to sort through a dilemma that percolated in his mind.

He had some good news and some bad news for his lord. Was this a good time to tell him? He could well be rebuffed and understandably so, with the wedding happening in a few hours time.

The border marshal had just visited him. He and his men had traced the death of Sir Roland Tavistock back to an old family of the Kerr Clan. That was the good news and he could see the look of surprise on the earl's face already, for the name of the Kerrs carried respect in some circles as lawkeepers in the land.

Personally, he hated all Kerrs. They wormed and ingratiated themselves into all manner of business and politics. They were scum! But he had to act prudently around the earl who had to be seen to be impartial to all but the law emanating from the south.

The bad news for the earl was that he was certain that his ward was going to marry one today!

A Kerr!

He was sure of it! And the more he thought about it, the more it made sense to him.

Was the earl innocent of this union? He had to be after what had passed between them many years ago.

The man whom he saw enter the gates twice this morning, and that was a strange thing in itself, also gave himself away by his left-handedness. All Kerrs were tainted with this impediment. It was renowned. *Yes,* he thought, *they must be Satan's spawn to all be made that way. He has the physique of the Kerrs, strong and tall, but his colouring is unusual, not fair skinned and blond, but dark, surely not the offspring of that Kerr who married the Flanders doxy years ago?*

The memory was more than fifteen years old or more and he thought that he had totally forgotten it until now. Yes, he remembered her. She had been a dark beauty, sable hair, dark eyes and fair, milky skin that had the texture of a pale peach. It had been the talk of the countryside, a crofter clan of the Kerrs marrying into a wealthy Flanders merchant family. It was a business arrangement of course, a shrewd move by the patriarch of the clan, but he had seen that there had been love as well.

He remembered that tortured night of raiding, the screams, the fire, the blood and the image of her, the dark French beauty and one of her twin sons tumbling into a fishing skiff. He could see her in his mind's eye running to save the boy as he drifted out to sea, the orange flames on the shore reflecting on the black surface of the sea. She managed to catch the skiff but the currant of the tide pulled them both out beyond of reach of her husband. She had screamed for him to save her. He stood on the shore, holding their other son, yelling helplessly. They were never to be seen or heard of again by all accounts.

He remembered the tortured look coming from their faces, the torture of separation. Surely that only comes with true love?

So they have wormed their way back from oblivion? He thought to dupe us, did he? Yes, he thought as the clamouring of Alnwich Castle came to the fore of his senses again, he was onto this Kerr usurper and he would deal with it in such a way as to keep his master above suspicion should he be implicated.

With his mind settled, he strode purposely away from the back of the carts of produce to scout out a good secluded vantage spot to execute his business.

***

Mary Talbot stared at her reflection in the beaten silver mirror that was held before her. She stood in the guest apartments of Alnwich Castle, where one day she would rule as Mistress of the North. One year ago, she would have been ecstatic at the image before her. She looked like a little ice queen, very regal in her ivory gown and with the Talbot jewels of pale sapphires, hanging like shards of ice at her throat. Months of anxiety had created shadows on her body where there were none before, hollows at her collarbones, lines where her ribs protruded, flesh had even fallen away from her hands, revealing bones like a birds. Her pasty complexion had been stretched to an untouchable white pallor. Her stepmother's cosmetic ministrations of lemon juice to her hair, to make it fairer, and belladonna to her eyes, to make them appear larger, had magnified her new fragility, but it was a cold beauty. There was no joy from within. No light of happiness danced from her eyes. Months of struggling with the fact that Henry did not love her, nor even like her, found her losing the battle of forgiveness. Bitterness encompassed her like a cage.

Though perhaps, she thought as she gazed at her reflection, *I have never looked so becoming; perhaps he might have a change of heart when he sees me coming down the aisle.*

She comforted herself that Henry would have to hold her in his arms in the marriage bed. It was the expected thing. Even emotions such as hate and dislike were put aside for everybody's greater good. Then she would show him the love she had for him and then he would know her.

***

Isabel was also gazing into a mirror held before her but her vision went through the polished metal and into her near future. What did it hold for her? What did he want from her? Why had they been so persistent in searching her out?

Come tonight she would know all she wanted to and perhaps all that she didn't want to.

She brought her eyes back to the present. Catherine, the Countess of Northumberland, had clothed her as if she were her own daughter. Her fingers lifted up the gold tissue of her wedding gown. It was like fine gossamer, beautiful and very becoming on her with her gold hair spread over her shoulders. Catherine had loaned her the jewels that she wore, topaz and emeralds set in gold hung from her ears and at her throat.

All Catherine's ladies stood back to admire their work. They *ooh'd* and *ahh'd* as they tweaked her sleeves, reset a jewel in her hair and told her to parade in front of them for any final adjustments. After they were satisfied and started to withdraw, Isabel reached out to grab Catherine's hand. Her eyes implored her to stay.

"I'll be out forthwith," instructed Catherine to her women, closing the bedchamber door behind them.

She led Isabel to the side of her bed and they sat side by side. Catherine took Isabel's hands in hers, trying to impart love and comfort. She waited for her to speak.

Isabel studied the floor as she tried to gather the right words to describe her fears without giving out too much information.

"Are you sure you know this man?"

Catherine threw back her head in a gentle laugh while patting Isabel's hands. She turned and looked into her ward's worried face.

"My dear, would we give you to somebody of no account? To be sure, he has not the lineage of Sir Roland, but a lot of merchant families are becoming gentry these days. And who knows, these families may well be the way of our economic future." She sighed. "It is true, we do not know him as well as we have our old friend, Sir Roland, but his family name is well known throughout the low country wool industry—very well known. You will not want for anything."

Isabel was still unmoved. She knew this already. She had asked the Northumberlands in all manner of ways to try and gather more information about this man who was going to marry her again, but nothing new was forthcoming.

"Where will I live?"

Catherine patted Isabel's knee. "Tibby, dear, it's going to be all right. You know all this. You are just nervous, which is totally understandable. All brides are nervous on their wedding day. Come now," she stood and drew Isabel with her. "Look at you. You are beautiful and I love you like my own. Hasn't Henry loved you just the same?" she continued, speaking of her husband.

Isabel nodded dumbly, unable to speak the truth of her situation in the light of all they had done for her.

"Would he give you to someone whose background he hasn't looked into?"

Isabel nodded again trying not to let her tears surface. She knew the financial background would be sound for both sides; the earl would make sure of that.

"And see, you are to be with us for an extra few weeks while Master Willem travels onto York for business. That will be wonderful, will it not? It will give us more time to add to your wardrobe, more time to be with each other? You will get to know Mary, too. It will be wonderful for Mary to have another young bride to share stories with. It will be her first time away from her family. She has not had the training that you have had being away from home. So, it won't be so bad after all. You'll see. You will be missing Willem while he is in York. You'll be waiting for him to come and take you away!"

Catherine kissed Isabel on her forehead. "It's just nerves, my love," she confirmed. "You'll see. Now, I think all of Alnwich awaits your presence."

Trying not to drag her feet, Isabel followed Catherine out of the chamber into the unknown.

***

Jennet Poll was horrified that the man of her dreams, the man who gave her the gold crown in the buttery, had been stuffed into a chest. She was confused. It looked like the man of her dreams had also hit the man folded in the chest. Who was who? They both looked the same! She couldn't figure it out and didn't spend any time trying to.

She had to help him!

When the man left the vestry to reply to a call from beyond the outside door, Jennet crawled forward through the back of the oak sideboard and slid ungraciously into the small room, with her skirts caught up about her waist. She clambered to her feet and stood stock-still, listening for any nearby sounds that might alert her to people approaching.

She feverishly grabbed the berries at the bottom of her apron and squeezed the juice into the goblet of wine, which sat with some honey cakes in the sideboard. She always carried them with her. The men who took advantage of her always woke up the next day with very bad stomach aches. She had seen the cows get very sick and some even die when they ate these berries. She grabbed another big handful and squeezed the juice into the wine. She'd knock him out for good!

He was coming! His hand was on the latchet at the outside door. She pulled aside and held the goblet of wine to him as he passed through. He grabbed it, downed the lot in seconds and handed the goblet back to her without a glance. In another second he was gone, waiting to receive his bride at the altar.

There was a background hum as guests started to arrive in the chapel and found seating for themselves.

She shuffled over to the chest and lifted the lid. The man lay still, like a crumpled rag doll. Jennet didn't know what to do. She rocked from side to side, plucking the edges of her apron with nail bitten fingers, as she tried not to voice her distress.

Making a decision, she stood still and tried to pull his arm from the box. It came free. She tugged on it a few times to try to wake him up. His head didn't budge.

Jennet dropped his arm and stood up. She was going to have to do what the Cook did to drunken retainers who slept at her door: smack them into wakefulness!

Hesitating with nervousness, never having slapped a man on the face before, Jennet lifted her hand to strike.

The first smite only caused him to turn his head some. She hit him again, this time harder. The man moaned and tried to open his eyes. Jennet wouldn't let him sink into oblivion again and tugged violently on his arm.

The man opened his eyes. As he turned his face up to her, she could see blood trickling down the side of his cheek where he had been hit. She tugged on his arm to get up out of the chest.

He did so with her help. When he eventually stood beside her, she encouraged him to dress with his clothes for the ceremony, which had been set out on various pegs. It seemed to break him out of the fog that he was in. He looked at Jennet, who looked back at him with wide eyes. He cupped her face with both hands and gave her a grateful kiss on her lips.

She looked on at him in wonder, touching her lips, as he dressed and wiped the blood from the wound to his head.

It was the first kiss she had ever received like that and she marvelled in it. She had been groped at and slobbered over by men who had had too much to drink and who wanted any port in a storm, but she had never been treated with respect in that way. This kiss imparted to her that she was someone of value.

She continued to look after him in awe as he dressed.

Through the stone walls, muted music struck up. The brides were making their way down the isle!

The man of her dreams rushed to the vestry door. As quickly as he left, he arrived back with his brother unconscious in his arms.

Jennet made as if to tidy up the wine and honey cakes as he entered the vestry. She very boldly turned to him and the man who came with him to help. She shooed them away after they laid him on a bench. "I shall revive him with some wine. Or maybe he has had enough already?" insinuating that all they had was a drunkard in their midst rather than a man asphyxiated by poisoning. The man who came to help didn't question anything; he only wanted the groom to get back at the altar.

Up in the choir's gallery, which looked down into the chapel, John Turnbull, confused, quickly slid his small bow and quiver of arrows behind an ornate tapestry on the wall. He slid unseen down a narrow back staircase; somebody else had already hit his target.

He didn't understand it, but that was more than fine, at least the ward of his master was free from the vermin Kerr. He hurried away before the ceremony started. He didn't want to be linked with skulduggery that might eventuate.

"One of Van der Veldt's supporters has fainted," went the ripple of whispers to the back pews. The groom had quickly dispatched the indisposed person to the vestry. An attendant quickly followed. After a quick few minutes, the groom, doing up the final button on his fine satin doublet, was looking composed and at the altar again. He nodded to the priest to start. The priest looked at the Earl of Northumberland for his permission to start. A curt nod was given.

The four faces in front of the priest showed no emotion as the vows were uttered. As the couples faced each other to exchange rings, they wouldn't have looked out of place at a funeral.

Immediately after the wedding, they celebrated Mass together. When the offerings were finished, a single trumpeter heralded the end of the solemn occasion and the couples were led to the great hall for the banquet.

The couples barely spoke to each other as they partook lightly of the sumptuous food. The guests more than made up for their lack of levity, eating and drinking well, with ribald jokes and innuendo getting louder as the time went on.

Just after dusk, it was announced that it was time for the bedding ceremony.

The priest led the way swinging his brazier of incense and holy water and everybody who could, followed.

Henry and Mary were first to be bedded. They were led off to separate antechambers by their attendants to undress and then dress again into their nightgowns.

Mary, gowned up to her neck in a drawstring affair was the first to be laid upon the sheets. She didn't have to wait long before Henry emerged, also trussed to the neck. The sheets and silk counterpane were pulled over them. The nuptial bed was blessed by the priest, with words of benediction and prayers of fruitfulness. When the priest drew back, the women came forward throwing petals and more words of blessing. One by one, people left the room onto the next bedding session. When the door was finally closed, the room echoed with silence.

Isabel and her groom suffered the same trial. Not a word was spoken between them as ribald laughter continued amongst the guests after the priest had finished. After some time, calling out their love and blessings, the wedding guests finally made their leave.

Mary took a sideways glance at Henry without turning her head. He was not moving and she didn't want to be the first one to initiate the consummation.

A rack of candles either side of the bed were their only light. Mellow yellow hues flickered over the bed curtains, walls and vaulted ceiling. It was very quiet. She could not even hear his breathing.

No action was forthcoming from Henry so Mary felt forced to lead. She undid the laces at her throat, which opened up the front of her nightgown. She had no cleavage to boast of but she was certain that the show of flesh might spark interest. Despite everything that he had put her through, she knew that she would toss it all aside and forgive him instantly if he came to her as a lover.

She felt Henry move. She looked at him quickly and was shocked. He was getting out of the bed! He turned to look at her. She could see no love or desire there whatsoever. Dread washed over her, as she perceived no change in his continued rejection of her.

"I will not lie to you, Mary. We may be husband and wife by law and the church, and I will honour it this night only, so you do not cry foul of my lack of manhood. No doubt the sheets will be checked in the morning.

"My body and heart belong to Anne Boleyn and it always will. We were betrothed before God and after this act, I will keep my vow."

Mary was stunned and unbelieving of what she had just heard. Her hands fell to her sides as her last hopes for their marriage relationship dissolved into ashes.

Henry proceeded to snuff out the candles until they were in complete blackness. She felt him crawl onto the end of the bed. He lifted up her gown from her feet and up over her legs.

She grasped at the sheets on both sides, fearful of what to expect next. It came suddenly.

"Turn over onto your front," Henry said without a scrap of warmth. He grasped her hips and forced her to turn over. He took her from behind. She screamed. The pillow she found in her mouth muffled her cries.

It was over very quickly and after a few moments she knew herself to be alone in the room. Suddenly the tears of heartache and sorrow poured out of her in a torrent of sobbing.

The intensity of it racked her little frame. She cried out for her dead mother, for herself and for the loss of her dreams. The pain felt like it might tear her in two.

In the wee hours just before dawn, cried out and empty of emotion, Mary curled herself into a little ball in the middle of the bed and finally fell asleep.

In another wing of Alnwich Castle, another groom alighted from the nuptial bed as the noise outside the door faded away.

Isabel watched her husband's movements with intensity, like a cat might stalk a bird.

He strolled to a side table and poured himself a fine red Gascony wine, imported especially for the wedding celebrations. His easy swagger shouted arrogance. So the words he spoke sent her into confusion. There was no guile, just frankness, if that were to be believed.

"You must be very frightened. Would you like a wine? Have no fear. You shall sup yours in the bed and I will sit here," he said motioning to a leather seat supported on a crossed oak frame.

Isabel dipped her chin in acknowledgement, but still remained silent. She accepted the wine from long tapered fingers.

Yes, she remembered his elegant hands, but to whom did they belong?

She found her voice. It was husky with the wine. Her eyes never deviated from his.

"And you are?" she asked.

Her husband threw his head back and laughed. He raised his glass of wine to her.

"Touché, my dear, touché!" he said appreciating her humour, despite the coldness of its delivery. He knew it was no more than he deserved.

He lowered his glass and looked at her.

He was still very handsome with his brown curls and amber eyes framed in dark lashes. It couldn't be denied; no matter what lack of character he may display, he was still a good-looking man.

He sat with his legs crossed. She tried not to look at his naked limbs underneath his nightgown.

She took another large sip of wine.

"My name is Gavyn Kerr. You have also met my first-born twin brother, Richard, I believe. In Colchester?"

Isabel didn't offer any comment.

Gavyn decided to go on in a different tack. He opened the collar of his nightgown and caressed the raised white scar between his collarbones. Above it was a thin red line that she hadn't seen before. It looked like the skin was broken in parts. Isabel tried to ignore it. Trouble seemed to follow this man wherever he went, whether he gave it or received it.

"I admire a fighting spirit." He didn't seem to be mocking her, but Isabel couldn't be sure. She clenched her jaw in her rising anger.

Yes, she was amazed that she had the ability to stab someone, but he had brought it on himself.

"I apologise for your inconvenience," she said with eyes blazing. "But if you had called on me through acceptable channels, that wouldn't have happened."

"No, indeed," he agreed. "But we were unsure of who we were dealing with. I apologise too. The whole thing could have been handled better, but we had to act quickly and there was no room for trouble."

It was Isabel's turn to laugh. It was harsh and held no humour.

Gavyn leaned forward in his chair, his arms resting on his knees as his face became serious. His shoulders dropped as if he had given in to something.

Isabel became wary.

"I am sorry, Isabel, for everything that we have caused you."

Gavyn dropped his eyes for a moment then returned them to her. Isabel could see real discomfort in them. "I'm ... I am sorry for violating you ... raping you in France. It was necessary to consummate the marriage. I had heard that my brother wanted to claim his inheritance and I couldn't let him take you."

The tension that Isabel held in her own shoulders from her anger dissipated somewhat. This was totally unexpected. He had a conscience? Unbelievably, tears welled in her eyes as his honesty touched the wound within that she had hidden from the world.

Before she could stop herself, she blurted out words that she had no intention of sharing. The unlocked emotion seemed to start down, deep in her belly. She could feel it shaking its way up and she was unable to suppress it. Tears tracked their way down her cheeks, blurring her vision.

Gasping through her great sobs she managed to throw out her words. "I - We ... lost ... a son ..."

"We what ...?"

Gavyn rose from his chair in bewilderment.

"What do you mean? We lost a son?"

Isabel wiped her eyes and gulped down her tears as she looked at him.

"I became pregnant. I miscarried him on the day your brother kidnapped me. Don't you remember? It was a wonder I didn't die from loss of blood." Isabel dropped her eyes to the bed as she thought about their little boy. "He was so tiny. He was so perfect ..." Tears continued. She had never had the time to mourn her loss.

Gavyn stood and sat on the side of the bed and reached out to take her hand. She snatched it back to her breast, angry with herself for opening up to him.

"Nobody knows this! Do you understand? You are not to tell a soul! How could I tell anybody? I was petrified! Do you know what you put me through? Why did you do it? Why?"

She was shaking with fresh anger. Every thought and emotion that had been suppressed since he entered her life bubbled to the surface. She was not going to hold back! She demanded answers!

"I am so sorry Isabel," said Gavyn again, "but a great wrong has been done to you and me. We are rectifying it."

"We? Rectifying it? Rectifying what?" she cried unbelievingly.

"You remember the battle of Flodden?"

Isabel continued to look at him but would not concede her acknowledgement either way.

He continued. "Well, that was caused by the murder of my kinsman, one Robert Kerr. He was a border warden; a Heron murdered him. In some respects, a lot of the battle is history, but for us Kerrs, the repercussions of the murder still live on. It apparently does for the Herons, too."

Gavyn looked down at the floor again and he fidgeted with the glass of wine in his hands.

Dread filled Isabel as she began to interpret his body language.

He eventually looked up. "Do you know who you are, Isabel?"

She tried not to look offended. "Yes. Of course."

"Who?"

"Isabel Percy, ward of the Earl of Northumberland. My parents, his distant relatives, died and he took me in."

"Half true," said Gavyn. "You are the ward of Northumberland but only because you were the payment of a debt that couldn't be paid by other means ..."

Gavyn broke off, clearly distressed. "Oh, God help me get this out ..."

He looked at her with miserable eyes. "You are so innocent of all of this, but at least I will tell you the truth, Isabel. It's going to hurt you. You probably won't believe it, but it's true."

Isabel had become very still and the colour had left her face.

"Well?" Her cold, steely eyes held his.

"You are Isabel Heron, heiress to the Dunningford holdings, the Heron lands due northwest, two day's ride from Alnwich.

"It was your uncle who murdered my kinsman, my second cousin to be exact, which started the war. But this was one of many tit-for-tat revenge strategies, murders and raids, which were going on before we were born. Many have happened since then. We Kerrs raided your lands and holdings to take back what was ours, even if we couldn't take back our flesh and blood.

"Nicholas Heron, Northumberland's aide, is your uncle. When he heard of the raid, he left Alnwich as fast as he could with a compliment of the earl's men and found you, the only person left standing. You were two years old; only child and now heir to the Heron estate of Dunningford.

"Heron saw his opportunity to pay back his gambling debt to the earl. Give you to him with all your lands and income.

"The earl restocked your land and under heavy guard, increases his wealth daily by your estates. Your wool is excellent quality and we give you or rather, Northumberland, a good price. I process the wool in the Low Countries. It is a profitable business.

"Your dowry was half your estate. We get back what should have been ours long ago. It is legal and there is nothing he can do about it."

"You duped the earl?" Isabel was stunned. Her eyes showed it, being as round as the gold plate that hung in the great hall below.

Gavyn didn't answer as he stopped to take a mouthful of wine. He looked at her as he swallowed. She had dropped her eyes to the silk counterpane.

He was right, she perceived. She didn't want to believe him. She found it hard to believe him. But what if it was true?

Where did that make her stand? Had her whole life been a lie up to now? It was too much to take in.

"Isabel, you are innocent of this affair. When I was instructed to find you and marry you, so that we could gain back what was ours, I never saw you as a person. You were a pawn on our border warfare chessboard. You were a …"

"An enemy to be conquered," whispered Isabel.

"Yes," Gavyn offered back.

Brutal honesty, thought Isabel.

Silence, for a time, weighed heavily upon them both.

At last, Gavyn spoke. "I release you from our marriage vows. Because the marriage has been consummated, the dowry is mine and there can be no annulment. But we can divorce.

"I suggest that while I'm away at York, you think where you would like to go from here. I can set you up anywhere you desire to be. Divorce should be easily enough obtained. You have enough evidence against me to be released. Money is no problem; I'll set up funds from your estates. You'll never be without. I can't guarantee what you're used to, Alnwich, the palaces in London and such like. But you'll want for nothing. I make that a personal promise."

"How very magnanimous of you," said Isabel, her voice laden with sarcasm. "Meanwhile, your brother has free rein to come and kidnap me again."

She noticed Gavyn tense up. There was a moment's pause before he spoke.

"You need not worry about him anymore. He is dead."

It was all too much information to take in. Isabel couldn't comprehend it. "Dead?"

"Yes, and it wasn't me. Somebody here, at Alnwich, wants me dead. Nobody, other than you, knows that I have a twin brother."

Isabel didn't know what to say. She should be glad that the threat of Richard was gone, but she felt nothing.

Gavyn was the first to speak. He looked tired as he ran his hand through his dark curls.

"I think we have had enough for the night. I'll leave you to sleep. I'll sleep in the cot at the end of the bed. To leave the room might raise suspicions that we don't need right now. You have my word that I won't touch you, but wake me if you have any concerns."

Isabel knew his word wasn't worth two figs, but she didn't gainsay him.

He pulled the bed curtains around her and she heard him settle onto his pallet bed without. After a time, as she listened hard, she heard his breathing change into a regular pattern as he fell into a deep sleep.

She stared into the blackness for ages. She could feel her body slowly relaxing but sleep would not come.

God where are you in all of this?

She was wide-awake with numbness. She couldn't even apply her brain to think through what Gavyn had said. It was all too over whelming.

As predawn crept in, Isabel eventually fell asleep, her wakeful uncertainties taking full flight in her dreams.

She woke up screaming.

***

"My lady! My Lady Van der Veldt!"

It was the shouting that caught her attention. Her new name was totally foreign to her. It wasn't a true one anyway. She spun around in her saddle. Behind her, from the distance of Alnwich Castle, a rider closed in.

When she had risen that morning, right on noon, she had found that Gavyn had left for York already. She didn't know how she felt about that, but she did feel heavy—heavy of heart, soul and body. After a light meal in her room, she made her way to the stables to gather a mount to ride. It was a beautiful day and she needed to think or clear her head or something. The castle felt claustrophobic. She passed Catherine through the great hall; they made pleasantries, but Isabel couldn't wait to get away. She felt Catherine's eyes lingering on her back and was grateful that she didn't follow.

She met Henry saddling up. They had given each other weak smiles of greeting and each saw the pain of the night before reflected in each other's eyes. They touched fingers lightly then mounted and ambled out through Alnwich's courtyards and gates in companionable silence; grooms followed at a discrete distance.

It was a beautiful day. The heat of the day was in full force without a touch of wind. Clouds as wispy as dandelion seeds meandered across the scorching vista of blue.

She and Henry had remained silent as they followed the peaceful River Aln, walking one in front of the other through the rushes that grew at its side.

Henry's larger mount had created a small distance between them when Isabel heard the shout.

A woman drew up. She recognised her as one of Gavyn's party at the wedding. She was an older woman who had a foreign, homely look about her. Her dress was of an outdated mode, though the cloth was excellent quality and her blonde hair, with occasional strands of grey, was coiled in plaits at the sides of her head. She had broad flat cheeks and her blue eyes, creased with laughter lines reached out to her with honesty and vitality.

"My Lady Van der Veldt, please excuse my intrusion, but may I ride with you for a short way? I believe it will be to your profit."

"Of course. I am afraid I'm not much company today but you are welcome to ride beside me. You are from the Low Countries by your accent?"

"Yes. I am Jacincka van der Veldt."

"Oh, you bear the same name as I do. How is that so?"

Isabel noticed Henry looking behind at her and Jacincka. She motioned him to keep walking forward. He smiled and gave them a slight wave.

A copse of trees loomed ahead. Isabel looked forward to the shade that they would bring as she had begun to feel the sun burn onto her shoulders.

"Please excuse my forwardness, but may I speak freely to you?"

Isabel frowned. What an unusual thing to say. Why wouldn't she speak freely?

"I don't understand."

"I am a very close confidant of Richard Kerr. I believe I am aware of things that you may need to know."

Isabel reined in her mount and looked hard at Jacincka, her suspicions aroused. "I heard Richard is dead," she said carefully.

To Isabel's surprise, Jacincka's eyes filled with tears. She dabbed them with a kerchief tucked into her sleeve. It looked well used, all twisted and damp.

"Please excuse me again. Yes, that is correct. Did Gavyn tell you?"

"Yes, of course. Nobody else I know knows of Richard."

"Yes, it's been a cat and mouse game that has ended badly for Richard."

Jacincka blew her nose on her kerchief. In that small action, which was rather blunt and unattractive but efficient, Isabel discerned instantly a practical, no-nonsense woman before her.

"What do you know of all of this," inquired Isabel, her interest growing.

With a deep breath, Jacincka was composed again.

"I was with Richard at the start of all of this."

"All of this?"

"Gavyn and Richard. The Kerrs and the Herons. What would you like to know? Richard has told me everything. If I can help you, perhaps it will help Richard to rest easy."

"Helping me would have gone against Richard's plans, surely?"

"Well, yes, you are right," said Jacincka ruefully. "But I loved Richard and although I supported him, I didn't condone what he was doing. I guess I have come to make restitution, if that is possible."

Isabel shrugged lightly; she gently squeezed her mare into a walk and guided her around a rotting tree stump. "Well, speak away. Tell me what I need to know."

"I am Richard and Gavyn's aunt by marriage. My dead husband was their mother's brother."

Jacincka laughed heartily at Isabel's quizzical eyebrows.

"Yes, I know, a bit hard to follow. He was twenty years older than I. An arranged marriage, but we were content enough. It brought together two parts of the wool industry: raw product from my husband's business, Gavyn now runs this, and the production of cloth from my father's business, dying and weaving. Van der Veldt Wool is growing from strength to strength. We have recently been offered at place on the Wool Guild, which governs the politics of the industry. It's very exciting."

Jacincka paused and cast a glance at Isabel.

"I'm sorry, I digress. It's my passion you see. Not that women can be seen to be moving in business circles. But I direct things behind the scenes as I can.

"Anyway, Richard came to us with his mother when he was about two. They arrived in a dreadful state. They were cast adrift in a fisherman's skiff during a horrific raid on their home on the coast by the Heron clan. Jamie, Richard's father, was trying to get the twins away with their mother when they were attacked. Jamie had to drop Gavyn at his feet to defend himself. When he had a moment to catch his breath, the skiff with Richard on board was halfway out to sea with his wife clutching the sides. It was the middle of the night and pitch black, I heard from accounts years later. A brewing storm broke and carried the skiff onto Belgium's shores. Marie-Anne, Richard's and Gavyn's mother, managed to make her way with Richard to the Netherlands, where we lived, but she didn't survive the journey. She was dead within six weeks of their arrival. Poor lamb, she was weakened by the whole ordeal and died with a fever; we know not what, to this day.

"Now here I was, just fresh out of the schoolroom at fourteen years of age and newly married, playing mother to my two-year-old nephew. We wrote to Jamie to tell him that his dearly beloved Marie-Anne had passed away and asked when he would collect his son. A message never came. I had heard later that his grief at the loss of Marie-Anne, for it was a love match you know, sent him into such despair that he couldn't even look after Gavyn. He never sent for Richard. Richard became bitter, as you can imagine. Over the years, he came to think that his father blamed him for his mother's death. If it hadn't been for him, they would still be together.

"My husband became very ill and I had to nurse him and help run the business. I had no time to pursue Richard's best interests of returning him home; in fact, I had come to rely on him helping me to run the wool business.

"Eventually, Jamie did come to see Richard but their relationship was always strained. After my husband died, we found comfort in each other's arms. Does that shock you?"

Isabel looked at Jacincka. Her close relationship to Richard seemed incongruous, with him so elegant and passionate and her so plain and homely.

Then she thought of how she would be tempted, right now, to fall into someone's arms if that person offered understanding and empathy. She smiled at her.

"No, not at all. It was wonderful that you found each other."

"We married secretly with no fuss, but Richard was unforgiving towards his father, even to the point of becoming a polygamist. Nothing I could say would deter him. So I insisted on coming with him to England to minimise the damage. After receiving your dowry, he was going to release you."

Isabel turned to Jacincka. "So, you know about France?"

"Yes, I do. I never approved. I tried my best to dissuade Richard but he was adamant. He knew he was the first-born you see. So he was determined to get what belonged to him— his father's inheritance—when that time came. He was eaten up with hurt by what he perceived was the lack of love or interest shown by his father. It warped his thinking.

"You saw that demented part of him, but I have lived with the sensitive, passionate side, that was truly him."

"How did Richard die?"

"It looks like poisoning by all accounts."

"Poisoning? When?"

"Just before you walked down the isle yesterday."

Isabel pulled up her horse again looking directly at Jacincka with unbelief.

"It is true. You see it was Richard's intention to stand with you at the altar. He had made arrangements to detain Gavyn. The only reason I came to England was to dissuade Richard from going ahead with this insane idea. He would not bend, not for a minute.

"But while you and Lady Mary stood at the back of the chapel getting organised, Richard collapsed. A man came out from the vestry. It happened so fast, we all thought it was his manservant; he told everybody all was well and he would loosen his collar as he carried him off into the little side room. Within a minute, Richard was back, making his apologies. He said it was exhaustion with the travel. I could see immediately that it was not my Richard.

"Oh yes, the twins look exactly the same to most people. But I know Richard so well. This man's walk was different, he stood differently; the turn of his head, a gesture of the hand, it was all different. I knew then, it was Gavyn that stood with you, not Richard.

"When everybody had their eyes on you and the Lady Mary, I slipped into the vestry. There was Richard, dead on the floor. I could tell he was dead. His lips were blue and his face was taking on the grey pallor. It must have been poison. His body was perfect. There was no wound on his body and he had been in perfect health. A maid, a simpleton, came to my assistance from the outside door immediately, with some gardeners of all people, to help take away the body. If I weren't so traumatised at the time, I would have thought it strange that someone was there so quickly to help. I followed the men to the back of the chapel. There was a room with a cot. They laid Richard there.

"A local doctor came to investigate this morning. He puts it down to poison—something he may have ingested or drunk.

"The gardeners and the doctor had never seen Richard or Gavyn before to know that he was the groom or groom twin, and I didn't want any trouble. I just told the doctor that he was my cousin and if he would box up the body I would have it taken to his home for burial.

"This morning, I have arranged for his body to be carted to the coast, to his home where he was born. I'll travel with him and bury him there tomorrow."

"Do you think Gavyn did this?"

Jacincka smiled. "No. He's not an innocent man by any means, but he doesn't have an evil bone in his body. He could no more kill his brother, no matter how he was treated by him, than you could kill Lord Henry ahead."

Isabel followed Jacincka's eyes to Henry who now waited for them under the shade of a giant ash.

"A simpleton you say?"

"Yes. A young girl, mop cap, lank brown hair with a nervous manner. Do you know of her?"

"Yes, I may. I'll investigate when we get back."

Isabel's gentle pull on the reins brought her mare to a stop and Jacincka pulled alongside.

"Thank you, Jacincka. Thank you for illuminating this nightmare for me. I'm sorry that it has ended in tragedy for you. What will you do now?"

Jacincka took a deep breath as she stared across the gentle rolling landscape drowsy with heat. Not a whisper of wind stirred the trees, even the birds and insects kept their calls to diminutive chirps, faint ticks, and languid trills.

The River Aln was the only thing that was not subject to the sun's wilting gaze. Its cool depths ran smoothly and invitingly as dragonflies played over its surface. They heard a plop as a fish darted for an insect hovering above the water.

"Well, I'll bury my love in his birthplace of Kinwelach and probably make my way home."

"Please come and call on me, here at Alnwich, on your way back through. I would like to talk some more, but I see Henry is waiting."

"Thank you, Mistress van der Veldt, er—Isabel, I should like that very much." She turned to go, then stopped and looked back. "I know Gavyn has probably said he would release you from your vows—if I know him at all. You ought to reconsider you know. He is one fine man, if you can get him away from border mentality."

Isabel watched Jacincka ride away with a final wave, parting the grooms that followed and left Isabel more unsettled than she was before she set out.

***

John Turnbull watched from the walls of Alnwich's outer bailey, as two of his personal henchmen cantered southwest toward York.

He had physically staggered to see that the Kerr had suddenly come back to life, holding Northumberland's ward on his arm as he entered the great hall for the wedding banquet.

He knew, he could have sworn that the Kerr's heart had failed him at the altar. He'd seen that look before. His own father had died right in front of him at the impressionable age of twelve. He had never forgotten the look on his father's face. It was if he had been immobilised by pain one minute and then collapsed and dead in the next. It would be forever etched into his mind.

However much he didn't understand it, he knew there was an answer and he set out to look into every person's comings and goings around Alnwich. Somebody knew something. Somebody had seen something and everybody had a price.

Living in and around the border country had honed his investigative skills to a knife-edge.

He smiled to himself as he stroked his wiry beard. Yes, it would only be a matter of time. He would be avenged and

225

these matters would be set straight, even for his master, whom he served with a fierce loyalty. If a Kerr had blinded the earl in his presence, then it was up to him to see that he was protected.

The two figures of his trusted right-hand men disappeared beyond the horizon. Yes, he may as well consider the Kerr scum dead already. His men were as passionate about a dead Kerr as he was and they weren't hampered by conscience. That had been seared from their souls in their cradles.

CHAPTER THIRTY-ONE

Mary was beginning to see that her mother-in-law ran her household with a strong moral hand. The house steward handled most of the day-to-day running of Alnwich, but the condition of the staff's souls was clearly directed by Catherine.

Sunday at home in Sheffield had always been a relaxed affair so her introduction to Sundays at Alnwich took a bit of getting used to. Mass was held twice a day and the times in between were for meditation. Not that family or staff were idle in these meditation times. No, even as she thought these thoughts, her hands were busy applying embroidery silk to an altar cloth. She didn't mind applying herself to the embroidery; it was the lack of choice to do what you wanted to do that was irksome.

She cast a quick look around. To the back of her, some housemaids were sewing baby clothes for the poor and gentlemen servers were polishing the plate that adorned the walls. They were silent at their work, as she was, for they were made to listen to the oratory from the local priest who, today, was expounding upon the psalms. His dry, papery voice was continually interrupted by an "ahem" as he cleared his throat.

Mary thought she was going to scream at any minute. She dare not, though, as Catherine sat beside the priest with her own embroidery in hands, occasionally casting her eye around to see that everybody was attending.

Mary shifted her eyes to Henry. Bitterness ate at her soul as she regarded him, his head bent close to Isabel's. They made out to be listening to the priest, but she could see them whispering together as they worked on a piece of prose. Once again jealousy stormed within her. How dare he whisper to Isabel like a lover when he hadn't even uttered two words to her since their wedding night? Even Thomas and Algernon were making mooneyes at her as they sat at her feet, half reading their books, half listening to the priest.

Tears pricked behind her eyes. She swallowed her pain down. If it weren't for Isabel, Henry probably would have been more attentive towards her. Yes, it was Isabel's fault! She more than likely put Anne Boleyn in Henry's path, seeing as they were friends in France. Yes, a cosy threesome they must have been at court! Just looked what happened then! They were brazen before the world and look where that got them.

Well, she wasn't going to put up with it! Not here at Alnwich, her new home now! She would bring Mistress Isabel down a peg or two!

Little Maud Percy stood up from her stool, where she sat with Margaret and their governess and brought her stitching to Isabel to untangle.

Mary hated Isabel's compassionate face, which shone with adoration towards Henry's youngest sister. She watched, seething with hatred, as Isabel sat Maud on her knee and with infinite patience, helped her to undo the knots that had been created.

Mary felt like snapping her embroidery frame and stamping on it. Maud should be coming to her, not Isabel! I am her sister-in-law, she railed silently to herself.

The morning after their wedding night, Mary had been sorely tempted to seek a friend in Isabel, despite what had passed between them. She wanted a friend to talk to. Had her wedding night been a success? Mary was dying to know. Or had it been a difficult time for her, too? But when, after seeking her, she found Isabel laughing with Henry coming back in through the Castle gates from a morning ride, Mary's heart hardened with total rejection.

She wasn't needed! Henry didn't need or want her and neither, it seemed, did Isabel. They should have married each other!

Isabel had put Maud down with a little peck on the cheek.

Mary boiled with dark emotion. Mistress Perfect was not perfect! She would watch.

She would be The Countess of Northumberland one day, so Mistress Nobody Isabel ought to have a care!

***

Isabel and Henry stood atop the crest of a hill on one of their early morning rides.

Isabel noticed that the deep hues of summer were looking dusty.

Summer is on the turn, she mused. The days were still warm, but the landscape looked tired. Oak leaves, though still green, hung dull and lifeless from their tired limbs. The wild grasses had gone brown since their seed cases had cracked and there was a general yellow tinge to the world.

They had ridden southwest. Isabel wondered what Gavyn was up to. When would he return? Would she go with him when he did?

She had no idea. Since Jacincka's visit, Gavyn and the whole Kerr scenario now piqued her interest. She found that she wasn't afraid of Gavyn or of her future anymore. She didn't feel like running or hiding, like she had done for the past year. Although she had suffered badly at the Kerr hands, she wasn't afraid anymore and even more than that, she was amazed that she didn't hold any malice towards them.

Was it that she understood them? Understood why they acted the way they did?

She didn't know.

She knew that her feelings towards the earl had changed. She felt uncertain around him now. She now knew that his mo-

229

tives towards her were selfish and any paternal displays were purely for his own gain.

She also felt odd around Sir Nicholas Heron. He was her blood uncle but nothing had been said. He knew she was his niece and she now knew he was her uncle. It was a strange feeling to know this secret and treat him as she had always done, with a respectful nod and a fleeting smile, nothing more than that. She could even see the hereditary likeness in their physical looks: blond hair, blue eyes, very fair skin and a tall, litheness of body. Part of her wanted to run to him and hug him. He was part of her real family—a family she thought was lost forever. But she had to remember he had sold her to pay his debts. What uncle would do that to a niece?

He was not to be trusted, that was for sure!

As she surveyed the hills of Northumberland, she was glad that she was only puzzled and not in fear of her life anymore.

She gave a satisfied sigh. Yes, things were working out.

Thank you God; I do not understand your ways. But I thank you for leading me where you want me to go. She found it very easy to draw close to God at Alnwich. They were all quite devoted to their religion, which meant Isabel was free to worship without being detected. Her murmuring lips as she prayed may as well have been English as it was speaking her strange language in tongues.

Although she had no idea of her future, at least she was not dreading it.

"Shall we turn back?" she asked Henry.

It was at that moment that she realised that she had never shared her faith with the one who probably needed it more than most right now.

She was surprised at the watery sniff that she heard and egged her horse forward to get a look at his face.

He didn't look at her.

"Henry?" Isabel ventured gently.

"You go back," he said.

Isabel grabbed his wrist and squeezed it. He immediately shook it off.

"Don't," he cried. "You'll only make it worse ..." His voice broke as he gave in to his heartbreak. Tears steamed down his face while his shoulders shook with silent sobs.

"I miss her so much, Tibs. I miss her so much. I just wish God would cut me down right now. I just don't know how I am going to stand it."

Isabel had no words to say. She could feel Henry's pain but was at a loss how to comfort him. How could anybody be comforted with the loss of a loved one? It was probably a loss worse than death. In death, you knew that a person was beyond normal communications, but if you were separated from somebody you loved, yet they still lived, that could send you addlepated if you let it.

They did say that time was the healer but Henry was much too raw to receive any verbal salve like that.

"Both you and Anne have been dealt a cruel blow in this life, but Anne will always love you Henry. If she could, you know that she would be with you."

Henry drew his sleeve across his running nose and finally turned to look at Isabel. He smiled a watery smile.

"I know. I know ... just sometimes ... it seems so hard. You go. You go back. I just want to stay here for a while."

"If you're sure ...?"

"Go." Henry turned his face from her as a dismissal.

Isabel smiled a sad smile and headed back to Alnwich, with the ever-present grooms riding behind her at their ever-respectful distance. She prayed for him under her breath.

She also prayed for Gavyn, that he would also find peace.

God took her further reminding her that she had to forgive him the hurts he had done to her. She baulked. Forgive all that suffering?

Just as I have forgiven you your trespasses, the Holy Spirit spoke back to her.

"I forgive Gavyn," Isabel said out loud, instantly obedient. She didn't feel any better for it but God loved obedience, she remembered Yves Briconais saying to her once. *Well let's see where that led her,* she mused, suddenly excited for no reason.

On her way into Alnwich, as Isabel passed the buttery, she paused then made up her mind to dismount. She tossed the reins to her groom.

As she entered the small wooden room the smell of pasture, butter and sour milk assailed her nostrils. She could hear the solid slap of the milk solids being separated from the buttermilk while the churn was being turned.

Cheeses matured in cloths hanging above her and on shelves about the walls.

The cook came through a door at the back where the cows were milked with a pail of cream in hand. She was surprised to see a lady of the house wandering in humble quarters.

"My lady!" she said shocked and frowning.

Isabel put up the palm of her hand to ward off any protest the cook might come forth with. She had heard that she was a woman who was very strong in her opinions.

The cook wasn't a tall woman, but what there was of her was round and solid. Her stern face, framed in a cotton cap, let Isabel know of her disapproval.

"I've come to have a word with Jennet if I may, Mistress Seton." Isabel barrelled on, not wanting to give the cook any room for comeback. "I'll only be a minute. Jennet can keep on working while I speak. You go on, Cook. I've just lost a ribbon out in the pasture. I wanted to ask Jennet if she'd seen it."

The cook harrumphed and grumbled ungraciously about butteries not being the place for gentleladies, then stopped to growl at Jennet. "Don't you stop that churning, my girl! Don't over churn it neither or it'll be your hide!"

Isabel grimaced at the cook's back.

Jennet was just as shocked as the cook at seeing a lady of the house in her menial place of work.

Isabel could see the fear that she created in Jennet eyes.

"It's all right, Jennet. Please keep on churning. I just wanted to thank you for helping a friend of mine."

Isabel was met by a blank stare. Obviously, compliments were not a language Jennet could understand. She tried a different tack.

"My friend's friend became very sick in the church."

Jennet's large brown eyes went up and down between Isabel and her hands, which gripped the churner handle.

Isabel didn't press Jennet but waited as the milk fat slapped its rhythm against the wooden paddles within. Slap-slosh, slap, slap-slosh, slap.

"He was hurting him," eventually came out.

"Who was hurting who, Jennet?" Isabel asked softly.

"I killed him. I couldn't let him kill my friend." Jennet shook her head as if denying what she had just admitted.

"Why, Jennet?"

"He was so nice to me, Miss Tibs – I mean Miss Isabel. He was so handsome. He could be my beau." She giggled like a six-year-old.

"He gave me a blue ribbon, Miss Isabel. That means he was sweet on me, doesn't it? Would you like to see it, Miss Isabel?"

"Sometime later, Jennet, after you've finished the butter. We'd better not make the cook angry."

Jennet's face changed to a sullen pout. "She's always angry."

"How did you kill the man, Jennet?"

"I feed him what makes the cows dead. It's the red berries what hangs over the walls into the pasture."

Yew trees, thought Isabel with a sinking feeling.

Tears filled Jennets eyes. "I saw them in the stables. The man was going to kill my beau, but men on horses rode in and the nasty man couldn't get to him. So I squeezed some berry juice into his wine. He put my beau into a trunk. He tried to kill him."

Little sobs were quietly put under control as Jennet concentrated on churning. Eventually she brought her hands to a stop.

"I better stop now. The butter's all done."

Jennet stood up and hugged the butter churn to her chest. She almost cringed as she passed Isabel on her way out of the door.

"You won't tell nobody, will you, Miss Isabel? I did it 'cause I love him, Miss Isabel. Nobody ever showed me any kindness before. How could I let a nasty man like that kill such a nice man like my beau? Please don't tell nobody, Miss Isabel."

Jennet's large brown eyes were imploring.

Isabel laid a gentle hand on Jennet's shoulder. "Of course not, Jennet. Your secret is safe with me. You go on now and don't you worry. Everything is all right."

Jennet bobbed up and down a few times, looking very uncertain. After a few furtive glances at Isabel, she made her way to the kitchen.

Mary could barely contain herself as she peeled her body away from the outside wall of the buttery. She knew that eavesdropping would eventually harvest some home truths – but murder! That was beyond her wildest dreams!

Isabel would pay dearly for taking Henry from her! She also knew that Henry would suffer through Isabel's suffering and she was glad.

Well and good, she thought. *He had it coming to him!*

CHAPTER THIRTY-TWO

York City, York

Gavyn was pleased with the conclusion of his business in York with a well-known weaving establishment. It was a small setup by European standards, but the quality was good. He organised a standing order, in season, for bales of cloth, which his business in the Netherlands would then finish with the fulling and dyeing processes.

He leaned back on his bench seat in a local tavern feeling very satisfied.

Despite every shutter being open in the taproom, the heat from the pressing but jovial crowd produced enough warmth to make sweat trickle. Peels of laughter and the occasional loud guffaw crested on the sea of merriment.

Pungent body odour, cheap wine, yeasty beer and roasting beef were inhaled as Gavyn savoured the cool wetness of his ale.

Nestled in a corner, half listening to conversations around him, his mind drifted to what waited for him back at Alnwich.

Isabel.

In the beginning, it had been an outrageous idea bandied around a crofter's table. It was a night like any other within a Kerr Clan family, the women settling the children into bed and the men sucking ale in front of the firelight.

The idea progressed to a plan and then it was delegated to the people who could best carry it out.

Scaring the daylights out of Heron's niece was a planned piece of encouragement to keep her quiet.

It worked, Gavyn conceded, but not with the lack of conscience within him that he desired. He had been happy to abduct and marry her. It was all in a day's work. She would be released from the contract—be glad of it too, no doubt—and he would get back to his routine of the family's wool business. She, at least, would be alerted to the truth of her situation, poor lass. But she was the enemy and retribution was needed to maintain the upper hand. They would never stand to be continually walked over by the Herons, or any other clan, for that matter.

When Richard showed up, his twin brother that he knew about but had never met, everything got messy.

Everybody knew Richard's intent: to gain his rights as the first-born son to the family inheritance when the time was right. This was known through letters of warning from his Aunt Jacincka.

By law, on the death of their father, everything would have gone to Richard. Second sons received nothing and had to make their own way in the world. Gavyn had worked all his life with his father building up their wool business and wasn't going to just hand it over to Richard when the time came.

He had kept his feelings to himself but he knew from the grumbling of other family members and kin that nobody wanted Richard to take over. He was an unknown quantity and he was foreign, despite being born on English soil.

But now that was all past history. His father was dead and now his brother was dead. Where to from here?

He had no intention of consummating the marriage with Isabel, but with Richard on the prowl, he couldn't leave the situation open to chance. He had to do what he did.

He wiped his brow. All of a sudden the day had lost its shine. There was no getting around it, he felt bad that he had taken advantage of Isabel. And she had gone through the miscarriage of their son!

He had a son and he never knew! He was responsible for a life! And a son ... all men dreamed of having sons!

Suddenly, he felt the impact of his actions. He couldn't seem to brush away the guilt like other times.

Why was that? He took another swig of ale.

Raids were commonplace in border country. You had to protect yourself and your family. The law of the land certainly couldn't; there was nobody to carry it out, at least to the satisfaction of its populace. The law of the land just didn't exist north, above Alnwich.

What was he to do? Why was this situation irritating him?

Instantly he knew the answer to the question as he asked it.

It was the smell of her skin.

He closed his eyes as he tried to recall it to memory. All the times they had been close, he had remembered the smell of her. Not the light overlaying fragrance of her clothes or hair, of lavender and lemon, but the essence of her.

Lying side-by-side in the nuptial bed, he had wanted to snuggle into her, to drink her scent in, to taste it with his lips, to taste it with his mouth. He was sure it would have made him feel complete. He just had that knowing. A feeling like he had come home.

Suddenly she wasn't just a Heron to exact his revenge upon for the sake of the generations that had suffered before him; she was a woman and a woman who was creating stirrings within him that he had never felt before. He knew lust and he knew good times, but Isabel had a mystery about herself that intrigued him. It was like he knew that no matter how long he spent with her, she would always surprise him.

Visions of Isabel flooded into his mind: a strand of hair, curling loosely down her cheek, the flash of anger in her stormy blue eyes, the delicacy of her wrists, her raw honesty.

Gavyn shook his head to try to eliminate these thoughts.

I must be going addlepated, he thought. *Too much ale!*

Well, the whole thing will be over after I've made a visit to Alnwich, and all this musing will have been a waste of time.

He needed something stronger to drink. *Did they serve a Scotch malt?* And he was getting hungry. *The beef sure smells good!*

CHAPTER THIRTY-THREE

Alnwich Castle, Northumberland

Isabel was in her bedchamber when they came to get her. She was reading at her window embrasure.

There was a sharp rap at her door. She didn't even have a chance to say "enter" before the door swung open. Catherine stood with an older, sombre looking man at her side.

Isabel looked blankly at them both. It was a surprise to have Catherine enter her room suddenly and unannounced. The Countess of Northumberland always believed that you led by example and she would press the point by teaching her daughters down to her maids that when one knocked at a door, you always waited for an invitation before you proceeded.

The dour man beside her looked nervous. It made her nervous.

"Lady Catherine?"

The Countess of Northumberland clasped her hands together. Isabel could see her knuckles turn white. Isabel tried to push the alarm down that she felt rising within.

"Isabel, dearest," said Catherine, with a waver in her voice. She cleared her throat. "Please come with us. You have some people who need to see you."

Isabel looked at the stranger beside Catherine. No introduction was forthcoming. Catherine turned to leave and it was obvious that this stranger waited for Isabel to follow. She did and closing her chamber door, he followed after them both.

Catherine led them both through several sets of stairs and narrow corridors that the servants used, to a small room away from the main hub of the castle. They didn't see anybody as they marched. It was as if the castle was deserted.

Isabel knew what it was about. She had been feeling a growing sense of unease over the last week as she had heard rumours floating in and around Alnwich.

They were malicious and also untrue. She had originally thought that the gossip would fade away, as there was no substance to the lie. But the talk would not go away. In fact, it got stronger. She had tried to push it to the back of her mind and as much as she tried to remain jolly on the outside, within her, fears pulsed with life.

They stopped outside a solid oak door with large black iron hinges. Catherine turned to Isabel and squeezed her hand. Her hazel eyes revealed her love and concern.

"Be strong, my dear. I'm sure this is all a misunderstanding."

She turned and left.

Isabel frowned at her but there was no time to say anything as the door swung open and the strange man at her side took her roughly by the arm and led her into the room. She looked wildly around, trying not to panic, as the door closed. She didn't even know where she was.

"It's all right, Isabel. I'm here."

Isabel immediately relaxed under the deep soothing tones that she knew so well—the Earl of Northumberland.

"Oh," said Isabel breathlessly, heart fluttering. "My lord, I didn't know you were here."

Her eyes finally settled on him. He stood to the side of some other men who were unknown to her. They were seated on the other side of a long table with official looking papers under their resting hands. The man at her side stood still, his fingers digging into her arm. A look from the earl discouraged her companion from his fierce grip and she was released. Isabel resisted the temptation to rub her arm. Maybe they would perceive it as a weakness and she needed to stand strong in a display of innocence and fearlessness.

The earl paced a little, his eyes searching the floor as his be-ringed hands held onto the edges of his finely beaded jerkin.

His still handsome face was now slightly florid with age. How strange that she had never noticed that before.

He offered no comforting smile.

"Isabel, it has been brought to our attention that some accusations have been brought against you."

Isabel held herself up straight with her hands folded lightly in front of her. "My lord?"

"Beside you is special constable Middleton. The gentlemen before you are Justice of the Peace Bartholomew Stonebridge and with him, petty constable Walter Whitten."

The men acknowledged her with a slight bow of their heads.

"Gentlemen, the lady in question, my ward, now Mistress Van der Veldt."

The Justice of the Peace stood up behind the table. He had the look of a dusty clerk about him with dry, wayward hair poking out from under his black cap and a grey wrinkled complexion, but his eyes, Isabel noted, as they fixed themselves on her, were clear, intelligent and piercing.

"Do you know of a Richard Van der Veldt?"

Isabel froze to the spot. What was she going to say? To admit to know him was to reveal her secret trials! Not to, was to lie! And although she had omitted information about her life to others, she never saw herself as a liar. The longer she hesitated, she realised, the more precarious her position would look. She chose to answer as vaguely as she could.

"Yes, my lords, I know … of him." Sweat broke out on her palms. With self-control she maintained her relaxed stance.

"Are you acquainted with his person?"

More pressure and infusion of sweat!

She hesitated again before stumbling forward.

"As—As I say, I know, of him. My lords."

Isabel felt her cheeks start to flush with nervousness. The wave of heat spread over her chest and between her shoulder blades on her back. It followed with another outbreak of sweat.

"And how do you know—of—him, Mistress Van der Veldt?"

"He is my husband's brother, or so I believe. May I ask what this is about? Why have I been summoned thus?"

"Mr Richard Van der Veldt is dead, Mistress. Murdered. Murdered here, right within these very walls and you were seen with him."

"I have never seen him here at Alnwich, upon my life," said Isabel, her voice ringing with true heartfelt sincerity, of which she was glad she could deliver.

"There will be an investigation and mayhap a trial. You will be contained within your chamber during this process. Special constable Middleton will be at your door should you desire to confess …"

Isabel's eyes widened with surprise at this remark.

"And his wife will sit in with you to see to your needs. Depending on the outcome of these events, you will either be released to your husband when he returns from York or you will be incarcerated for imprisonment or death.

"Is this understood?"

Nervousness had given way to absolute terror. The blood drained from her face. As she reached out her hand to the Earl of Northumberland, the only person who could offer her any comfort, her eyes blacked out and she let out a little cry as she staggered towards him to faint on the flagstones.

Only her body never reached the ever cool, polished stone. The Earl of Northumberland quickly moved in to scoop her up in his arms as she fell.

Nobody saw the expression of intense grief and suffering in his face as he carried Isabel back to her room.

He whispered some words in her ear, which if she had been conscious to hear would have cast aside all her worries and concerns and indeed enlightened her anxieties of her existence.

As he made his way to exit her chamber door, the tears that were in his eyes dissipated, as if they had never been.

***

Henry paced the hall as he waited for his father to come forth from the chamber, which had been made into a makeshift examination room.

An unsettling presence had descended upon Alnwich since Isabel had been charged with the murder of Richard Van der Veldt.

Whisperings were rife in the stables, kitchens, and servant's quarters, even in the town of Alnwich itself. Henry's manservant had been diligent to report back the general gossip and mood of Alnwich.

"How was it that their golden girl, their adopted darling had come to an end such as this?"

"Who was behind such an act? It's an injustice I tell you!"

"Wasn't she a virtuous young woman? Why would she jeopardise her brand-new future?"

"She's a witch! Just you mark my words! She'll be hanged! Like all other of her kind!"

"I swear I've seen animals follow her! Do you see the control she has over the birds? And I've seen the shadow of a familiar."

Henry had gleaned from his mother that Isabel remained true to her original confession, that she declared that she remained innocent of any charge.

His father, although not able to be a part of the trial procedure, dragged out things as long as possible by making sure all parties adhered to the law. He made sure that they followed steps that were only taken in cases of high treason. He wanted to see that detailed questionnaires, known as interrogatories were carefully dissected before being applied. Verbatim transcripts were then to be painstakingly looked over by two clerks in case someone had missed something.

Last night, Jacincka Van der Veldt had made good on her word by calling back to Alnwich to visit Isabel. Henry helped mop up her tears of horror at finding her sister-in-law under lock and key with the suspicion of murder.

Henry frowned as he remembered Heron's comments over dinner. They were directed rather nastily at Jacincka. He had insinuated, very loudly before everybody, that the reason for Jacincka's travels north was to hide the poisoned body.

Jacincka handled the situation well, he thought. She had looked affronted by his bad behaviour towards a guest and held to her story that it was her cousin who had died and that he had died of natural causes. Her boldness in declaring Isabel's innocence shamed some into silence. Others agreed with her, arguing how could there be accusation of murder without a body to be examined?

His father took control of the wayward conversation, saying that they had all better keep their counsel to themselves if they valued their own lives.

Jacincka left Alnwich the next day, laden with apologies from Catherine and an assurance that her message of farewell would be given to Isabel.

It didn't make sense to Henry. Something or someone was missing. Why would Heron accuse Jacincka of hiding a body? Why was any of it connected to Isabel? Henry couldn't understand it. Somebody must be spreading a web of lies and it was capturing the minds of all involved.

On top of all this, there was some new evidence that couldn't be disputed. Henry shook his head to himself as he recalled the information that had been delivered to him by his mother earlier this week. Yew berries had been found in her room. Just a branch hidden behind a tapestry but it also came with fresh fowl entrails, which everybody knew was for divination. Poison and witchcraft, this was proof enough to stand her atop of a witch's pyre, innocent of murder or not.

Isabel couldn't move a step to the left or to the right without somebody monitoring her moves. Somebody must have planted this evidence but who?

Henry stopped his pacing to stare out of a latticed window. It was the first day that seemed to acknowledge summer's entrance into autumn. Grey clouds had spread themselves across a colourless sky, releasing veils of drizzle. Even the river Aln had lost its velvety blackness as the rain pocked its surface to reflect the drabness above.

Henry heard footsteps behind him. He spun around to see his father surrounded by a handful of men walking briskly through the hall from the examination room. He called out to him.

"Father!"

The earl raised his head and then signalled for the party surrounding him to go on ahead.

Henry just looked at his father, his eyes expressing all the pain and anguish that his mouth couldn't quite articulate.

The earl gave his son a squeeze of encouragement on the shoulder but the message in his eyes only mirrored his own.

Henry gulped back a sudden whoosh of fear for Isabel and forced back a weak smile. He reached out his arm under his father's hold and gave his father's arm a return grip, affirming his rarely felt love and confidence in his abilities.

They held each other's eyes only for a brief moment but in those fleeting seconds, they communicated in a way that they never had before. Abruptly, his father walked off.

Henry watched his father as he strode away. He was filled with a kind of elation. They had connected. For the first time in their lives, they had conveyed their innermost thoughts to each other and had connected heart to heart. In those few seconds, there was a mutual understanding and support.

Henry felt stunned … amazed and wonderfully stunned!

Did it take the imminent death of a loved one to bring them together? His elation instantly dissipated as he thought of Isabel's future, or rather the lack of it.

"Father!" he called out, remembering something.

The earl stopped in his stride and turned around.

"Should I dispatch someone to York? To find Willem?"

The earl smiled. It was a strange smile that Henry could not fathom. "A good thought, son. Be at rest, I have already sent someone." His father turned and left.

Wearily, he made his way back to his apartments to think.

He heard some faint footsteps behind him. He turned to see his wife, Mary, following carefully, at a distance.

He ignored her but to his annoyance, she followed him to their rooms and closed the door behind her.

He knew she stood behind him as he gazed out of their chamber window.

"What is it Mary?" he said ungraciously, irritated at her presence. He wanted to meditate on what transpired between him and his father. What did his father's smile mean? He wanted to think of solutions to help Isabel; God willing that would be possible. He –

Thud!

Henry spun around at the unusual sound. He found Mary on her knees on the floor. He was untouched at her apparent misery. He rolled his eyes with impatience to the elaborate domed ceiling. "What is it Mary?"

Mary lifted her face to his. The rims of her eyes and the tip of her nose were red with shed tears.

"I am so sorry," blubbed Mary, her voice nasally with crying.

Henry stood with his legs wide apart and hands on his hips looking down at her. His irritation was turning slowly to anger.

"Sorry for what?" he demanded.

"I'm so sorry …" A fresh wave of weeping interrupted her words. She tried to control herself by wiping the back of her hand across her nose, wiping away mucus and tears, her chest heaving. Her voice, when she found it, came across high and thin. "Please, my lord. Please forgive me. I-I was so j-jealous …"

Mary dropped her small hands to her sides, nervously clenching and unclenching her silk skirts that ballooned around her.

"P–Please forgive me. I was so jealous of her relationship with you … yours with her … I – I was so angry with you. Because of her and Anne Boleyn and their hold over your affections. There is no room for me …"

Suspicion slowly dawned upon Henry as the seemingly disjointed words started to paint a picture in his mind. His anger boiled over into intense rage. It was unbelievable that she would do such a thing! How could anybody do such a thing?

He lunged forward, grabbed her by the wrist and yanked her violently up from the floor. Mary cried out in pain. He shook her.

"Tell me what you did!" he roared.

"I –I planted the yew branch and the fowl entrails in Isabel's room. I did it. I didn't start the rumours … you have to believe me. I just used the opportunity, Henry–Henry, please forgive me …"

Henry's lips trembled as they curled in a sneer, hatred trying to find its voice through the unbelief.

"You—You—ungodly whore!" Totally disgusted with her and reviled by her touch, he flung her away from him. She fell heavily with a grunt and sprawled backwards across the floor, winded.

As soon as she could, Mary brought her knees up to her chest to protect her stomach. She had missed her monthly course and the last two mornings she had skipped breaking her fast because of the nausea.

"Our baby … our baby … " she whispered.

Henry never heard. The door had long since slammed as he stormed his way to his father's presence.

CHAPTER THIRTY-FOUR

York City, York

In the city of York, Reeth, one of Turnbull's men, awoke around noon on their fourth day in town. He awoke sober for the first time since arriving. The harsh light of day, coming in through a small square of window above, made his head throb. He gently opened his eyelids a bit at a time so that the pain wasn't so intense. He could see dust motes hanging in the sunbeams of light.

He became aware that his body was entangled with other limbs. Some dressed, most undressed. Heads, bodies, arms and legs crossed and recrossed each other so that there seemed neither beginning nor end to them. The stench of sour wine, unwashed bodies sticky with last night's secretions and old unaired straw mattresses made him gag.

He groaned and went to hold his head but found one hand was captured between a pair of mountainous thighs and the other trapped under locks of dirty red hair. He could feel the lice crawling on his palms.

His twisting to extricate himself brought forth some muffled protests as the local doxies from the Wool Pit Tavern tried to maintain deep sleep. The voluptuous beauties of the night looked decidedly seedy in the light of day. He wondered if they might be witches to keep him mindlessly seduced for almost half a week.

He and his mate, Hogg, had set to work to find the dog, Kerr, as soon as they hit town. They found his whereabouts with ease and more enquiring enlightened them to the fact that he would be around for the rest of the week.

Making the most of the opportunity of some newfound freedom, away from Turnbull's rigid routines at Alnwich, they delighted themselves in some self-perceived, well-deserved off-duty time.

Reeth was vaguely aware that he and Hogg should be moving. Today was the day they agreed upon, or was it yesterday? Or maybe they had agreed on tonight? He couldn't remember.

God's teeth but his head hurt! Maybe a little rest will help. Just keep the eyes closed until the pain eases …

CHAPTER THIRTY-FIVE

Alnwich Castle, Northumberland

Isabel sat at her window embrasure staring into the unknown.

She had had a terrible night's sleep. Grey-blue shadows haunted the delicate skin around her eyes. Her cold bloodless fingers fidgeted with a devotional in her lap. She had tried to read it for encouragement. One moment she was transported into God's presence, with peace and acceptance, and then the next, she was struggling to maintain decorum, wanting to scream and cry, to rant and rage.

Catherine, the Countess of Northumberland, had spent most the previous evening with her. They had wept together over the verdict of her trial. She had been found guilty of witchcraft. Mary's sudden confession to Henry was brought before the jurors, but it came to nothing. They saw it as a last minute emotional outburst from a tormented relative. Mary's testimony was dismissed. Isabel was to be burned at the stake on the morrow.

Mistress Whitten, her mouse-like jailor, sat up from her seat by her chamber door. She ventured to see if Isabel's breakfast tray was finished. She came up silently and nervously, wringing her hands together, not wanting to disturb. As soon as she saw that it was untouched, she bowed low and backed away looking at the floor as if Isabel were Queen Katherine herself. Isabel could see that Mistress Whitten was very uncomfortable in her new role. She felt sorry for her. It wasn't her choice to play jailor to the Earl of Northumberland's ward. Isabel imagined that she had been living her simple life of quiet contentment, serving her husband, a local businessman in the township of Alnwich, delightedly industrious and happy with the little things in life. Now because of this, she had been snatched from her comfortable four walls and thrust into this strange world of wealth, power and evil witches. Her husband, being a law-abiding citizen, was also probably pulled unwillingly into this scenario himself to play a petty constable by the local justice of the peace.

Isabel studied her as she made her way back to her needlework. Mistress Whitten was round like a mouse, short, only reaching to Isabel's chest, curved back, round hips under her spotless apron and round rosy cheeks in her little round face. She never spoke directly to Isabel but always deferred to Isabel's instruction, scant as it was.

Isabel watched Mistress Whitten settle into her chair, pick up her needlework and work the fine stitching. She was aware that after a while, her head would turn, just ever so slightly, to surreptitiously take in Isabel's movements.

Isabel was well aware that every action would be reported and interpreted to see if all the hearsay could be validated into real occult activity.

Isabel turned her eyes back to the window. All manner of thoughts flooded her mind. The injustice, wondering how she found herself here, sorrow at the lack of real help and above all, the very real feeling of terror.

Terror threatened her very sanity. She felt at any moment that she would start screaming and never be able to stop. Under her breath, she had started to whisper psalms and verses of the Bible to herself. It calmed her somewhat until she thought of the flames that would lick at her body. How would she be able to stand it? Weeping now threatened. She shook with controlled emotion, her eyes burned with the torrent of suppressed tears. The afterlife didn't worry her. She knew that God would be waiting to receive her.

But how was she going to deal with the pain of being burned? How would she stop herself from screaming? How would she stand the heat? How would she stand it, her mind still working while her flesh melted?

She started to shake in large jerks.

Wine! She needed wine!

Isabel grabbed a pewter wine jug and goblet, which rested on a wide ledge in the window embrasure. She had to hold the hand holding the goblet to her mouth, she was shaking so much. She downed the entire contents in a few swallows. Her hand continued to shake as she poured herself another. The rich liquid warmed her insides and quickly made her light-headed on an empty stomach. That was better. It took the raw edge off the terror.

A jangle of keys in the lock caused Isabel to quickly swing around to face her chamber door. Mistress Whitten was already there, allowing somebody to enter.

It was Mary. The door was locked again from without and Mistress Whitten took her seat, with needlework back in hand.

Mary walked slowly toward her. She looked awful. Nights of crying and days of loneliness with only the torment of guilt for company had rendered her to a shadow. The whites of her eyes were as red as their puffy surrounds.

Isabel put down her goblet with an amazingly steady hand. She felt really tired now with the wine and lack of sleep. Maybe it was that which dulled her senses toward the person who had signed her death warrant with one spiteful act.

Isabel looked upon Mary and amazingly felt no animosity towards her. It surprised her. The words that God had spoken to her many months ago, "if you know there is God then follow him," drifted slowly into her mind. Instantly she realised that the Holy Spirit was letting her know that she had been obedient in following God, even though she had questioned it at the time. She now knew that she had been following God in the attitude of the heart, if not literally following him by the way of entering an abbey for the cloistered life of a nun. She got the impression that God was saying, "well done, my good and faithful servant."

Gazing upon Mary, she could see her personal growth. Where once she had been irritated beyond distraction whenever Mary walked into a room with her, she now felt pity, sorrow and an unconditional love for her. She could see right through Mary; her lack of confidence in herself and her desire to be loved, but without wisdom, had turned her into a disagreeable monster—a monster that Jesus had also died for.

"Hello Mary," said Isabel softly.

Mary fell to her knees and grabbed at the hem of Isabel's gown. She started to kiss it with an unnatural fervour.

Isabel reached down and grabbed Mary's forearm.

"Stop, Mary, stop this."

Mary stopped and looked up into Isabel's face. "I'm so sorry. I'm so sorry ..." Mary's face crumpled as hot tears started to fall again. "I'm so sorry. I'm so sorry. I'm ..."

Isabel withdrew her hand, wondering how she was going to bear this load as well as the one she was already carrying. "If you don't stop crying, I'll have to have you removed."

Mary tried to choke her emotions back with sniffing and swallowing. Her words rushed out between great heaves shuddering in her chest.

"I'm so sorry. Can you ever forgive me? I've done you a terrible wrong. I've tried to undo it but they won't listen. They–They won't listen ..."

Isabel felt sorry for her. She could also see that Mary was innocent of basic people skills. Mary's world revolved around her. She was a product of her society—bred for marriage but having no training in dealing with real issues that arose in life.

Isabel poured herself another wine. She wouldn't be here tomorrow night. Tomorrow night she would dine with God and she needed to forgive because God had forgiven her. Isabel reached out to Mary and gently touched her hot cheek. She smiled wanly at her.

"You are forgiven, Mary. Tomorrow I go to God, a little earlier that I would have anticipated," and released a rueful grin. "But then his word does say that he numbers our days. So rest and have peace, Mary. As God forgives you, so I forgive you."

Mary fell into fits of weeping as the weight of her guilt slipped away. "Oh, bless you. Bless you. Bless you. I'm going to name our little baby after you if she is a girl."

"On, Mary, you are pregnant so soon? How wonderful! Does Henry know?"

"No, He will not come near me, for me to be able to tell him."

"Well, if he is allowed to come to me, I will tell him to go to you. This is wonderful news. Let's hope it is a son. There will be great celebrations, you know."

Mary mopped her wet face with her sleeve. She started to smile. "Yes," she said, allowing herself to dwell on happy thoughts. "There will be, won't there?"

Isabel could see that Mary's head was soon full of herself again. Her death tomorrow was entirely forgotten.

Isabel put a hand to her lower stomach. She had almost forgotten that if she were going to live, she wouldn't be able to bear children again. She recalled Richard's words to her that seemed like a lifetime ago, now. The physician had said she would never have children again after losing her Henry, a brief smile came to her lips, and she would meet him soon!

When Mary left, Isabel finished her wine and lay on top of her bed. Sleep claimed her swiftly.

After a time, she had another visitor. The clanking of the keys in the lock never woke her. Mistress Whitten bowed right down to the floor as this visitor entered the room.

He made his way to the bed and sat on its side. Gentleness softened his face. He started to talk to her. His voice was low but unbeknown to him, it drew her back up from oblivion. His words came to her like a dream before her eyes had a chance to open.

"Fret not, my daughter."

She felt his departure from the bed and forced her eyes open as she struggled to sit up. When she did she saw the back of the Earl of Northumberland.

CHAPTER THIRTY-SIX

York City, York

He could hear the ringing of a hammer. The sound reverberated into the still, expectant air. It filled him with a sense of foreboding and he didn't know why. The hammering continued and his unease grew. Then suddenly he knew.

It was a scaffold! And it was being built for him! A wave of sweat drenched him, waking Gavyn with a start. He sat up in his hired bed. He felt disoriented as the dream, so real in his mind, didn't correlate with what his eyes were taking in. He was safe in a well-appointed room, not an icy, stone-walled prison, but still the hammering continued.

As the fog of sleep receded, he realised that somebody was banging on his door. A quick glance to the window told him that it was still the middle of the night. Perplexed, he went to open his door. The floor was cold beneath his bare feet.

He was surprised at the face that greeted him.

"Jacincka!"

His young aunt fell into his arms harassed and exhausted.

Something was wrong. He drew her to his bed and propped her up on a pillow. Jacincka found some energy to take off her gloves and untie her hood. Her normally relaxed, friendly face was strained and white.

"Jacincka, what brings you here? How did you know where to find me?"

Her worried blue eyes fixed their stare on his. She grabbed his forearm with an iron grip.

"Northumberland sent me. But I come endorsing his message. You have to race back to Alnwich as fast as you can. Don't delay. Go tonight!" She paused to take a breath.

"What is the urgency, Jacincka?"

"It's Isabel. You are not the only one claiming back your lost inheritance! Someone else fights for it, too, but in this case, Isabel's death is needed to make a way for him! It will be her then you. I've thought about it all the way here and the more I think, the more I am sure ..." She broke off. "You do want to save her don't you Gavyn? You have some fondness for her?"

"Fondness for Isabel?" Gavyn repeated to gather some time.

"Of course," he said absently, but as he said it, he knew that his feelings were growing uncomfortably deeper day by day. He didn't want to acknowledge that, even to himself, in case when he returned, he would be rejected.

He recognised that he had given her that choice, but now he was regretting it. Should she choose to go her own way, he would be disappointed. Be honest, another part of him said. Devastated was the real word that welled up from his gut.

He battled to dismiss the raw thought. Nobody had ever made him feel like that before; no reason to take it on board now. His own cheeks flushed red at this lie to himself.

"Is she in mortal danger?"

Jacincka didn't answer his question.

"I know you two can make a go of it, Gavyn. I've seen her character. She is strong and has integrity. She would be a wonderful wife at your side. She's bonny and has a wonderful heart. You need to settle down. Take yourself away from these borderlands. Leave these conflicts and revenge to others. Have a life, Gavyn."

Jacincka's eyes welled with tears as she pulled on his arm again. "Have the life that Richard and I will never have now. Don't end up like him. Where did revenge get him? Dead. What can you do when you're dead? Live your life, Gavyn. Live it for good things. A wonderful woman, the children you might have. Family. Take your business away from here. Come to the Low Countries."

Gavyn sat beside her on the bed.

"I'm so sorry, Aunt Jacincka. I'm sorry for your loss."

Not one to fuss and dwell on herself, Jacincka sniffed and sat up off the pillows. Her blue eyes bore into him with her no-nonsense look.

"Now, what are you going to do? She is being held under house arrest. The trial is no doubt being held as we speak."

"Trial?" Gavyn felt fear blanch his face and embrace his heart with a cold fist.

"You pack and I'll fill you in. Do you want me to finish off any business you have here in York? I am rather exhausted; would you mind if I just slept here for the night? I can pay for your lodgings first thing tomorrow. No use in waking the land-lord now. You need to be gone before dawn. And I just pray to our sweet lord Jesu that you are not too late!"

Jacincka collapsed back onto the bed and closed her eyes. Sleep. She needed sleep. She could feel herself drift off as Gavyn rustled around the room preparing to travel light for his journey back to Alnwich.

CHAPTER THIRTY-SEVEN

Alnwich Castle, Northumberland

Jennet was agitated. She had found it hard to concentrate on her tasks that day and had bourn some heavy blows for it. But in her present state of mind she barely felt them.

What was she going to do?

She sat, hugging herself and rocking on a low rock wall just below the castle. The pre-dawn light gathered momentum in the clear sky above, first violet, and then a wash of dove grey and now streaks of primrose yellow.

Her sleep had been fitful. Her tossing and turning had been interspersed with nightmares and sticky sweats. She decided to rise early to her cows and watch them as the herd boy brought them into the stalls. There was still no sign of the boy, so she sat on the low wall. The stones pressed uncomfortably through her fustian skirt into her bottom and beneath the soles of her feet as she hugged her knees to her chest. She welcomed the pain, for it was pain that was due to her for what she had done.

As she rocked, she gazed at the cows. They munched the grass eyeing her warily. A few lifted their heads.

Creatures of habit, they knew when something was out of order. She hoped her unusual, early morning presence wouldn't stop their milk from flowing for there would be more cuffs and blows to her head and arms. Some more bruises to add to her bruises!

The cold pressed in through her cotton sleeves bringing out goose bumps on her tanned arms and she hugged herself more tightly.

Jennet knew that it should be her going to the stake, not the beautiful lady from the castle. She knew that most people didn't think that she was much better than a dog. She may not be smart and proper like other people but she knew what she knew and that was: she had sent an innocent person to her death.

She could barely handle the burden of it and rocked herself harder as she tied to shake off the guilt. A pre-dawn passer-by would have sworn that she was arguing with an invisible person.

"He was going to kill my beau," her face was contorted with her agony. "I couldn't let him kill my beau. He had to be stopped. Oh, all the saints above help me …" She cradled her face in her hands. "What have I done? What have I done?"

Suddenly she pulled her hands away from her face.

The agony had been replaced with anger. She poked a finger into the air, her eyes wide, the fading moon mirrored in the whites. "I saw what he did! I saw! No one else did, but I saw." Her face changed again, a mask of fear. Her voice came out like a whine. "What shall I do?" Jennet started to squirm, not from the uncomfortableness of the stones, but from the knowledge rising from her gut of what she must do.

She shook her head. "No, no, no," she whined. "Don't make me … don't make me. He won't listen to me. He's everybody's master. How is he going to listen to a dairymaid?" Her voice strengthened and became more resolute. "I saw him. Yes, I did. He was up to no good. I have to for Mistress Isabel's sake … it should be me. Yes, it should be me. Yes," she finally conceded. "I will go. I will meet him outside the gates when he takes his hounds for a run. Oh, my–the sun is nearly up! He will almost be there! Oh my, don't let me be late!" Jennet jumped off the wall and started to run towards the outer gates of Alnwich Castle in her lumbering gait.

CHAPTER THIRTY-EIGHT

York City, York

The latch on the inn window, which had been unhooked during the height of the day on the pretext of checking the leaky roof, swung outward without a sound.

It was the quietest time of the night, a few hours before dawn, just as most people were entering their deepest state of sleep, when the black silhouette entered the room. Standing absolutely still, getting his bearings and waiting for his eyes to adjust to the darkened interior, he tried to spy the bed.

Ah, there it was against the wall. He could just make out a slumbering form as the moon's rays contoured a woollen counterpane.

There was not a sound to be heard as the figure silently crept over to the bed.

He withdrew his weapon seamlessly from within his tunic, drew up his arm slowly then quickly plunged it into the unmoving body. The dagger felt spongy in his hand. That was strange. He'd never come across a spongy body before. The mound that he had pierced appeared to collapse.

Puzzled, he grabbed the night-capped head of the body and yanked it to see the face. He was taken by surprise again as the cap came way in his hand and its filling, a nightshirt, unravelled itself across the bed.

It wasn't a body! There was no body!

He stripped the bed of its blankets and in frustration stabbed at the horsehair mattress through the sheet, in case somebody was hiding in there. He stood up and looked around. As his eyes adjusted even more to the dark inner recesses of the room, he became aware with growing anger and some fear that the apartment was empty. No clothes, no traces of last night's supper … nothing.

The scum, Kerr, had escaped! How? he wondered. *He was to have remained in York for another two days? Somebody must have alerted him, but whom?* His mind drew a blank.

Turnbull's face loomed large in his mind's eye. There would be repercussions! They shouldn't have dallied so long!

Hogg stood outside the door just in case of a scuffle. Reeth went to let him into the room. They were now going to have to plan their way out of their blundering. Turnbull was a ruthless man. They could not return back to Alnwich empty handed.

Reeth opened the door a crack expecting to see Hogg's shadow to one side. The whisper that was ready on his lips disappeared as opening the door found some opposition. His eyes fell to the blockage. Hogg's body lay sprawled across the hall floor. He lay face up; his eyes were wide open, gazing sightlessly to the ceiling. Further inspection brought clarity to his friend's demise. Hogg's throat had been cut. Blood was still pumping out. A fresh cut! It had happened only moments before. Reeth looked up sharply, his senses keen. The killer still had to be around. He went to step over Hogg's body but found himself sliding to his knees. Surprised and slightly disorientated, Reeth saw that he had slipped in the widening pool of his friend's spilt blood.

He had no time to react.

The sound that came from behind him was almost an intuitive thought rather than a physical vibration to the ear.

It was his death knell and he knew it.

He cursed himself for not being cautious. He knew that he had broken all the rules for this type of warfare. He had succumbed to the very thing that he taught against.

He suddenly remembered his grandmother's words from long, long ago. He could even smell the salty tang of the sea air as he sat on his granddame's lap.

He had been a very young lad holding a piece of driftwood that he used as a sword. His wispy blond hair had been buffeted by the strong breeze. "Live by the sword, die by the sword," she had said admonishing him of the lifestyle of their menfolk. How true, she was ...

He barely felt the blade on his throat as it rendered his airways open to the infilling of his own blood. With his fading eyesight he caught the gold pattern worked on the offending blade as it flicked in front of him. It was the Northumberland crest.

CHAPTER THIRTY-NINE

Alnwich Castle, Northumberland

Jennet just made it to the gate as the Earl of Northumberland clattered out of it with his hounds, a few personal attendants and some grooms. She rushed up to his mount, startling it so that it reared. Swords were pulled and she was surrounded within seconds. After some immediate cussing, the earl brought his gelding under control.

"Who goes there?" he demanded at Jennet as she appeared in silhouette before him.

"A young maid," called out one of his attendants.

One of the grooms drew close, turning his steed in tight circles to get a closer look. "It's young Jennet, the milkmaid, my lord," he said. "Out of the way! You imbecile!"

Jennet fell to her knees in the dust. She knew that she had to speak loud and quick if she were to get the earl's attention.

Before he could move on she turned her face up to him and spoke. "My lord, I saw Sir Nicholas Heron pays some money to the Justice of the Peace, six pieces of gold, sir. Just last night sir, behind the buttery, my lord ..."

She had the earl's attention now. His annoyed stance left him as he held his mount tighter and leaned over his reins to inspect her closer. "What is that you say, girl? Is this true? By the Virgin, you shall not be lying to me or you shall be burning at the stake this morning!"

Her knees turned to jelly and her mouth went dry. "No, sire, 'tis true, 'pon my oath, my lord!"

Northumberland nodded to one of his attendants to grab the maid and haul her close to him. The attendant slithered down the side of his mount and quickly drew Jennet closer to the earl.

Her heart thumped in her chest as she beheld the mighty lord of all the north only inches from her face.

"And what did you hear them say, little milkmaid?" he inquired.

"Just that he had done a good job, my lord, ah, Sir Heron said and that nobody would know and more money to his account would be on the way after he had his land back." Her strength of determination started to fail as fear set in and her voice had faded to a whisper.

"What is that you say? Speak up! Speak up, girl!"

The roar of the earl's voice in her face made her realise that her bladder needed emptying.

She opened her mouth but nothing came out.

Northumberland sat up and barked some orders to those around him. Jennet felt confused as the man clutching her elbow let go. She staggered, not realising that she had wholly leaned into him in her fear. There was a blur of activity as horses took off in all directions, hands flicking reins, spurs in hindquarters, rumps bared as horse tails arched and flicked. Within seconds, Jennet was alone. She stood uneasily, hands outward at her sides as if she needed to balance herself. As the dust settled, she saw the sun's rays stretch up from the horizon into the sky. Her eyes followed the beams of light until they disappeared—sunrise and the start of a new day.

But it wasn't going to be a new day for Mistress Isabel and Jennet realised that she hadn't told the earl that it was her fault. That it had been she who had killed the man, not Mistress Isabel. Agony started to bubble in her soul again. There wasn't much time left! Oh, what to do? What to do? Jennet started to mewl like a newborn kitten. Her hands wrung upon each other in her lap. She still hadn't told anybody the truth! She had to save Mistress Isabel!

A new sound started to ring out on the cold clear air of the morning. It came from the township of Alnwich just down the hill. Her hands became still as she realised what it was. Hope sprung up within her, dispelling her agonies. The milking forgotten, she sped off into the town through one of the four gateway towers that cornered the town like silent sentries; redemption was near!

***

Isabel sat still as her hair was being shaved off. She could feel the blunt blades of the scissors scraping off a layer of skin with her tresses. It stung. She tried not to wince. The pain she would be feeling later would be far greater than this small imposition. She should try to embrace it.

Her long blonde locks fell like veils to her feet.

Mistress Whitten tried to be careful and was full of apologies when she accidentally drew blood. Isabel was beyond answering. She was readying her mental state for the trial to come, the burning of her flesh at the stake.

A dribble of blood ran beside her eye and down her cheek. She barely noticed it. The drop fell onto the ruffled collar of her white cotton shift, an adornment of death.

Last night, they all came to say their goodbyes, one by one, under intense guard. There were more tears, encouraging words, pieces of scripture thrust into her hands to take her through her last night on earth. It was the last time she would ever see them. She never had a chance to say goodbye to Maud and Elizabeth, which she felt sad about. She had wanted them to know that she loved them.

Algernon choose to stay away, Thomas had said. Isabel said to tell him that she understood and still loved him. She found it hard to see the pain in Thomas's eyes. She grabbed his hand and squeezed all the love into it that she could. She loved his heart of passion. He walked away, tears rolling down his cheeks.

Henry had broken down almost immediately. He had to be carried from the room. She had to be dragged from him as she held his face in her hands, as she tried to encourage him.

She told him to talk to Mary and that she had something wonderful to tell him; that in death there would be life. He had good things to look forward to.

The earl was the last to leave. During the whole time of this last visit, she tried to speak to him through her eyes. Was he indeed her father? How strange if he was. Was she an illegitimate child, a love child? Or had she merely heard wrong? Maybe she was delusional? Who could blame her of that, if that was truly the case?

Now, here she was, ready to meet her God and it would not matter one way or another if she was Northumberland's daughter or not.

Mistress Whitten picked up her silky hair and smoothed it in her hands.

"Such beautiful hair God has blessed you with, my lady."

Isabel didn't answer. She just rose gracefully from her stool and very slowly, walked to the window embrasure.

It was a dry autumnal day. The sun was still close to the horizon, but rising, the long shadows of the night quickly disappearing.

A jangle in the lock announced the local priest.

She could see him in her mind's eye, crossing himself so that he would be protected from the evil that she supposedly carried, as he approached her. She had explained to him, from his first visit in her dire circumstances, that she was innocent of all accusations. He had not believed her at first, believing that she was in denial, but eventually, he began to see the real Isabel Percy through all the lies and gossip. He wasn't totally convinced for she could be casting a spell to bring down his guard as they spoke, so he had best be wary. Everybody knew that a witch could transfix a person's liver by stabbing it with needles by a mere thought! His nervousness betrayed the doubt that he would not voice and Isabel could see right through him.

Never mind, Isabel comforted herself, he was only a man and perhaps the only human comfort she would have until the end. He would ride with her in the cart that would take her into the town square.

She didn't turn but continued to watch the dry brown leaves circle below. She felt strangely detached. Her mind was already journeying into the face of the unknown.

CHAPTER FORTY

Alnwich Town, Northumberland

Jennet skidded to a stop on the outskirts of the square. It was empty, bar one man making the noise that rang out over the town. A hammer was being welded to build the stake to be used at the burning. Movement across the way revealed another man coming through a narrow alleyway, walking a cart full of faggots and kindling, bags of gunpowder swung freely from hooks on the sides.

The centre of the square, also known as the marketplace, seemed very barren at dawn. It was usually a bustling place, a hive of activity, full of the noises of people and animals coming and going, people selling their wares from the baker to the butcher, the clothier and the tinker. People travelling north into Scotland, people travelling south to London mingled with roaming players, children running truant, maids gossiping and men doing business.

Jennet crept back under the shadow of some low-slung eaves to remain out of view. She could see the stake. It was being built on the ground. Soon it would be erected into place. She was hoping that it was going to be erected over the spot where the butcher had his stall.

That would be just perfect! If it wasn't going to be erected there, she didn't know what she would do. She just had to make it so that the stake was erected there! How she was going to make that happen was a bit beyond her at the moment, but

God would make a way, she believed. She may be slow and dim-witted, but she knew when she had done a wrong. Her heart had only wanted good; how had it turn out so bad? She had said she was sorry to God but she had to make it right.

***

The Earl of Northumberland, the richest man in England after the king, looked aloof and imperious, sitting upright on his horse as he looked from afar off.

Nobody would have guessed the feeling of panic that was rising in his bones for the third time in his life.

Hurry, hurry, hurry, he mentally urged one of Turnbull's younger men and his personal guards as they approached the Justice of the Peace's home.

He had long since been suspicious of Heron's motives and movements of the last few years. Now the situation to deal with him appropriately had arisen. He was glad, as this would also release Isabel from this madness, this farce of murder by witchery. He would have loved to intervene, as all the border families seemed to do, by taking the law into their own hands—*or to be truthful,* the earl thought, *create their own laws altogether*—but he had to be seen to be upholding the law of the land, even in his own tragedy. He dare not do anything else if he was to keep his head and assets.

He could see the fresh young man knocking on the front door. A serving girl opened the door. She quickly disappeared into the back of the house after the guard questioned her. The young guard didn't wait and followed her in with his men.

Good! Good, thought the earl. His nervousness was also on account that Turnbull was not available to help him. He would have known exactly what to do. He knew the law, he knew people and most importantly, he knew what his liege lord would have wanted. Turnbull had an uncanny knack of reading his thoughts and producing results that he would have produced himself. And Turnbull had displayed loyalty continually over the years, whereas Heron, it seemed, was another matter.

The earl had received orders from the King's Council that the guarding of the English border had to be strengthened now that England was at war with France. Northumberland wanted the job to be done well and had sent Turnbull, his trusted servant in matters of warfare, with a team of scouts and a large retinue of soldiers to make sure invasion from the Scots, if France won, would come to nothing.

As Northumberland surveyed the empty door, which continued to gape wide like a slack mouth, his impatience grew. He almost dug in his spurs and raced down to see what was taking so long.

After a time, his men came to the door and helped a lady onto a horse.

Northumberland frowned. What was going on?

He watched them make their way to the castle. Where was Bartholomew Stonebridge?

The earl wheeled his mount around on the spot and returned to the castle. There he would hopefully have the constable and special constable waiting to receive him to arrest the bribed justice of the peace. Had Stonebridge slid silently away under the darkness of the night, knowing that his crime would eventually be found out? Had Heron helped him?

His face grew grim as he contemplated Heron's treachery.

Years ago, it had never been like that. He would never have dreamt it would be like this now.

Sir Nicholas Heron was the second brother from the Herons of Dunningford. His older brother, Lord Dunningford, had inherited the Keep and holdings on the death of their father. Second sons from any good family were always promised to the church. Nicholas was saved from this "fate worse than death" as he had put it, by the arrival of the Henry Percy, who was helping to keep the peace on the borderland front.

He had arrived at Dunningford to amass some more men to stop a nearby skirmish from developing into another war. Nicholas' strategy to ambush was a success due to his knowledge of the area. Henry Percy valued it and invited him to join his ranks as a soldier. For Nicholas, there was no comparison from the glory of ecclesiastical duties to the glory of successful warfare. He went with his family's blessing.

A night of revelling at Dunningford Keep, celebrating their success, produced an heir for Nicholas' brother and his wife. It was a cause for more celebration than usual on these occasions because the older couple had been thought barren. Only three people knew the truth.

Nicholas found a very drunken Henry rolling on a hay mattress cot with his brother's' older but still beautiful, inebriated wife. His older brother was out cold, looking very much like an old man, with dribble in his salt and pepper whiskers. He was slumped, unconscious with strong drink in the corner. They all looked into each other's eyes, their sin uncovered for Nicholas to see.

Nicholas chose to see nothing.

There wasn't anything he wouldn't do for the man who saved him from a life of the living dead, as he perceived it.

He pulled a blanket over them both, to keep them from other eyes that may pry, then threw his older brother over his shoulder and took him to his own bedchamber.

Northumberland didn't remember too much of that night, only that he had been intensely satisfied by a woman who wasn't his and wasn't there with him when he woke.

Knowing that he had committed a great wrong, he left without saying goodbye.

Dragging his thoughts away from the past, the earl entered the gates of Alnwich Castle. It was a hive of activity with more assembled soldiers making their way to the border.

Turnbull's young protégé was shouting out last-minute strategy and instruction before releasing groups through Alnwich's gates. The horses, which had been cooped up in stalls for a few days, were stamping, sidestepping, snorting and shaking their bits with impatience to be gone. The polished metal on their bridles glinted like new in the sun. Their experienced riders held them in check as they jostled against each other.

He would be joining them soon with his son Thomas.

It would be Thomas' first excursion of a military manner and he could barely hold him back with his enthusiasm. Henry should be with them, too, but he had taken to his bed. Northumberland shook his head at his firstborn's behaviour. How was this son going to govern his wealth that he had carefully amassed over the years? He was loath to really think about it. If he died tomorrow, he didn't know how Henry would cope. He had no ability to cope with the realities of life. Everybody suffered pain of some sort or another; it was a fact of living this life. Most people got on with their lot. But his son, his firstborn, oh, no; he caved in at the slightest bit of pressure. He sighed a heavy sigh, which expressed his internal groaning. Hopefully this news of the faulty trial would rouse him from his sick bed. But first he would have to deal with this matter of the Justice of the Peace and make sure that Isabel was released from the confines of her prison. Hopefully Willem would be well on his way back to Alnwich from York and would whisk her away from this place.

Heron had been trustworthy in one way, Northumberland conceded: he never breathed a word to anybody of that night. Northumberland promoted him to one of his right-hand men.

It was a rare thing for people of any elevation in life to have someone that they could trust with difficult affairs that needed dealing with. Heron, it seemed, was one of these.

The only time Heron ever mentioned that night of madness was nine months later, as they both surveyed Northumberland's soldiers at practice mock battles.

"You have a daughter, my lord, a bonny wee thing. Everybody celebrates the miracle baby, now heir to considerable lands and assets. Congratulations."

Heron had sauntered away as though the words carried no import. Northumberland had no idea of the bitter jealousy that had obviously grown like a cancer within Heron's mind over the years. Only now was he able to perceive the vile hatred that had grown silently over the years toward him. Yes, Heron had been glad to be relieved of a life in the church, but he had stolen Heron's legacy by laying with his sister-in-law. He should

273

never have lain with her. It was a sin and no good had come of it, except for Isabel. Men made mistakes, but children were often the innocents caught in the web of their sins.

Because of Isabel, Heron had been cheated out of his inheritance. And it was because of him that Isabel was.

When the raid by the Kerrs wiped out the Heron family, he thought Isabel to be lost.

It was only on the last reconnoitre of the Dunningford Keep and hamlet by Nicholas, that he heard Isabel crying. She had snuggled up to her dead mother. Her face had been streaked with tears that had created trails of mud down her cheeks. Heron had picked her up and brought her to him.

Herons hidden bitterness towards Northumberland expressed itself in other destructive behaviour, gambling for one. He owed Northumberland a small fortune but now there was a way out, only he had to give up all hope of his dreams of becoming the Heron heir to do it. It was to give Isabel to him as a ward, together with her lands and assets. It paid off his debt to him but Northumberland could see that it just about tore Nicholas in two. Heron's behaviour had often bordered on madness or insanity after that. Northumberland couldn't understand it at first, but over the years, it had become clearer and he began to be wary of all Heron's actions. This latest one had just sealed his fate for him, Northumberland decided. To kill his own niece for his own gain was indeed madness. He had to be stopped and he would stop him.

Shouts made their way over the general melee of noise as mounted soldiers made their way through Alnwich's gates.

It brought his attention fully back to the present. He relaxed his hands on his reins and his mount came to a standstill. He could see the constable and petty constable pulled up in the courtyard with their scribes waiting to dismount.

Northumberland decided that it didn't matter whether the Justice of the Peace was found immediately or not. Isabel would be able to go free. It would soon be public knowledge that the trial was false.

And Heron, he continued to muse, Heron's fate lay in his hands. His eyes glinted hard like flint and his mouth turned up in an ugly grimace. Maybe, just maybe, he was tainted by border warfare after all. His wants, desires and motives were no different than the crofter in the fields.

The shouts continued. The persistence of them caused him to focus. Somebody was calling to him. It was somebody that he knew. He looked over the press of soldiers continuing to find their way through Alnwich's gates and saw two people making their way to him. He dismounted. As a groom came to his side and led his horse away, he recognised the Catherine wheel plaits that could only belong to Jacincka Van der Veldt. Willem walked beside her.

Northumberland felt some of his burden for Isabel slip away. Willem was a shrewd businessman, by the Flanders Wool Guild accounts upon investigating him, and if he could run a business well, he should be able to run a wife well. Isabel would be well looked after and her dowry of half the Heron lands would stand them in good stead. Willem would take her away from all of this and he could rest easy that his oldest child was safe.

"Mistress Jacincka and Sir Willem. Fortuitus timing. All is well! Come!'

Jacincka's small dip of a curtsey was cut halfway through execution as Gavyn took her arm and followed the swift moving earl into Alnwich's great hall.

The earl threw his short cloak to a manservant scurrying at his side. He clicked his fingers to Jacincka and Gavyn.

"Come this way. We will release Isabel to you." He whipped his head around as he walked. "It's all been a farce!"

His hands gestated in agitation before him. "Heron bought the justice of the peace for a price, an act of revenge. A Pilate and a Judas! Nothing new under the sun, the Lord's book says! God's teeth, how true that is!"

Northumberland led them up stairs, down corridors and along closed-up wings to the rarely used parts of the castle. His pace did not let up.

When he did suddenly stop, Jacincka ploughed into the back of Gavyn as she had been studying her steps on the uneven stone floor. An oath exploding from Northumberland made her look up.

"Where is she?" demanded the earl of a little bowed serving woman tidying up the last evidences of Isabel's imprisonment.

Flustered, the woman curtseyed and stammered out what was requested. "G—gawn, my lord, the guards took her. She must be almost at the marketplace now, my lord. You must not worry, my lord. Lots of guards came. She'll be getting her just desserts, spawn of the devil ..."

"You hold your tongue!" the earl roared, cutting her off. "Be gone with you! I never want to see you at Alnwich again!"

The old serving woman looked like she'd been slapped in the face.

All three were gone again before they could see her start to tremble and hyperventilate. With no family of her own, she had just been cast down to beggar status.

***

As they arrived in the marketplace, the flames were well under way. On their mounts, they were well able to see over the large group of people that had gathered.

The crowd was made up of a good cross-section of the community. The local gentry had also come to see the earl's ward go up in flames. Hoots and catcalls were yelled up into the air as people vented their feelings toward witches.

Gavyn could just see the top of Isabel's shaved head. It was turning this way and that, trying to escape the inhalation of smoke and heat. His heart dropped through the soles of his feet and a lump developed in the back of his throat. He blinked to clear the tears that had formed in his eyes as he tried not to cry. He failed.

The woman he loved was going up in flames. He didn't expect the sudden slam of emotions that rose up from his gut. A sob was out of his mouth before he was aware of it. Tears rose in his eyes and coursed, unchecked down his cheeks.

He could not, now, deny the realisation that he loved a Heron, a sworn enemy of his family for generations. And it was all too late!

The flames grew so high that he could no longer see Isabel. The roaring of the fire was all consuming now. People had to step back for the heat of it.

Beside him, Jacincka sobbed quietly, a kerchief at her face. The earl was swallowing his tears, eyes glittering.

***

Isabel couldn't help but cough as the smoke rising from the faggots wafted across her face in heavy plumes. Her eyes stung and immediately started to water. Through the blurriness and growing flames, she could see the crowd jeering and mocking her. She couldn't hear them though. It was like she was in a world of her own with her crackling walls of flame. Their faces appeared wavy and wobbly through the intense heat. She could see the flames starting to lick her gown as she looked down against the rope at her neck. Patches were being scorched brown, and then they burst into flame, one patch after another.

Terror rose to full flight! Under her breath, "Oh God, oh God, oh God," trembled from her lips as the horror of burning drowned out all meditations that she had previously dwelt on. God help her, she could feel the flames on her skin! Screams tore from her throat as the pain and unspeakable terror deepened. The sound of sizzling came to her ears as her bladder voided down her burnt legs.

Suddenly she felt herself falling. The flames must have her whole body now as a different burning sensation seared down her back.

As instantly as it came, it went. She fell down into hell itself. It was full black confusion, just like people had described it. She felt disorientated. Demon hands were grabbing at her. Her terror magnified, even more than being tied to the stake! Hell was for eternity! The words that spiralled through her

Amanda Hawken

mind were exactly the same as her Lord's. My God, my God! Why have you forsaken me?

The utter blackness that surrounded her suddenly took her consciousness, as another type of pain shattered all thought.

***

Suddenly there was an almighty explosion as the gunpowder, which would have been tied around her waist and under her armpits, ignited. Everybody ducked and shielded heir faces with their forearms. Blue flames spiked powerfully into the air, quickly followed by clouds of billowing yellow fire and smoke. The crowd drew back with gasps of horror being torn from their throats.

"My God! She did not deserve this!" exclaimed Gavyn, between sobs, settling into a state of shock.

Even the jeering crowd had grown quiet. The most experienced burning witches' watchers had never been party to an explosion like that! Most times the gunpowder was too damp to really ignite. Whether it was God rebuking them for their sins or whether it was the witch trying to take one of them with her, it was a bad omen. People started to slink away silently. The whole affair had gone sour.

The ashes were to go totally cold before locals ventured willingly into the marketplace again, with thumbs placed between fore and second fingers to keep at bay any evil.

Gavyn felt an incessant tugging at his sleeve. Eventually he managed to tear his head away from the fire that had now devoured the whole platform and the stake and had even scorched the cobbles surrounding it.

As he looked down into a very grubby face from his seat on his mount, his nostrils were assaulted by the stench of dead meat. His first instinct was to pull away, but the dirt on the face was not just the ordinary grime of the unwashed. Thick smears of green slime and days old blood, which had turned brown, were all over her face, her bodice and skirt wet. It was Jennet, the milkmaid from the Alnwich Castle dairy.

"Jennet?" he inquired, frowning with disbelief.

278

By this stage, both the earl and Jacincka had noticed the reeking creature at Gavyn's side. Jacincka pressed her kerchief harder to her nose to keep out the offensive stink.

"Come, Master, come," she whispered urgently, still pulling on his sleeve.

"Why, Jennet?"

"Mistress Isabel, Master ..." She kept her eyes averted so as not draw attention to herself.

"Be off with you!" cut in Northumberland, wheeling his horse around to face back to the Castle. The whole scene now made him sick to his gut. Changing his mind, he careened haphazardly out of the town and charged in a westerly direction, with dust flying.

Gavyn leaned down and grabbed Jennet's wrist to stop from bolting like a scared rabbit. Knowing that Jennet would not approach anybody without a reason, he leaned down to her, breathing through his mouth.

"Yes, Jennet? What is it?"

Jennet looked furtively from side to side, so that nobody near could hear. She whispered up to him. "Follow me, Master. It's very important!" She turned and looked back to see if he was following.

"Come," she mouthed silently, beckoning with her grubby hands. "Come."

Gavyn turned to Jacincka. "You go on ahead. I'll catch up with you soon."

Happy to leave the stench and get away from the tragedy that was played out before them, Jacincka made her own way up the slope from the township into the castle gates.

Gavyn had to bring his horse to a trot to keep up with Jennet, who skirted the town to the banks of the river Aln. There were not many people about; they had all opted to go back indoors despite the clear sky, afraid of the evil that might taint them.

As Gavyn started to dwell on what Heron had done, his anger grew white hot until he was shaking with it. His first thought was to get rid of him. The situation called for revenge!

Another voice, weaker than the other, instantly reminded him that Isabel was now dead because of revenge. Hadn't Jacincka told him as much? He had laboured for revenge and now he was receiving its wages. Emptiness! His labouring was for nothing! For the first time in his life, as he felt his anger dim, he knew the loss of something that was infinitely precious.

Picking his way through a rough part of riverbank as he followed Jennet in an easterly direction, leaving the town of Alnwich behind, Gavyn found himself falling into depression. He felt like he had come to the end of himself. He reined in his mount to a standstill, lifted his hands to his face and began to sob. His mount stamped his legs to rid himself of the insects as they started to settle in the stillness.

After a moment of what felt like a total loss of self-control, he gathered himself, wiping the tears on his face away with his hands and sniffing down the rest.

It suddenly occurred to him that he was grieving. It was a new sensation that he had never felt before, even at the loss of his twin brother.

He had lost someone he loved, something that was dearer to his heart than anything else in the world, and he never got a chance to tell her.

He looked up to see how far Jennet was along. She was now scrambling back up a small creek that flowed back from the town in the river. He pulled his horse up from cropping the lush grass at the rivers edge and followed her back to Alnwich along the creek.

The creek was like a sludgy drain. Some surface water flowed through it, but mostly it filled with piss pot slops that trickled there from the front doors of homes around the market place.

Jennet got down onto her hands and knees and let herself down into the drain crevasse. As she stood in it, the bank came up to her chest.

Gavyn pulled his horse up and dismounted. "Jennet?"

Jennet didn't answer, but dipped down from his sight.

Gavyn tied his horse to a nearby tree. It immediately started to graze. He walked to the creek's edge.

He couldn't believe what he saw.

Isabel lay in the stinking drain with Jennet crouched at her side.

They could have been sisters with the same muck all over them. Mud and sludge streaked from Isabel's shaved head to burnt toes.

"I saved her. I saved her," said Jennet. "I won't go to hell now, will I? I saved her. She didn't kill that man ..."

Gavyn could see tears in Jennet's eyes. She looked straight at him, voice wavering with emotion. "I killed him. I killed the man. I should have been burned ... Mistress Isabel is a fine lady. She wouldn't do no bad thing."

Jennet turned her attention back to Isabel, wiping the mud and sludge form her face.

Stunned at what he saw before him, Gavyn jumped down into the bottom of the creek and crouched down on the other side of Isabel. He wiped the mud from the base of Isabel's throat.

A pulse!

Not satisfied with believing his own eyes, he put an ear to her chest. The steady rhythm of a strong heartbeat thrummed back at him.

Tears instantly filled his eyes. "Oh, my God! Oh, my God!" he cried into the air, not quite believing his good fortune.

"I won't go to hell, will I?"

Gavyn looked up at Jennet. For a moment he had forgotten that she was there. He continued to look blankly at her.

"I killed him, my lord. I killed him. Not Mistress Isabel."

Jennet started to whimper, wringing her hands as her mental agitation grew. "It's all right, isn't it? I won't go to hell now. Will I? I saved her."

Gavyn looked back up into the drain. "How did you do it Jennet? How did you save Mistress Isabel?"

"I made sure they built the scaffold over the butchers drain. I moved the grate for my lady. It weren't nothing to kick the faggots away for her to fall into the drain. Her legs be a bit burnt and hers head be banged. Can you make them better?"

Gavyn smiled at Jennet and reached across Isabel to still her writhing hands. "You did well, Jennet. You did very well

Jennet had never heard those words spoken to her before.

It was her time to feel amazed. Grinning stupidly, she sat back, hugging herself in silence, watching him at his work while she basked in his praise.

Gavyn sat back on his haunches to undo the rope at Isabel's neck and then untie her hands behind her back. He would bathe her in the river.

His senses were heightened as a deep peace came over him. A grey warbler's keening cry above came sharp and sweet to his ears. He could almost hear the rustle of feather on feather as its wings flitted, darting for insects above the river. The trickle of water from the drain sounded like a melody from heaven as it made its way bubbling and gurgling over the stones and re-fuse.

Feeling the autumnal sun on his back made him want to stay like this forever. He felt like he had been reborn.

He had been given another chance at life. He wasn't going to let go of it easily. He hoped with all the hope that was within him that Isabel wouldn't let go of him either, but he remem-bered that he had left that decision up to her before he left for York and he said that he would honour her choice–even if it meant a certain type of death for him.

CHAPTER FORTY-ONE

Flanders Coast

Ah, I love the sea! Isabel thought to herself as she opened her winter cloak to catch the icy air. Frigid tendrils sliced across her throat and down into her chest. She could also feel the cold caress her ankles and feet. She revelled in the freedom of it. After the burning at the stake, she felt almost suffocated when she became too warm. Even though winter had arrived, she was only sleeping with a sheet for covering. Any hint of heat or sticky sweat on her body brought out the sensation of flames licking her skin.

She stood on the top of a sand dune just a small way from a little cottage where she had been living for the past few months. It was a wild piece of lowland coastline. The untouched white sand dunes met the sky at both the northern and southern horizons. Behind the cottage, once a fisherman's croft, the land was abundantly flat, a vivid green, dotted with the occasional milk cow and windmill, segregated by its infamous dykes.

Immediately behind the low hung house, a few sheep grazed in a rough paddock, and to the right, a small stable housed four horses.

Gavyn and Jacincka had brought her to her new home in the Netherlands while she healed. It was Jacincka's home that she used sometimes in the summer when she took time away from the wool business.

This morning, Jacincka left for Flanders for the close of the Wool Guild before the twelve days of Christmas. She took with her, her secretary—her male voice for her business—and a bodyguard. Women could never be admitted into the inner sanctum of the wool guild, even a widow who had the freedoms of most men.

Forever practical, she encouraged Isabel to have a walk outside before the bad weather set in.

Isabel stood looking northwest out over the English Channel toward the North Sea. A misty grey snow cloud, dense with smudges of violet and purple, blanketed the entire sky. Close to the earth, it seemed to brood over the dark, sullen swells of the sea. The strong blustery wind had died away and with it the cresting foam on the tops of the waves. It looked like the sky and sea waited for a command before it unleashed its pent-up fury. Gulls still soared majestically overhead, seemly impervious to the icy expectancy in the air.

Isabel's burns were all but healed now.

They were mainly on her legs, and walks in the sea with her skirts bunched to her knees to soothe the continual heat she felt there had definitely aided to the new pink flesh coming through.

Jacincka said it was the immediate plunging into moisture, despite its unsavoury nature, that had stopped the burns from being worse than what they were. They had told her the story of what Jennet had done to free her: that she had pushed the beginning of the frame of the platform over the butcher's drain, while pretending to be slightly crazy. Because it was she, the local dimwit, her actions were not suspected.

While the carpenters began to build the main structure of the platform, Jennet hightailed it to the drain, which opened out at the river and crawled through the filth and slime to the grate, which was now immediately under the platform. When the last board was on, she huffed and puffed to lift the grate and push it aside, so that when Isabel fell through the burnt faggots and boards, her exit through the drain would be unhindered.

After washing Isabel in the river and encouraging Jennet to do the same, Gavyn had left them drying in the sun before he set off to the castle for help. Northumberland did everything. After some words with Gavyn, he quickly and efficiently made provision for them to cross the channel. It was all done in secrecy, only the family knowing of their flight to the Low Countries. It was best that way, said the earl, a fresh start for all of them. He gave Gavyn a letter to give to Isabel when she had recovered. In it Isabel read the true story of who she was. So, she had a father who was alive after all. She had been conceived in a night of passion. Well, that wasn't so bad; who was she to judge? Her father had loved her and had done all he could for her despite the difficulties for him in hiding her true identity. She refused to make room for those burgeoning questions of why didn't he tell his wife Catherine? She could have grown up knowing she was part of a real family and not just an orphan taken under their wings. Asking questions that she knew she wouldn't get answers to weren't worth pressing into and would only produce bitterness. Families weren't perfect because they were made up of imperfect people. There was only one who was perfect and her fulfilment was in him.

Isabel sighed contentedly as she continued to open herself to the chill. She saw the first few snowflakes of the season flutter down from the sky. She turned and made her way down the grass-tufted sand dune and back into the white cottage, fishing baskets and old nets attached to the whitewashed walls like barnacles to the hull of a ship.

"How is your head today?" asked the cook and resident housekeeper. She turned her head up from stirring a pot as Isabel entered the back door.

Isabel smiled at Claudette, the young French wardrobe mistress. She had been stunned but then not surprised to find her in Gavyn's employ. She had assisted Gavyn in Isabel's transfer from the ruined abbey back to the Duchess of Alençon's châteaux. Her silence in which she had assisted Isabel on that morning after all made sense now.

285

She touched the back of her head where the swelling had been going continually down. It was surmised that she had whacked her head on something in the drain as Jennet tried to pull her out. Her fingers testified to her head being almost back to normal, a slight bump but hardly any pain and she hadn't had any headaches for the last few days.

"Very well, Claudette. Much better, thank you."

Isabel held her hands out over the cooking fire. "It looks like snow soon, Claudette."

"Yes, I can smell it in the air. Now go and sit by the fire and I'll bring you in a mulled wine. Mind, Louis!"

She spoke to an absent-minded, white and brown spaniel, which sniffed at Isabel's feet.

Isabel bent down to pat him. "It's alright, Claudette. He's no trouble. He's adorable"

"Adorable, maybe. But Madam Van der Veldt won't thank me if you are flat on your back again for falling over my dog."

Claudette settled Isabel into a cushioned chair in front of a cosy fire and lifted Isabel's legs onto a small footstool with great care. She went to pick up a fur covering to put over her legs, but Isabel stayed her with her hand and protested kindly. "Claudette, I am so much better now. I can do these simple things for myself."

Claudette clucked disapprovingly. "You'll let me be the judge of that one, Mistress Kerr. I'll not have Madam Van der Veldt telling me that I am slipping in my duties."

"Claudette, you would never be blamed for that, but no furs for me. I cannot bear to be too hot now."

Claudette lifted her eyebrows to let Isabel know that she was doubtful of her actions, but decided not to say anything and went back to the kitchen.

Isabel gazed blankly into the crackling fire, comforted by its warmth and constantly moving colours. Louis settled at her footstool and appeared to sleep.

It was strange to be called by her husband's name. She had barely gotten used to being called Mistress Van der Veldt at

Alnwich. Now, Gavyn introduced her to others as Mistress Kerr.

Her looks were somewhat marred now. She wasn't the untouched beauty that he had married. She was now scarred in body and in mind. Nightmares tortured her nights and the skin on her legs, although growing back healthily would never be smooth again. And there was the fact that she would never be able to bear children again after the rough ride she had after delivering little Henry. The only thing that was returning to normal was the hair on her head. It was growing back in tousled, blonde curls, with wispy tendrils spiralling delicately at her neck.

She recalled Gavyn's words before he left Alnwich for York.

He had said that she could choose to annul their marriage if that was her heart's desire.

As she gazed, slightly mesmerised by the flickering flames, she wondered if he might want to annul their marriage.

She was a different woman now, slower in thought and movement, bruised of heart and soul. What were his thoughts?

Gavyn had been so attentive and caring since they had come to the Netherlands, but never once had he tried to get familiar with her. Not even a chaste kiss goodnight. He was constantly busy outside, fixing things that Jacincka never had time for, so there had been no time for deep conversation.

Dinner table talk was about the wool business and plans for its future, and the day-to-day running of the cottage and the care of its animals. Despite the lack of conversation about her future with Gavyn, the atmosphere was always cheerful, focusing on the positives of life and interspersed with jokes and laughter.

Claudette entered the room with a pewter goblet of mulled wine.

The spicy scent of cinnamon and orange peel lifted her spirits. Isabel inhaled it with great pleasure.

"Ah, Claudette," sighed Isabel, leaning back with her eyes closed. "Who is going to make me mulled wine like this when I go?"

"Go, madam? Oh, you must mean to the new house? Well, you may rest your thoughts on that account. Madam Van der Veldt has promised Master Kerr that I shall stay on.

"I must say that it will be no hardship for me. I love the country, especially the sea, and the sea air will do wonders for Louis's rheumy legs. We will be getting new staff, so I will be overseeing that Madam Van der Veldt has good servants. I won't suffer any lazy people about her new establishment.

"There now, that's enough chat from me. Master Kerr will be back from town soon and dinner is nowhere near ready."

Isabel tried to keep the surprise of this new information from her face as she sipped and nodded pleasantly. What did this mean? What were these plans being made without her knowledge? What did he intend to do with her? The whys and wherefores brought her no answers.

Isabel was almost dozing off when she heard the clip-clop of horses along the side of the house. There were the sounds of muffled voices as Gavyn gave his groom last minute instructions. She watched the door for his entrance. He came in with a gust of wind and a flurry of snowflakes. He had just closed the door when Claudette was at his side hanging up his cloak and doublet as he shook the snow from his cap.

From the sideboard, she thrust a mulled wine into his cold hands.

"You warm up by the fire, Master Kerr. I'll see to Hans when he comes in."

Isabel watched him take his seat in silence. Through the closed door into the kitchen, they could hear Claudette pounding dough.

Part of Isabel felt an excitement and a warm affection as she gazed at Gavyn as he stretched himself before the fire, but another part of her still felt hurt as memories of the abduction and rape flared fresh in her mind. She had yelled out to God that she had forgiven him, for she knew that is what she must do, not only in obedience to her faith but also to release herself from constant emotional suffering. But the memories were still there, fresh and vivid at times.

She had accepted his apology on their wedding night, but where would it all go from here? She couldn't wipe away the past.

After another sip of the spiced wine, she decided to venture into the unknown. She leaned her goblet against her chin as she spoke. "So, I hear that you are building a new house."

She turned her face to him from gazing into the fire, her grey-blue eyes resting evenly upon him.

She noticed that he had the grace to look slightly embarrassed.

"Claudette?"

She nodded.

"We didn't want to excite you. Your health is paramount in our thoughts."

"You and Jacincka, I presume?" Isabel wasn't going to be sidetracked.

Gavyn sighed, with a gesture of giving in. "Yes. Jacincka wanted to add a wing onto this cottage but I suggested building a new house altogether," he looked at Isabel.

"I have decided to leave England and live here. Oh," he shrugged, "I will go back for business, but to stay there would be to keep myself amid border politics. And we all know where that has led. Jacincka, in her wisdom, has encouraged me to settle here," he flicked Isabel a quick look. "To raise my family and future children here, in relative safety."

Isabel tried not to gulp aloud as tears sprung into her eyes. *I am to be cast off,* she thought. *As soon as I am well, I'll be shipped back—to where?* She couldn't go back to Alnwich or anywhere in England probably.

She buried her head in her goblet of wine, so that he couldn't see her tears. Where would she go? She was all alone.

Suddenly Gavyn was kneeling at her side, putting his hands on hers to bring down the goblet. She knew that he could see her shimmering tears.

He swore to himself as he could feel her trembling.

"God's blood, it was too soon! That Claudette! She should keep her business to herself! Now look what has happened. You are not well enough to cope with this yet."

"Do not curse Claudette. You should have told me yourself!" said Isabel, angry with herself for displaying her weakness to him.

He pulled back, holding the arms of her chair. "For this reason, I have not told you, for look how upset you are!"

Isabel conceded, sniffing. "Well, maybe so. But where do I go?"

"Go?"

"You'll pack me off when I am well again. To England, I presume?"

Gavyn frowned in disbelief. "You want to go back to England?"

Isabel looked at him, not understanding him at all.

"What do you mean?"

Gavyn took her feet from the footstool and sat on it himself. He kept her elegant white hands in his as he leaned in towards her. "Isabel, I didn't want to discuss this until you were better. But it seems this conversation needs to be discussed now. Do you want to have our marriage annulled?"

Isabel blanched and her head spun out. She tried to focus her eyes again. The moment of her future was here. She had to be strong. She owed it to herself. "You do, by what you have said."

"What have I said?" said Gavyn, confused.

"You said you want to raise your children here. You must remember Richard telling us both that I couldn't have children, so I presume you want the marriage annulled to re-marry to have children."

Gavyn's face grew dark with anger. "Even in his death bed he tries to ruin my life! God's teeth!"

"Who?"

Gavyn turned his flashing amber eyes onto Isabel. "Richard, of course!"

"What has Richard to do with all of this?"

"He lied to you Isabel! After I sent Richard packing, off to the Norfolk coast in Colchester to be delivered back to Jacincka, I went back to your room to bring you home with me, but you had mysteriously disappeared. While I was wondering what to do, Mistress Simcock came in thinking I was Richard and started to relay the doctor's findings that you would be fine. She was regaling me with recipes to keep your good humours up, so that we could bear many more fine children."

Isabel sat up, shocked and surprised. She pulled a hand up to her bosom. "I'm fine? I am able to have children?"

Gavyn leaned into her more, her other hand still in his. "Yes. You are absolutely fine! You will be able to bear many more children. Richard just wanted to unsettle me, to make me let you go. He wanted your dowry. Half the Heron lands, which back onto Kerr lands. He was determined to put his stake in as first-born son."

Isabel settled back into her chair. She couldn't believe it! She had believed a lie all this time. She put her hand to her stomach. She could have another little Henry if she chose!

She wasn't a barren woman; she was a woman of promise again! She would be able to enter the marriage market full and whole. Next question was, when would that happen?

"You haven't answered my question, Isabel. Do you want a divorce?"

Isabel didn't want to reveal herself for fear of rejection, so she threw it back to Gavyn. "Do you?" she asked quietly.

They both saw the hesitancy in one another's eyes as uncertainty, lack of trust and self-preservation kept them from totally opening up to each other.

Claudette came in from the kitchen, interrupting the crucial, intimate moment. In her floury hands, she held forth some letters held together with string. She showed no surprise with the closeness in which they sat.

"You must have forgotten these, sir. Hans has just brought them in from your saddle bag." Claudette handed them down to Gavyn. "Dinner will be in about one hour," she called over her shoulder before closing the kitchen door and leaving them quiet again.

"Ah," said Gavyn, sitting back onto the stool. He looked up at Isabel. "Letters for you."

He untied the string and gave them to her one by one. "One from Mistress Anne Boleyn; it has the Boleyn crest on the seal. It looks like it's been delivered to Alnwich. And one from the Countess of Northumberland and one from Henry."

Isabel was thrilled to receive the letters, but Gavyn was surprised when she put them aside.

"Do you want to annul our marriage, Gavyn?"

Surprised at the forthrightness of her question and thrilled that she wasn't going to let the subject drop, he revealed to Isabel his heart, casting caution aside without another thought. "No, I don't want to annul our marriage. I know we have started off very badly, and it is entirely my fault, but through it all, I have come to see that the person you are is everything I need. You are exciting and strong, wise and tender and above all beautiful."

Isabel laughed with nervousness and anticipation of good things. "Beautiful? Fire damaged and terrified of dark places, I would have thought."

Gavyn fell to his knees from the footstool and gathered both Isabel's hands to his lips as he looked across at her. "Do you feel the same way, Isabel? Do you want to continue living with me, as man and wife?"

Isabel tossed away all thoughts of playing emotional hide-and-seek now that Gavyn had revealed his true feelings toward her. A cheeky smile crept onto her face creating her adorable dimple. "Don't man and wife share a bed?"

Isabel's roguish smile touched his soul like a healing balm. "I'm sure we can remedy that. If you are sure."

"I'm sure."

Isabel's smile suddenly became serious as she looked deeply into Gavyn's concerned amber eyes. "Part of me really wants to—wants to abandon myself to you. Another part of me finds it hard to trust you. I have forgiven you over and over, you must know that, but I still see pictures of you hurting me."

"Oh, God," whispered Gavyn, full of agony and sorrow for what he had done. Isabel held up his chin, so that they could look at each other.

"You'll have to help me, all right?"

Gavyn looked unbelievingly into her face, which held no hint of anger or resentment, only openness and a willingness to move on from where they had been; tears filled his eyes, words were beyond him. He was forgiven. How sweet was the knowledge. It set him free.

Slowly they moved towards each other and as their lips touched, a feather of a kiss, their souls touched. Gavyn pulled away.

"God, I love you more than life itself. You are too good for me, but dammed if I'm going to let you go. "

Trembling, Gavyn cupped his hand behind Isabel's head and drew her to him as if she were made of Venetian glass.

The kiss started gently, promising commitment, love and honour.

As it deepened, they tasted each other's warmth and explored each other's tenderness. Neither of them wanted the moment to end.

In one swift movement, Gavyn swung Isabel out of the chair and carried her upstairs, above the tiny bedrooms and into the loft. There, he laid her on the recently dried straw and they loved each other with a tender abandonment that went beyond all thought.

EPILOGUE

The Tower of London, May, 1536

The Tower Great Hall was tiered with makeshift stands to allow room for the populace to view, what many were calling, the trial of the century.

Henry Percy, now Earl of Northumberland upon his father's death, sat against one wall with other peers of the realm. Below him Anne Boleyn's uncle, the Duke of Norfolk presided over the proceedings as Lord High Steward for the day.

Henry felt really ill. He felt sick to the stomach, mentally and physically. He knew that the dousing of cold to his body some six years before, to end his days after being separated from Anne, had finally arrived. Even before he was summoned down to London for his beloved's trial, he was coughing up blood. Seeing Anne again or the first time after six years caused him both elation and anguish. She hadn't changed much. She was still the beautiful, elegant woman that he had known before. Her hair was still black and glossy and she held herself well, despite all that had been thrown at her.

Lies, the lot of them, he seethed!

She never wavered once with the barrage of accusations that was fired at her. She had answered respectfully deflecting all insinuations with the clarity of simple truth. It kept the indecisive people whispering into their sleeves.

He, on the other hand, felt like he was dying as he stood on the stand. He felt so dreadfully ill. His palms were sweating and the fever that racked his body, tortured it so much that he could hardly carry himself upright. Answers were demanded of him about his betrothal to Anne. To release Anne from any more tribulation, he had said there had been nothing between them. As he spoke those lies, he looked directly into Anne's eyes. He released all the love he had left to give into that gaze. His heart broke as she looked back at him without any emotion at all. He could have been anybody, a stranger from another country. He brought the back of his hand up to his mouth to choke back a sob.

He needed to be helped from the stand.

Now the moment had come for the Anne's uncle to demand the verdict from the peers of the realm.

The word "guilty" was uttered one after the other without hesitation, until it came to Henry. He was too weak to go against the flow. His beloved had not given him any encouragement.

After mopping his brow, he mumbled "guilty" at his shoes.

"Speak up, Northumberland!" came a loud, cutting demand into the expectant air.

Henry felt he was living hell on earth. He had to make a decision and follow it whole-heartedly. He made it quickly and without thinking, to reduce the agony.

"Guilty!" he called loud and clear.

The same word continued though the tiered rows until they reached the Duke of Norfolk's chair. It was now his job to declare the sentence. He cleared his throat before commencing. Halfway through, his voice broke and wavered.

Despite all the injustices, there was enough heart left in the congregation to offer the duke a look of sympathy as he condemned his niece to death. Henry watched as the duke wiped his mouth, whether by misery or distaste he couldn't tell.

Anne was manhandled from the stand.

Henry couldn't stand it a moment longer. It was all wrong! If only they had been allowed to marry all those years ago, this scene would not be happening. The king hadn't even loved her!

It was just lust and now he lusted after another. Dispose of the old and on with new like a suit of clothes!

May he rot in hell, Henry smouldered.

The pain of that could not be compared to the real issue here and that was that he had let her down.

When she needed him most, he was as bad as the rest. It was an emotional pain that he couldn't bear. Together with the sickness raging in his body, it was enough to cause him to collapse. The gentlemen beside him pored over him in concern. He had to be carried out.

Six months after the beheading of the love of his life, he was dead.

Flanders Coast

Isabel stood at the first floor window, which faced out onto her new formal garden. Below she watched the playful scene with great contentment as Gavyn rolled on the grass with their two older children, three spaniels leaping and romping on top of them. Her third was in a crib at her side and a fourth now grew within her womb.

They had grown prosperous. Their marriage was prospering too. It wasn't perfect but they were quick to communicate their differences knowing that their future was built on right choices.

She had heard about Henry's death through a letter she had received from Thomas Percy, Henry's lovable brother, now the new Earl of Northumberland, some weeks ago. She would miss Henry's letters, although they had become quite morbid in the last year. But she would love Henry always, with all of his faults.

She remembered that Mary had been delivered of a stillborn and left Henry after two years of marriage. The last she had heard of her was that she had returned to live with her parents. She wondered what she was doing now.

The Earl of Northumberland, her father, had always written to her on a monthly basis when he was alive. God truly was a God of restoration.

God was good. He was seeing to it that the latter part of her days was better than the former.

She patted her rounded belly, her fourth child kicking furiously, making it's presence felt.

Gavyn looked up from the play in the garden with his golden amber eyes. He blew her a kiss. She caught it and placed it on her cheek. He laughed and turned his attention back to their older children.

Yes, she was blessed. Very blessed, indeed.

LaVergne, TN USA
28 September 2009
159199LV00002B/62/P